SHE LOVES ME NOT

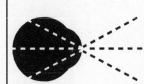

This Large Print Book carries the
Seal of Approval of N.A.V.H.

SHE LOVES ME NOT

NEW AND SELECTED STORIES

RON HANSEN

THORNDIKE PRESS
A part of Gale, Cengage Learning

GALE
CENGAGE Learning®

Detroit • New York • San Francisco • New Haven, Conn • Waterville, Maine • London

GALE
CENGAGE Learning

LIBRARY OF CONGRESS CATALOGING-IN-PUBLICATION DATA

Hansen, Ron, 1947–
    [Short stories. Selections]
    She loves me not : new and selected stories / by Ron Hansen. — Large Print edition.
        pages cm. — (Thorndike Press Large Print Reviewers' Choice)
    ISBN 978-1-4104-5729-5 (hardcover) — ISBN 1-4104-5729-X (hardcover) 1. Short stories, American. 2. Large type books. I. Title.
    PS3558.A5133S48 2013
    813'.54—dc23   2012049535

Published in 2013 by arrangement with Scribner, a division of Simon & Schuster, Inc.

for my mother, Marvyl Hansen
and my mother-in-law, Hester Caldwell

CONTENTS

WILDE IN OMAHA

The Record of an Acquaintance

Since the overseas reports of Oscar Wilde's premature death, in Paris, at age 46, I have experienced pangs of grief and loss, and have felt the need to memorialize our gladsome meeting eighteen years ago in a fuller way than the exigencies of newspaper journalism permitted at the time. I shall leave to posterity this record, hoping that some may consider it a fitting tribute to a man of literary genius who achieved greatness and also disgrace, but whose hours in Omaha still constitute, for many of us, a high point in our lives.

Initial Impressions of the Aesthetic Poet

I originally sought out the famous Mr. Wilde just after his lecture on "The English Renaissance" at the Academy of Music in Sioux City, but some of Iowa's finer sort spirited him off like a *petit roi* to some Lucullan feast of the night and it was left to this reporter to find him in the Hubbard House at his rising in the morn. So it was in the milky light of sunup on Tuesday, March 21st, 1882, the first day of spring, that I first met the aesthetic poet and leader of the so-called Artistic Movement.

Wilde was lolling in the gray haze of a cigarette on the hotel's patch-quilted bed, but was fully dressed in patent-leather shoes and a great, green, ankle-length coat whose collar and cuffs were trimmed with an otter fur that also formed the turban on his head. Underneath his coat was a white linen Lord Byron shirt and a sea-blue scarf he'd tied at his neck like a sailor. On his right, littlest finger was a great seal ring with a cameo of a classic Athenian face. Wilde was then a soft, pleasant innocent of 27, though he only owned up to being 25. I was 23.

I handed him my card from the *Omaha Daily Herald.*

"Oh, I'm so glad you've come," he averred in a sigh, his timbre deep, his pacing languid. "There are a hundred things I want not to say to you." Reading the card again, he said, "Robert Murphy. Are you called Bob?"

"Mostly."

"I shall call you Bobby. Reporters so often

remind me of the Metropolitan Police."

"I do hope you won't think I'm prying."

"Certainly not, *Bobby.* I am the only person in the world *I* should like to know thoroughly. But I don't see any chance of it just at present."

Entering his quarters was a strong, young, Negro valet whose name was W. M. Traquair or Traquier. I failed to spell it out in my notes. But I recall that as he in haste filled Wilde's gripsacks and portmanteau, Wilde introduced us and speculated that the name's origin may have been in the French noun *traqueur,* for those who thrash out game in a hunt. Wilde shook his fist in a facsimile of irritation. "But I shall thrash *him,* if he's not deferential!"

His valet continued his folding and cramming.

Seeing my shorthand, Wilde took the opportunity to say his own name was properly Oscar Fingal O'Flahertie Wills Wilde. (At Oxford, I learned, he signed his papers "O.F.O'F.W.W.")

"And here I was going to call you plain Oscar."

"Don't be ridiculous. Would anyone, least of all my dear mother, Speranza, christen me plain Oscar?" He tapped his shortening cigarette's ashes into a Japanese teacup. "I

11

suppose as I continue to rise in lofty eminence I shall shed my names, just as a bal-
loonist sheds ballast, and finally be called
simply Wilde."

"We're ready for the train, Mr. Simply,"
said Traquier.

"Oh, how could I function without him?"
Wilde asked this reporter. "In a free country
one cannot *live* without a *slave.*"

Surprisingly, his valet found that amusing.
But it was possibly an old joke, for they'd
been journeying westward together since
the Irishman's first lecture on January 9th
at New York City's Chickering Hall.

When Wilde got up and stabbed out his
cigarette, I saw that he was far bigger than
I'd imagined from eastern press reports
where he was so often caricatured as a sissy
because of his florid manner, his fat, fishy,
voluptuous lips — one critic called it "a
carnal mouth" — and the feminine efflu-
ence of his undulant, shoulder-length,
chestnut-brown hair. Wilde was a hefty six
foot three — six inches taller than me —
rather wider at the waist than at his chest,
but with large, farmerish hands to go with a
large, pallid, slack-jawed face, a face that
was akin to Billy the Kid's. "China-blue
eyes," say my notes, "hooded, dreamy,
debauched, and half-asleep" — a fact I

12

chalked up to his being a confessed noctur-
nal who disliked waking in the forenoon.
Walking out of the room, he revealed a
pigeon-toed gait, and I noted that his hips
swayed in a way that once caused an English
ladyship to determine his sex as "undecided."

We were to be cheek by jowl the whole
day.

The Tyranny of Facts

Mr. J. S. Vail, Wilde's traveling business
manager, greeted us as we got to Sioux
City's railway depot. Although Vail was less
than wildly enthusiastic about a reporter
eavesdropping and recording the hithers
and yons of "His Utterness," he was but a
grousing employee of Colonel Morse in
England, who was himself merely the
American tour booking agent of the fabu-
lously successful London impresario Richard D'Oyly Carte. I presumed I was invited
until someone had the gumption to say
otherwise, and they didn't find the grit.

Wilde and I shared a first-class compartment on the hundred-mile ride south to
Council Bluffs. Traquier hunkered with the
colored porters near the caboose and Vail,
as was his habit, wandered off. The *Omaha
Daily Herald* ambassador sought this advan-

tage to have some particulars confirmed.

Wilde yawned at the notion.

"Don't you appreciate some occasional accuracy in reporting?"

"It's simply that one can't escape the *tyranny* of facts. One can scarcely open a newspaper without learning something useful about the sordid crimes against greengrocers or a dozen *disgusting* details relating to the consumption of pork. On the other hand, I *do* like hearing myself *talk*. It is one of my greatest pleasures." Our railway car jerked forward into a screaking roll and Wilde looked outside. Watching soot-blackened shanties slide past, he said, "I find railway travel the most tedious experience in life. That is, if one excepts being sung to in Albert Hall, or dining with a chemist."

I sallied forth recklessly by asking, "Was this outré persona of yours concocted at Oxford or earlier?"

Wilde forgot himself momentarily and grinned with buck teeth of a smoker's yellow hue. And then he superimposed his mask again. "I behave as I have always behaved — *dreadfully*. And that is why people *adore* me." After a little reflection, he added, "Besides, to be authentically *natural* is a difficult pose to keep up."

Oscar was the son of the late Sir William Wilde — a distinguished Dublin surgeon, archaeologist, man of letters, and gossiped sire of three illegitimate children — and Lady Jane "Speranza" Wilde, a large, flamboyant poet, translator, and Irish nationalist who called herself "a priestess at the altar of freedom." She was a fabled hostess who claimed to be above respectability, and once, Wilde told me, "considered founding a Society for the Suppression of Virtue." Disappointed that she'd given birth to a boy instead of a girl, she dressed Oscar in flounces and petticoats until he was nine, schooled him extensively with private tutors, spoke to him in German and French. In childhood Oscar taught himself to read two facing pages at a glance and could finish a three-volume novel in an hour. "I'm so well informed," Wilde told me, "that my mind is like a horrid bric-a-brac shop, full of monsters and dust, and everything priced above its proper value."

At Trinity College in Dublin, where he felt "like a carrier pigeon in a nest of sparrows," Wilde majored in classical languages and literature for three years, then won a scholarship to Magdalen College at Oxford. There he affected whimsical costumes, was nicknamed Hosky, studied

15

aesthetics and art with John Ruskin and Walter Pater, earned a rare double First in Latin and Greek — Aeschylus was his favorite playwright — and was awarded the prestigious Newdigate Prize for his long, lachrymose elegy "Ravenna," its rather trite rhyming couplets describing the vanishing glories of the Italian city.

Soon Wilde was living on fashionable Tite Street in the Chelsea area of London and was a swank man about town, friendly, he said, with that finest of the English painters, James McNeill Whistler, as well as the international beauty Mrs. Lillie Langtry, with whom he was fruitlessly in love, and even the Prince of Wales, who'd said of Oscar to "not know Mr. Wilde is not to be known." The London actress Ellen Terry said of Wilde that "about him there is something more instantaneously individual and audacious than it is possible to describe." Just so.

Owing to his increasing celebrity, the British magazine *Punch* twitted him in a number of cartoons and criticized his art with the note "The poet is Wilde. But his poetry's tame." Wilde and the vogue of aestheticism were lampooned in such theatrical entertainments as *The Grasshopper, The Colonel,* and *Where's the Cat?* And then W. S. Gilbert and Arthur Sullivan created the opera *Patience,* in which the fatuous characters of Reginald Bunthorne and Archibald Grosvenor were both modeled on Wilde. A great financial success in London and New York for its producer, Richard D'Oyly Carte, *Patience* was what conveyed Oscar Wilde on a speaking tour through the heartland of America, not his wretched and unproduced drama *Vera* nor his sixty-one shuffled-up and self-published *Poems.* Even his booking agent disparaged Wilde as simply "the latest form of fashionable madness."

Wilde and I talked about all these things, and lastly the plays, most of which he dismissed as insipid burlesques. But of Gilbert and Sullivan's *Patience* Wilde would only say, "Oh, Bobby. Satire is the *usual* homage which mediocrity pays to genius."

And then he turned to pull down the green window shade, shutting out the cloudless blue serene and the plowed Iowa farm fields we were trundling past, their even rows of earth and sillion shining glossily in the sun.

"You're missing the view," I said.

Wilde lit another cigarette. "I hate views," he said. "They were only made for bad painters. And thus far the prairie has only reminded me of a sheet of blotting paper."

There was a novel entitled *Mirage* in which Wilde starred as a character with the name of Claude Davenant — which Wilde enjoyed mispronouncing as "Deviant." The authoress wrote of Claude speaking "in a low voice, with peculiarly distinct enunciation; he spoke like a man who has made a study of expression. He listened like one accustomed to speak."

Oxford erased much of Wilde's Irish accent, but encouraged his gift for epigram and taught him a rhythmic oratory full of inflection and rhetorical pauses, of heightening pitch falling off into monotone so that it could rise precipitously again. One reporter swore that Wilde spoke in hexameter lines, another that he accentuated every fourth syllable, and his affect was such that it was not uncommon for newspapers to record his diverting visits in verse. It was a tendency I would resist. Yet I did find myself ever leaning forward in his company, scribbling shorthand across the tablet on my knee, half-fearful my pencil would break and I would miss a stray jest or opinion. But after a while he fell into a silent and sullen mood, for he thought "only dull people are brilliant at breakfast," and Omaha was his thirty-eighth stop on an American tour that would not end until October 13th. Wilde was conserving himself for the entertainments of the afternoon and evening.

We changed to a Union Pacific train in Council Bluffs, and Wilde stood between the rocking cars with me and Vail and Traquier and the baggage for the short shuttle across the Big Bridge into Nebraska. Seeing the wide Missouri River, Wilde called it "disappointing"; he thought it had "a want of grandeur and variety of line." But as we continued our screeching way high above it, Wilde held so tightly to the iron railing that his knuckles whitened and he excitedly praised its "majesty," "the sheer physical force of its currents," even "its tawny color and green, aesthetic shadings."

"Are you trying to buy it off with flattery?" Vail asked. "You *do* know that if you fall you'll still drown."

Wilde turned to his valet. "Who needs song and sunflowers when one can have the solace of Mr. Vail?"

The "Peasantry" of the West
Waiting for us at the Union Pacific depot on Tenth Street were three pillars of Omaha City: Dr. George L. Miller, 52, was a graduate of the New York College of Physicians and Surgeons, a former member of the Nebraska Territorial Council, a former

19

sutler at Fort Kearny, holder of wide real estate interests in our fifteen-year-old state, and joint proprietor and editor-in-chief of the *Omaha Daily Herald*. With him was Lyman Richardson, 47, of the University of Michigan, a captain on the staff of General Steele in the War of the Rebellion, and joint proprietor and business manager of the same cynosure of journalism. The affable financier with a mustache as wide as a house-painting brush was Mayor James E. Boyd, also 47, from County Tyrone, Ireland, the owner of the Omaha Gas Works, the Central National Bank, the Omaha and Northwestern Railroad Company, a cattle ranch in Wyoming, an Omaha pork packing company, and Boyd's Opera House on the northeast corner of Farnam and Fifteenth Streets, where Wilde would lecture that evening. Each man zealously shook Wilde's hand, and then Wilde said, "I'm so very glad to meet the *peasantry* of the West."

My editor-in-chief glared at me, as if to say, "What have you gotten me into?"

I could only shrug. I recalled Wilde saying that a gentleman is one who never hurts anyone's feelings unintentionally.

Though it was little more than a bracing walk from the depot, we took carriages to the Withnell House on Fifteenth and Harney Streets, where Wilde and his party would be ensconced. Wilde inquired innocently about the origins of the city, and Dr. Miller expatiated on the Omaha Claim Club, a score of men who each purchased from the Omaha Indian chief Logan Fontenelle, for ten dollars, three hundred twenty acres of hilly wilderness on the west side of the Missouri River. Within twenty years some of their city lots were selling for one hundred dollars a foot.

"So you have done rather nicely in your investments," said Wilde.

"Indeed," said my employer.

"We now have a population of thirty-two thousand," said the Irish mayor to his Irish guest. "And one hundred sixty-five saloons, should you find yourself parched with a Saharan thirst that needs slaking."

"I shall inform Willie, my older brother."

My employer inquired, "And what does this Willie work at?"

Wilde sighed. "At intervals," he said.

Eddies of dust fishtailed down the newly bricked streets. Water trickled toward our just-installed sewers. The steel tracks for our horse-drawn trolley cars winked silver in the noonday sun. Everywhere I looked there were hints of beauty and civilization and new limestone commercial buildings

21

with ornate cornices and tall plateglass windows and ceilings of painted tin fleur-de-lis. But Wilde observed, "The fault in American architecture is that most of the buildings are mere constructions of incongruous anachronisms."

We heard the clopping of the horses' hooves in the silence.

Wilde asked innocently, "Are there industries here?"

The mayor noted with pride there were many. And more to come.

"Industry is the root of all ugliness," Wilde said.

Dr. Miller tilted until he could lock a cold stare on my floor-seeking eyes.

Mayor Boyd folded his arms in high dudgeon. "I can only disagree."

"Oh good," said Wilde. "When people agree with me I always feel that I must be in the wrong."

The Withnell House, so named for brothers who also owned the brick factory, was the former headquarters for the military during the Indian Wars and the finest hotel in Omaha until the Paxton and the Mercer were built. (President and Mrs. Ulysses S. Grant were hosted at a Republican banquet in the Withnell House in 1879.) While the Omaha greeting delegation repaired to their mansions to get their wives, we cooled our heels in the hotel's sumptuous lobby and Vail registered at the front desk. Surprised by Wilde's rudeness, I mentioned to him, "Aren't you a little ornery with the citizenry?"

Wilde played surprise. "But I *love* the public," he said. "I *patronize* them as often as I can."

I could see Vail flinging a hand with demands, and I was irked when the Omaha registrar tractably accommodated him. Traquier pressed his high-buttoned shoe into a vermilion Persian carpet and judged it soft as angel food cake. Wilde lit a cigarette and admired the lovely dadoes, plinths, and flutes on the Athenian columns. My shorthand recorded a wide-eyed darling toddling to the dining room and too loudly whispering to her mother, "Why doesn't his wife cut his hair?"

Wilde laughed and called to the girl, "I'm too poor to have a wife! I can afford nothing but self-denial!"

"But not for long," said Vail, holding out to Wilde the skeleton key to his suite.

"Are you wangling more engagements?" I asked the traveling business manager.

"On the morrow we head to San Francisco and a contract at Platt's Hall for four lectures." Vail grinned and wrung his hands as I had imagined Fagin doing in *Oliver Twist.* "Two weeks in California for a fee of five thousand dollars."

I was stunned. I made just over four hundred dollars a year.

Wilde said, "Mr. Vail also received a wire from some odious village called Griggsville demanding that I instruct them in aesthetics."

The other shoe failed to drop so I tipped it. "And what did you say?"

"Begin by changing the name of your town."

"And the threats," Vail hinted.

"Oh yes. Elsewhere, the owners of an opera house wanted my performance and insinuated *violence* against Mr. Vail were it denied them. I told them that nothing that they could do to my traveling manager would intimidate *me* in the least."

Vail chortled and shook his head.

Wilde turned to his valet. "Shall we go up?"

A Grand Luncheon Held for Him

Wilde's visit was sponsored by the Social Art Club of Omaha: seventy-five of our finer women who took classes in sketching, watercolors, and oils to eradicate their

24

lonesomeness and loss of eastern culture. Worrying that they'd get too little of him in just an evening's entertainment, they were holding a grand luncheon for him in the Withnell House. While he was changing, I stayed in the lobby to watch the guests saunter in. Entering first was Edward Rosewater, the Bohemian owner and editorial director of our rival paper, the *Omaha Daily Bee.* In the instant I seem to have been rendered invisible to him. Then a liveried footman held open a glass and brass door for the shy Mrs. Emma Doherty, who smiled gently my way, and the Reverend Doctor Robert Doherty, 38, originally of County Cavan, Ireland, and just installed as Canon Residentiary of Trinity Episcopal Cathedral. Immediately after them came Mrs. Mary Jane Paxton in a fashionable Sears, Roebuck dress and a wide veiled hat, holding the hand of her husband, William, 45, owner of an ironworks company and a wholesale grocery, a stockholder in the First National Bank, and the president of the Union Stockyards. Walking in alone was Dr. Amelia Burroughs of Council Bluffs, a recent graduate of the Cleveland Homeopathic College; Miss Mary P. Allan, the head librarian of the Omaha Public Library; and Miss Lizzie Pennell, who taught water-

25

color painting to the club and was wearing a form-fitting dress in Wilde's preferred shade of café au lait.

The Honorable James M. Woolworth, 53, helped his wife, Elizabeth, with her mink coat and handed it to the bellman, then saw me note-taking and headed over. A graduate of Hamilton College in upstate New York, he'd practiced law in Syracuse before moving to Omaha at age 27. Since then he'd fathered three children, represented state and railway interests before the United States Supreme Court, and became the first Omaha city attorney as well as chancellor for the Episcopal diocese. Woolworth was honored with a doctorate in law from Racine College, founded the Nebraska Historical Society, spoke occasionally on such topics as "The Philosophy of Emigration," and was a major book collector of English and American classics. Wiping his small oval spectacles with his handkerchief, he asked in a spy's whisper, "Would you happen to know if Mr. Wilde is available for dinner?"

Woolworth owned a magnificent residence on St. Mary's Avenue and was a gracious host to many visitors of eminence, most recently King Kalakaua of Hawaii.

I told him I hadn't heard of any plans, but that Wilde's traveling business manager was

Mr. J. S. Vail and just over there.

Woolworth scanned the dining room where Vail was flirting with Miss Pennell, and he patted my shoulder in thanks. I watched the city attorney cross to Vail, introduce himself with a card, and offer his courteous invitation. Vail's fledgling effort at a smile failed and he said something that made Woolworth's face fall. Woolworth spoke with concern and tilted an ear forward. Vail spoke again. Reddening with fury, Woolworth shut his back to the manager and stormed to his wife, saying as he passed me, "The scoundrel wants me to pay *fifty dollars* for the privilege!"

Soon after that Wilde shouted "Howdy, pardnuhs!" from the mezzanine and heard a smattering of welcoming applause that dissipated as he descended the staircase in a halting, mincing, queenly way, his mane of dark hair still tangled and wet from his bath, a lily held to his nose as his other hand squeaked in its slide along the brass balustrade. Clothed now in his valet's high-button shoes, a charcoal bow tie, and a Wall Street sort of dull gray suit whose color, he was to insist, was that of "moonlight gleaming on Lake Erie," Wilde was taunting Omaha's virility by treating their accustomed business attire as the most droll of his fanciful costumes.

I scowled at his cheekiness, certain that his teasing strategy of affront and parry would not serve him with this frontier audience, and, I confess, half wishing that some man of importance would dress him down for his impudence. But most of the invitees had already entered the dining room, and the others so desperately wanted the afternoon to meet with the aesthete's approbation that they overlooked his ridicule.

We were seated at a dais in the dining room, I on his right hand by dint of my newspaper assignment and Reverend Doherty from County Cavan on his left by dint of his blessing before the meal and his introductory remarks about their very talented guest from across the water. Three minutes into it, Wilde interrupted the Irishman by shouting, "You are so evidently, so unmistakably *sincere,* and worst of all *truthful,* that I cannot believe a word you say!"

Though many laughed, Reverend Doherty did not immediately get the joke and flushed with apology as he explained that he'd gotten all the information on Wilde from eastern newspapers.

Wilde replied, "It is a sure sign that newspapers have degenerated when they can be relied upon."

Adopting the pretense that I was deaf, Wilde spoke so loudly throughout the luncheon that even the kitchen help could hear him, and he continually gave uncensored expression to whatever entered his mind. A Cornish hen was served to him and he held his head as he whined, "Oh why are they always giving me these *pedestrians* to eat?" A Merlot from California was poured and he hesitated before trying the American vintage. But after he sipped it, he thought "the hooch" quite good. "I have learnt to be cautious," he explained. "The English have a miraculous power to turn *wine* into water."

Reverend Doherty resisted when Wilde tried to refill his wineglass, smiling as he said, "I ply the caution of Juvenal: 'A sane mind in a sound body.'"

Wilde said, "But nothing is good in *moderation*. You cannot know the good in anything till you have torn the heart out of it by excess."

The dining staff removed our entrées, and I could see Wilde craved a cigarette, but with ladies present it was impossible. We overheard one of the fairer sex say to a waiter, "Would you please put that lamp out? It's smoking." And Wilde loudly fumed, "Lucky lamp."

The forty luncheon guests were now ignoring each other to concentrate on hearing Wilde's comments. Seeing that, he smiled and leaned toward me to confide, "I could deny myself the pleasure of talking, but not to others the pleasure of listening."

I flattered myself that I was as educated as he, but I was certainly not a celebrity and neither extroverted nor witty nor especially talented, so I frankly felt honored by his intimacy and was proud to have been included as a player in his afternoon entertainment, even though I was alert to his puppetry. And, as was habitual with Wilde, what earlier seemed an Oxonian's scorn and derision gradually began to take on the character of simple puckish joie de vivre. We know now that as he continued to court controversy this would not always be the case.

"The Poet Is Wilde. But His Poetry's Tame."

With the dessert course, he was requested to speak — as if he had not been speaking throughout the meal. And by then the hostilities of those he'd earlier insulted had felt the balm of his humor and charm, and when Wilde rose up it was to smiling faces. His first act was to present to the Social Art Club of Omaha his *Poems,* cautioning,

"Books of poetry by young writers are usually promissory notes that are never paid off. But I do hope this may be an exception." And then he talked about the book's binding of white parchment, which he admired, and the printing on Dutch handmade paper that disappointed him, maligning one fouled page as "a curious toadstool, a malodorous parasitic growth."

Soon many were vocalizing the desire that he actually read one of his sixty-one poems, and after some demurrals and much false-seeming embarrassment, he relented. "But I must limit it to just one, or my own artistry may so captivate me that I'll find it impossible to stop."

Choosing the sonnet "The Grave of Keats," he lingeringly read:

Rid of the world's injustice, and his pain,
  He rests at last beneath God's veil of
    blue:
  Taken from life when life and love were
    new
The youngest of the martyrs here is lain,
Fair as Sebastian, and as early slain.
  No cypress shades his grave, no
    funeral yew,
  But gentle violets weeping with the dew

Weave on his bones an ever-blossoming
   chain.
O proudest heart that broke for misery!
   O sweetest lips since those of Mitylene!
   O poet-painter of our English Land!
Thy name was writ in water — it shall
   stand:
   And tears like mine will keep thy
   memory green,
   As Isabella did her Basil-tree.

Whiffs of other, finer poets made his sonnet resemble a schoolboy's plagiarism, but Wilde hung his head as if faint from his own artistry, only to be revived upon hearing enthusiastic applause. Smiling, he said, "If I may be fetchingly immodest, I congratulate you on your good taste." Looking at the book's page again, he said, "I feel I should provide a gloss. The sonnet was written in Rome shortly after I visited the shabby grave of John Keats, that divine English boy who died prematurely at age twenty-six. I thought of Keats as of a priest of beauty slain before his time; and a fantastical vision of Guido Reni's *Saint Sebastian,* my favorite painting in the whole world, suddenly appeared before my eyes. I'd just seen the picture in Genoa: a lovely, muscular, all-but-naked boy, with dark, clustering hair and red lips, bound by his evil enemies to a tree and, though cruelly pierced in the chest by arrows, lifting his divine, impassioned gaze toward the eternal beauty of the opening heavens."

Some in his audience stirred uneasily at the shocking indecency of Wilde's description, and I sought to rescue him by asking, "Would you tell us something of your impressions of America so far?"

Wilde turned to me and opined, "The journalism is unreadable, and literature is not read." There was a good deal of laughter at my expense, and then he went on. "I find less prejudice and more simple and sane people in the West. But I have noticed in too many places that art has no marvel, and beauty no meaning, and the past no message. In this and other regards, Americans have really everything in common with the English — except, of course, language."

Wilde waited out the jollity and continued, "Also, in marked contrast to England, where the inventor is generally considered crazy, in America an inventor is honored, assistance is forthcoming, and the exercise of ingenuity is here the shortest road to great wealth."

Out of the blue, Mr. Rosewater of the *Daily Bee* asked, "Are you a hunter?"

"Are you asking if I gallop after foxes in the shires? Indeed not. I consider that the unspeakable in pursuit of the uneatable."

"What about tennis?" Rosewater persisted, jotting his notes. "Cricket?"

"I hate all sport," Wilde said. "Each requires one to assume such indecent postures." Scanning a dining room of raised hands, he said, "Oh, I'm afraid I really must quit now. I'll empty myself of all thought and opinion and find I've become electable."

With their laughter Wilde sat, fluttering a hand in gratitude as he heard their ovation. I took the opportunity to bid my adieus and exit to my office in the Herald Building, where I spent the afternoon transcribing my shorthand notes on my Remington typewriter. At home I performed my ablutions and changed into my swallowtail and white tie, then hurried to meet Wilde and his entourage at the Withnell House.

His Earnest and Instructive Lecture

Seeing me, Wilde told his valet, "With an evening coat and a white tie, anybody, even a journalist, can gain a reputation for being civilized."

Wilde wore a silk maroon scarf and peeping handkerchief, but was otherwise wholly in black, with a velvet smoking jacket and vest, silk breeches that reached just past his knees, snug leg hosiery, and what looked like gleaming patent leather ballet slippers faced with sizable bows. (In four years' time F. H. Burnett would give such an outfit to his title character in *Little Lord Fauntleroy*.) Affecting a placid pose against the Withnell's sculpted wainscoting, Wilde crossed his feet like a dandy, gently tilted his head, and held still for a photograph.

We strolled silently to Boyd's Opera House, which was just a block away on the northeast corner of Fifteenth and Farnam. The opera house was gloriously ornate and effulgent, a mere six months old, could seat seventeen hundred, and was constructed at a staggering cost of ninety thousand dollars. The high society of Omaha, Lincoln, and Council Bluffs were streaming through the main entrance as Wilde slumped in a chair in his dressing room and his valet softly dusted Wilde's bloodless face with stage makeup and rouge. Judge James W. Savage, 56, rapped the door before sauntering in, the cold, fragrant air of a March night floating off his formal coat. Shaking my hand with vigor whilst giving Wilde a sidelong glance, the judge genially announced that he would be introducing the speaker to a full house. Lest Wilde consider him unequal to the task, Savage managed to steer our fleeting conversation toward the data that he was distantly related to the English poet John Dryden; graduated from Harvard University, seventh in his class; and was associated in legal practice with Charles F. Manderson, our junior United States senator.

Quaffing a full glass of water, Wilde handed it to Traquier and said nothing as he warily stood just as the stage manager called the friendly Savage out.

We watched the judge's histrionic introduction of "the Oxford aesthete and poet of note" from the wings. Wilde did not joke about his exaggerations, and as Savage got to his concluding paragraph, Wilde turned to me with wild eyes and held up hands that were trembling.

"Are you that nervous?"

"Dear sir, my speech is so very, very *dull*. Omaha will be convinced I have a coma of the mind."

Savage finished eloquently and shook Wilde's hand as the large Dubliner sashayed out, curtsying in gratitude for Omaha's considerable applause, then seating himself at a Louis XV secretaire that was on loan from Lininger's Art Gallery. The gas footlights tinctured him in golden tones, while behind him was a green-tasseled fireproof asbestos curtain with the name BOYD'S OPERA HOUSE emblazoned on it in circus lettering.

Squaring his pages, Wilde commenced by announcing his subject as "The Decorative Arts." And then he read: "In my lecture tonight I do not wish to give you any abstract definition of *beauty;* you can get along very well without *philosophy* if you surround yourself with beautiful *things;* but I wish to tell you of what we have done and are doing in *England* to search out those men and women who have knowledge and power of *design,* of the *schools* of art provided for them, and the noble *use* we are making of art in the improvement of the *handicraft* of our country."

House decoration, for gosh sakes! The topic was not especially inert, nor his overly inflected and cautious presentation necessarily stupefying, but his lecture was so much less clever and pungent than his amusingly insulting conversation that I wanted to shout out to the simulacrum, "Stop, Oscar! This is not you!" And then I was forced to confront the urgency of my dyspepsia. Was I afraid that he seemed foolish, or that I did? That he seemed dull, or

37

that my high hopes of enterprise and wealth in Omaha had descended into simply holding a job? *This is not you* and its hundred variations had afflicted me often since this daredevil tyro made the three-week journey west to the rich possibilities of Nebraska, but there was no *This is you* as its complement. Amid my hearty and prosperous cohort, I felt like a poseur.

And there was Wilde no longer reading his pages to say from memory, "Do not mistake the *material* of civilization for civilization itself. It is the *use* to which we put these things that determines whether the telephone, the steam engine, or even electricity are valuable to civilization."

The stuff was so close to the seemingly sincere editorials I was called upon to write on occasion that I found myself drifting into shorthand notes on the intricate song of his performance and the British oddities of his pronunciation: "poo-ah" for "poor," "yee-ahs" for "years," but also "Oma-har" for the city, and "moo-say-um" for "museum." Wilde graphically described cheerless rows of American houses, glaring billboards, and streets that were no more than gumbos of mud, and the seventeen hundred in the audience responded with ripples of subdued laughter. But Wilde could not have been satisfied with such small beer, and as he stood at the conclusion of his talk and modestly accepted a din of applause, I noted that he seemed rattled and frail and sick of himself. Walking past me in the wings, Wilde muttered with self-loathing, "Moths were flying from my lips."

A Throb of Joy

Wilde was in such a dismayed mood in his dressing room that I hesitated to invite him out, but he seemed only too happy to avoid an early return to the Withnell House, where perhaps the Irishry of Omaha would be waiting to hurrah him, and we two strolled alone that cold, blustery night to my humble abode on Thirteenth Street.

My lodgings were just a front room, sleeping room, and kitchen, with an outhouse in the yard. I took his turban and ankle-length coat from him and flung them onto my slovenly bed even though they reeked of stale tobacco smoke, then got out of my swallowtail coat and white tie. My four chromolithographs were hung too near the ceiling, which Wilde had flouted in his lecture, but he seemed to take no notice of them. Wilde had said that there was one article of furniture that confronted him wherever he journeyed on this continent and that "for absolutely horrid ugliness surpassed anything he'd seen — the cast-iron American stove." I owned one that was precisely what he'd snidely described: ornamented with wreaths of grimy roses, and with a sooty smokestack shaped like a funeral urn. I found myself ill-at-ease and defensive, and it forcibly struck me that forebodings of his criticism must have stifled many friendships. But Wilde calmly looked at the stove without comment as I got a bottle of the Macallan Scotch whisky from the kitchen cabinet and filled two shot glasses. Wilde held his in both hands like a chill-slaying candle as he sipped and peered about him, mentioning no excellencies of style in the décor — hardly a surprise to me — but spying my copy of Mrs. Browning's *Aurora Leigh,* a book of poems whose quality he exaggerated as being greater than the sonnets of Shakespeare.

"Shall we sit?" I asked.

"Another, please."

I filled his shot glass.

Wilde lounged on my sage-green sofa as if it were a fainting couch. Berliner's Gramophone was not yet in manufacture, so we lacked the idylls of music as I trimmed and lighted two kerosene lamps and took a seat on my Brewster chair. Continuing in the interrogatory mode we'd earlier established, I said, "You have plans for future work, I presume?"

"For my future life, do you mean?" Wilde held a cigarette to the kerosene flame before falling back against the sofa. "Well, I'm a very *ambitious* young man. I want to do everything in the world. I cannot conceive of anything that I do *not* want to do. I want to write a great deal more poetry. I want to study painting in oils more than I've been able to. I want to write a great many more plays, and I want to make this artistic movement the basis for a new civilization. Are we done with the *Quotidian Herald* interview?"

"If you wish."

Wilde took the liberty of filling his shot glass again. With a consoling measure of respect, he said, "*Cask* strength."

"Specially ordered from a shop in Glasgow."

Wilde stared at me for a confusing moment. "So, *Bobby,*" he said, "you're not married."

"I have a fiancée in Connecticut. She's a trifle afraid of the West. She's waiting for me to get more established. Or flee."

"The hard life on the *frontier,*" he said. "It's just as well. Modern women understand everything except their husbands. And where do *you* hail from?"

"Connecticut. Yale, actually. Were you there?"

"I have no idea. While sowing my 'Wilde oats of aestheticism,' I've been signing my letters to London 'Somewhere and sometime.' "

"Was that a newspaper quotation?"

"Wilde oats? Certainly. And don't forget the coming dances: 'The Oscar Wilde Quadrille' and 'The Too-too Waltz.' "

"We can be cruel."

"Oh well. Half the world does not believe in God; the other half does not believe in me." Wilde finished his third Scotch whisky and held his shot glass out.

I filled it. Embers from his cigarette fell onto his velvet vest and he flicked them off with irritation. "Are we at all near the hideout of Jesse James?"

"Don't know. We hear rumors he's in or around Kansas City." (On a Monday, two weeks hence, Jesse James would be killed by Bob Ford in Saint Joseph.)

"Americans are great hero worshippers," Wilde said. "And you have an intriguing tendency to take your heroes from the criminal classes."

I sought a riposte and came up empty. There was a silence in which it seemed my turn to sally forth with a conversational gambit, but my habit of stalling on such things was more than equal to the short term of his patience.

Wilde laid a hand to his forehead as if swooning and said, "The most graceful thing I ever beheld in the West was a construction worker outside the Mercantile Library in Saint Louis, Missouri, driving a new shaft of some sort with a hammer. At any moment he might have been transformed into marble or bronze and become noble in art forever." Wilde was silent for a minute and then assessed me. "Are you an *art* fancier?"

"I have so little free time," I said.

Wilde sighed with dissatisfaction. "Aren't you the will-o'-the-wisp."

I am abashed to admit that I felt so adrift in our colloquy I could only find the craft to top off my shot glass with whisky.

Seeing me, Wilde drank and held out his shot glass again. I indulged him. Wilde said, "I find it perfectly *monstrous* the way people go about nowadays, saying things behind one's back that are absolutely and entirely true."

We listened to the floor clock ticking in the quietude. Waiting for me to say something was an agony for him. So it was with a sense of emergency that I finally risked, "Would you mind an impertinence?"

Wilde softly rested an inquisitive gaze upon me.

"It's my stab at some good advice."

"It is always a *silly* thing to give advice, but to give *good* advice is absolutely fatal."

But I perdured. "Don't give all these lectures," I said. "Don't let audiences feed on you like this. They'll lay waste to your talent. And don't dissemble. Even poetry is wrong for you. It feels trumped up. With your fluency and flair for humor it's far better you concentrate on fiction and plays."

At first Wilde seemed shocked and disturbed by my outburst, but then he smiled wryly and sat up and shook his hair free of his face. "What excellent whisky!" he said. "And how perfectly *splendid* of you to accompany me through this wonderfully *exciting* day. This is the first pleasant throb of *joy* I have had since Mr. Vail last took sick."

"Only too glad to oblige," said I. I confess with shame that the acquittal and relief I felt was greater than my frustration at his tone of farewell.

Wilde stood to his full height and tilted, slightly off balance with drink. Smiling down at me, he said, "I have discovered that alcohol taken in sufficient quantity produces all the effects of drunkenness."

I got up as well and indicated my book-case. "Would you like some volumes to take with you to California?" I was hoping, I suppose, to compel some contact with an international celebrity in the future.

But Wilde said, "Oh, no worry. I never travel without my *diary*. One should always have something *sensational* to read on the train."

I helped him get into his ankle-length green coat, thinking that *this* was my only diary moment. Oscar Wilde would be my sole claim to fame. Even marriage and children would be as nothing compared to our fifteen hours together. "We're on Thirteenth Street," I said. "Walk north to Harney, turn left, and the Withnell is in the second block."

The customary expectation was that I escort my houseguest back, and my lapse in etiquette pinked his face. "I shan't get lost," he said. Wilde had his hand on the door handle when he halted a moment and squared toward me so that I fell back a little, fearing a fist. "Most people are other people," he said in good-bye. "Their thoughts are someone else's opinions. Their lives a mimicry. Their passions a quotation."

And he was gone from me and from

Omaha before I could nag him with the reminder that it was Oscar Wilde who said the first duty of life is to be as artificial as possible.

WICKEDNESS

At the end of the nineteenth century a girl from Delaware got on a milk train in Omaha and took a green wool seat in the second-class car. August was outside the window, and sunlight was a yellow glare on the trees. Up front, a railway conductor in a navy-blue uniform was gingerly backing down the aisle with a heavy package in a gunny-sack that a boy was helping him with. They were talking about an agreeable seat away from the hot Nebraska day that was persistent outside, and then they were setting their cargo across the runnered aisle from the girl and tilting it against the shellacked wooden wall of the railway car before walking back up the aisle and elsewhere into August.

She was sixteen years old and an Easterner just recently hired as a county school-teacher, but she knew enough about prairie farming to think the heavy package was a

47

crank-and-piston washing machine or a boxed plowshare and coulter, something no higher than the bloody stump where the poultry were chopped with a hatchet and then wildly high-stepped around the yard. Soon, however, there was a juggling movement and the gunnysack slipped aside, and she saw an old man sitting there, his limbs hacked away, and dark holes where his ears ought to have been, the skin pursed at his jaw hinge like pink lips in a kiss. The milk train jerked into a roll through the railway yard, and the old man was jounced so that his gray cheek pressed against the hot window glass. Although he didn't complain, it seemed an uneasy position, and the girl wished she had the courage to get up from her seat and tug the jolting body upright. She instead got to her page in *Quo Vadis* and pretended to be so rapt by the book that she didn't look up again until Columbus, where a doctor with liquorice on his breath sat heavily beside her and openly stared over his newspaper before whispering that the poor man was a carpenter in Genoa who'd been caught out in the great blizzard of 1888. Had she heard of that one?

The girl shook her head.

She ought to look out for their winters, the doctor said. Weather in Nebraska could be the wickedest thing she ever saw.

She didn't know what to say, so she said nothing. And at Genoa a young teamster got on in order to carry out the old man, whose half body was heavy enough that the boy had to yank the gunnysack up the aisle like sixty pounds of mail.

In the year 1888, on the twelfth day of January, a pink sun was up just after seven and southeastern zephyrs of such soft temperature were sailing over the Great Plains that squatters walked their properties in high rubber boots and April jackets and some farmhands took off their Civil War greatcoats to rake silage into the cattle troughs. However, sheep that ate whatever they could the night before raised their heads away from food and sniffed the salt tang in the air. And all that morning streetcar mules were reported to be acting up, nipping each other, jingling the hitch rings, foolishly waggling their dark manes and necks as though beset by gnats and horseflies. A Danish cattleman named Axel Hansen later said he was near the Snake River and tipping a teaspoon of saleratus into a yearling's mouth when he heard a faint groaning in the north that was like the noise of a high waterfall at a fair distance. Axel looked toward Dakota, and there half the sky was suddenly gray and black and indigo blue with great storm clouds that were seething up as high as the sun and wrangling toward him at horse speed. Weeds were being uprooted, sapling trees were bullwhipping, and the top inches of snow and prairie soil were being sucked up and stirred like the dirty flour that was called red dog. And then the onslaught hit him hard as furniture, flying him onto his back so that when Axel looked up, he seemed to be deep undersea and in icehouse cold. Eddying snow made it hard to breathe any way but sideways, and getting up to just his knees and hands seemed a great attainment. Although his sod house was but a quarter mile away, it took Axel four hours to get there. Half his face was frozen gray and hard as weatherboarding so the cattleman was speechless until nightfall, and then Axel Hansen simply told his wife, That was not pleasant.

Cow tails stuck out sideways when the wind caught them. Sparrows and crows whumped hard against the windowpanes, their jerking eyes seeking out an escape, their wings fanned out and flattened as though pinned up in an ornithologist's display. Cats died, dogs died, pigeons died. Entire farms of cattle and pigs and geese and chickens were wiped out in a single night. Horizontal snow that was hard and dry as salt dashed and seethed over everything, sloped up like rooftops, tricked its way across creek beds and ditches, milkily purled down city streets, stole shanties and coops and pens from a bleak landscape that was even then called the Great American Desert. Everything about the blizzard seemed to have personality and hateful intention. Especially the cold. At six a.m., the temperature at Valentine, Nebraska, was thirty degrees above zero. Half a day later the temperature was fourteen below, a drop of forty-four degrees and the difference between having toes and not, between staying alive overnight and not, between ordinary concerns and one overriding idea.

Ainslie Classen was hopelessly lost in the whiteness and tilting low under the jamming gale when his right elbow jarred against a joist of his pigsty. He walked around the sty by skating his sore red hands along the upright shiplap and then squeezed inside through the slops trough. The pigs scampered over to him, seeking his protection, and Ainslie put himself among them, getting down in their stink and their body heat, socking them away only when they ganged up or when two or three presumed

51

he was food. Hurt was nailing into his finger joints until he thought to work his hands into the pigs' hot wastes, then smeared some onto his skin. The pigs grunted around him and intelligently snuffled at his body with their pink and tender noses, and Ainslie thought, *You are not me but I am you,* and Ainslie Classen got through the night without shame or injury.

Whereas a Hartington woman took two steps out her door and disappeared until the snow sank away in April and raised her body up from her garden patch.

An Omaha cigar maker got off the Leavenworth Street trolley that night, fifty yards from his own home and five yards from another's. The completeness of the blizzard so puzzled him that the cigar maker tramped up and down the block more than twenty times and then slept against a lamppost and died.

A cattle inspector froze to death getting up on his quarter horse. The next morning he was still tilting the saddle with his upright weight, one cowboy boot just inside the iced stirrup, one bear-paw mitten over the horn and reins. His quarter horse apparently kept waiting for him to complete his mount, and then the quarter horse died too.

A Chicago boy visiting his brother for the holidays was going to a neighbor's farm to borrow a scoop shovel when the night train of blizzard raged in and overwhelmed him. His tracks showed the boy mistakenly slanted past the sod house he'd just come from, and then tilted forward with perhaps the vain hope of running into some shop or shed or railway depot. His body was found four days later and twenty-seven miles from home.

A forty-year-old wife sought out her husband in the open range land near O'Neill and days later was found standing up in her muskrat coat and black bandanna, her scarf-wrapped hands tightly clenching the top strand of rabbit wire that was keeping her upright, her blue eyes still open but cloudily bottled by a half inch of ice, her jaw un-hinged as though she'd died yelling out a name.

The one a.m. report from the chief signal officer in Washington, D.C., had said Kansas and Nebraska could expect "fair weather, followed by snow, brisk to high southerly winds gradually diminishing in force, becoming westerly and warmer, followed by colder."

Sin Thomas undertook the job of taking

Emily Flint home from their Holt County schoolhouse just before noon. Sin's age was sixteen, and Emily was not only six years younger but also practically kin to him, since her stepfather was Sin's older brother. Sin took the girl's hand and they haltingly tilted against the uprighting gale on their walk to a dark horse, gray-maned and gray-tailed with ice. Sin cracked the reins loose of the crowbar tie-up and helped Emily up onto his horse, jumping up onto the croup from a soapbox and clinging the girl to him as though she were groceries he couldn't let spill.

Everything she knew was no longer there. She was in a book without descriptions. She could put her hand out and her hand would disappear. Although Sin knew the general direction to Emily's house, the geography was so duned and drunk with snow that Sin gave up trying to nudge his horse one way or another and permitted its slight adjustments away from the wind. Hours passed and the horse strayed southeast into Wheeler County, and then in misery and pneumonia it stopped, planting its overworked legs like four parts of an argument and slinging its head away from Sin's yanks and then hanging its nose in anguish. Emily hopped down into the snow and held on to the boy's coat pocket as Sin uncinched the saddle and jerked off a green horse blanket and slapped it against his iron leggings in order to crack the ice from it. And then Sin scooped out a deep nook in a snow slope that was as high and steep as the roof of a New Hampshire house. Emily tightly wrapped herself in the green horse blanket and slumped inside the nook in the snow, and the boy crept on top of her and stayed like that, trying not to press into her.

Emily would never say what was said or was cautiously not said that night. She may have been hysterical. In spite of the fact that Emily was out of the wind, she later said that the January night's temperature was like wire-cutting pliers that snipped at her ears and toes and fingertips until the horrible pain became only a nettling and then a kind of sleep and her feet seemed as dead as her shoes. Emily wept, but her tears froze cold as penny nails and her upper lip seemed candle-waxed by her nose and she couldn't stop herself from feeling the difference in the body on top of her. She thought Sin Thomas was responsible, that the night suited his secret purpose, and she so complained of the bitter cold that Sin finally took off his Newmarket overcoat and tailored it around the girl; but sixty years later, when Emily wrote her own account of the ordeal, she forgot to say anything about him giving her his overcoat and only said in an ordinary way that they spent the night inside a snowdrift and that "by morning the storm had subsided."

With daybreak Sin told Emily to stay there and, with or without his Newmarket overcoat, the boy walked away with the forlorn hope of chancing upon his horse. Winds were still high, the temperature was thirty-five degrees below zero, and the snow was deep enough that Sin pulled lopsidedly with every step and then toppled over just a few yards away. And then it was impossible for him to get to his knees, and Sin only sank deeper when he attempted to swim up into the high wave of snow hanging over him. Sin told himself that he would try again to get out, but first he'd build up his strength by napping for just a little while. He arranged his body in the snow gully so that the sunlight angled onto it, and then Sin Thomas gave in to sleep and within twenty minutes died.

His body was discovered at noon by a Wheeler County search party, and shortly after that they came upon Emily. She was carried to a nearby house where she slumped in a kitchen chair while girls her own age dipped Emily's hands and feet into pans of ice water. She could look up over a windowsill and see Sin Thomas's body standing upright on the porch, his hands woodenly crossed at his chest, so Emily kept her brown eyes on the pinewood floor and slept that night with jars of hot water against her skin. She could not walk for two months. Even scissoring tired her hands. She took a cashier's job with the Nebraska Farm Implements Company and kept it for forty-five years, staying all her life in Holt County. She died in a wheelchair on a hospital porch in the month of April. She was wearing a glamorous sable coat. She never married.

The T. E. D. Schusters' only child was a seven-year-old boy named Cleo who rode his Shetland pony to the Westpoint school that day and had not shown up on the doorstep by two p.m., when Mr. Schuster went down into the root cellar, dumped purple sugar beets onto the earthen floor, and upended the bushel basket over his head as he slung himself against the onslaught in his second try for Westpoint. Hours later Mrs. Schuster was tapping powdered salt onto the night candles in order to preserve the wax when the door abruptly blew open and Mr. Schuster stood there without Cleo and utterly white and petrified with cold. She warmed him up with okra soup and tenderly wrapped his frozen feet and hands in strips of gauze that she'd dipped in kerosene, and they were sitting on milking stools by a red-hot stove, their ankles just touching, only the usual sentiments being expressed, when they heard a clopping on the wooden stoop and looked out to see the dark Shetland pony turned gray and shaggy-bearded with ice, his legs as wobbly as if he'd just been born. Jammed under the saddle skirt was a damp, rolled-up note from the Scottish schoolteacher that said, Cleo is safe. The Schusters invited the pony into the house and bewildered him with praises as Cleo's mother scraped ice from the pony's shag with her own ivory comb, and Cleo's father gave him sugar from the Dresden bowl as steam rose up from the pony's back.

Even at six o'clock that evening, there was no heat in Mathias Aachen's house, and the seven Aachen children were in whatever stockings and clothing they owned as they put their hands on a hay-burner stove that was no warmer than soap. When a jar of apricots burst open that night and the iced orange syrup did not ooze out, Aachen's wife told the children, You ought now to get under your covers. While the seven were crying and crowding onto their dirty floor mattresses, she rang the green tent cloth along the iron wire dividing the house and slid underneath horse blankets in Mathias Aachen's gray wool trousers and her own gray dress and a ghastly muskrat coat that in hot weather gave birth to insects.

Aachen said, Every one of us will be dying of cold before morning. Freezing here. In Nebraska.

His wife just lay there, saying nothing.

Aachen later said he sat up bodingly until shortly after one a.m., when the house temperature was so exceedingly cold that a gray suede of ice was on the teapot and his pretty girls were whimpering in their sleep. *You are not meant to stay here,* Aachen thought, and tilted hot candle wax into his right ear and then his left, until he could only hear his body drumming blood. And then Aachen got his Navy Colt and kissed his wife and killed her. And then walked under the green tent cloth and killed his seven children, stopping twice to capture a scuttling boy and stopping once more to reload.

Hattie Benedict was in her Antelope County

schoolyard overseeing the noon recess in a black cardigan sweater and gray wool dress when the January blizzard caught her unaware. She had been impatiently watching four girls in flying coats playing Ante I Over by tossing a spindle of chartreuse yarn over the one-room schoolhouse, and then a sharp cold petted her neck and Hattie turned toward the open fields of hoarfrosted scraggle and yellow grass. Just a half mile away was a gray blur of snow underneath a dark sky that was all hurry and calamity, like a nighttime city of sin-black buildings and havoc in the streets. Wind tortured a creekside cottonwood until it cracked apart. A tin water pail rang in a skipping roll to the horse path. One quarter of the tar-paper roof was torn from the schoolhouse and sailed southeast forty feet. And only then did Hattie yell for the older boys with their cigarettes and clay pipes to hurry in from the prairie twenty rods away, and she was hustling a dallying girl inside just as the snowstorm socked into her Antelope County schoolhouse, shipping the building awry off its timber skids so that the southwest side heavily dropped six inches and the oak-plank floor became a slope that Hattie ascended unsteadily while ordering the children to open their *Webster Franklin*

Fourth Reader to the Lord's Prayer in verse and to say it aloud. And then Hattie stood by her desk with her pink hands held theatrically to her cheeks as she looked up at the walking noise of bricks being jarred from the chimney and down the roof. Every window view was as white as if butcher paper had been tacked up. Winds pounded into the windowpanes and dry window putty trickled onto the unpainted sills. Even the slough grass fire in the hay-burner stove was sucked high into the tin stack pipe so that the soot on it reddened and snapped. Hattie could only stare. Four of the boys were just about Hattie's age, so she didn't say anything when they ignored the reading assignment and earnestly got up from the wooden benches in order to argue *oughts* and *ought nots* in the cloakroom. She heard the girls saying Amen and then she saw Janusz Vasko, who was fifteen years old and had grown up in Nebraska weather, gravely exiting the cloakroom with a cigarette behind one ear and his right hand raised high overhead. Hattie called on him, and Janusz said the older boys agreed that they could get the littler ones home, but only if they went out right away. And before she could even give it thought, Janusz tied his red handkerchief over his nose and mouth and jabbed his orange corduroy trousers inside his antelope boots with a pencil.

Yes, Hattie said, please go, and Janusz got the boys and girls to link themselves together with jump ropes and twine and piano wire, and twelve of Hattie Benedict's pupils walked out into a nothingness that the boys knew from their shoes up and dully worked their way across as though each crooked stump and tilted fence post was a word they could spell in a plainspoken sentence in a book of practical knowledge. Hours later the children showed up at their homes, aching and crying in raw pain. Each was given cocoa or the green tea of the elder flower and hot bricks were put next to their feet while they napped and newspapers printed their names incorrectly. And then, one by one, the children disappeared from history.

Except for Johan and Alma Lindquist, aged nine and six, who stayed behind in the schoolhouse, owing to the greater distance to their ranch. Hattie opened a week-old Omaha newspaper on her desktop and with caution peeled a spotted yellow apple on it, eating tan slices from her scissor blade as she peered out at children who seemed irritatingly sad and pathetic. She said, You wish you were home.

The Lindquists stared.

Me too, she said. She dropped the apple core onto the newspaper page and watched it ripple with the juice stain. Have you any idea where Pennsylvania is?

East, the boy said. Johan was eating pepper cheese and day-old rye bread from a tin lunch box that sparked with electricity whenever he touched it. And his sister nudged him to show how her yellow hair was beguiled toward her green rubber comb whenever she brought it near.

Hattie was talking in such quick English that she could tell the Lindquists couldn't quite understand it. She kept hearing the snow pinging and pattering against the windowpanes, and the storm howling like clarinets down the stack pipe, but she perceived the increasing cold in the room only when she looked to the Lindquists and saw their Danish sentences grayly blossoming as they spoke. Hattie went into the cloakroom and skidded out the poorhouse box, rummaging from it a Scotch plaid scarf that she wrapped twice around her skull and ears just as a squaw would, and snipping off the fingertips of some red knitted gloves that were only slightly too small. She put them on and then she got into her secondhand coat and Alma whispered to her brother but Hattie said she'd have no whispering, she hated that, she couldn't wait for their kin to show up for them, she had too many responsibilities, and nothing interesting ever happened in the country. Everything was stupid. Everything was work. She didn't even have a girlfriend. She said she'd once been sick for four days, and two by two practically every woman in Neligh mistrustfully visited her rooming house to squint at Hattie and palm her forehead and talk about her symptoms. And then they'd snail out into the hallway and prattle and whisper in the hawk and spit of the German language.

Alma looked at Johan with misunderstanding and terror, and Hattie told them to get out paper and pencils; she was going to say some necessary things and the children were going to write them down. She slowly paced as she constructed a paragraph, one knuckle darkly striping the blackboard, but she couldn't properly express herself. She had forgotten herself so absolutely that she thought forgetting was a yeast in the air; or that the onslaught's only point was to say over and over again that she was next to nothing. Easily bewildered. Easily dismayed. The Lindquists were shying from the crazy woman and concentrating their shame on a nickel pad of Wisconsin paper. And Hattie thought, *You'll give me an ugly name and there will be cartoons and snickering and the older girls will idly slay me with jokes and imitations.*

She explained she was taking them to her rooming house, and she strode purposefully out into the great blizzard as if she were going out to a garden to fetch some strawberries, and Johan dutifully followed, but Alma stayed inside the schoolhouse with her purple scarf up over her mouth and nose and her own dark sandwich of pepper cheese and rye bread clutched to her breast like a prayer book. And then Johan stepped out of the utter whiteness to say Alma had to hurry up, that Miss Benedict was angrily asking him if his sister had forgotten how to use her legs. So Alma stepped out of the one-room schoolhouse, sinking deep in the snow and sloshing ahead in it as she would in a pond until she caught up with Hattie Benedict, who took the Lindquists' hands in her own and walked them into the utter whiteness and night of the afternoon. Seeking to blindly go north to her rooming house, Hattie put her high-button shoes in the deep tracks that Janusz and the schoolchildren had made, but she misstepped twice, and that was enough to get her on a screw-tape path over snow humps and hillocks that took her south and west and very nearly into a great wilderness that was like a sea in high gale.

Hattie imagined herself reaching the Elkhorn River and discovering her rooming house standing high and honorable under the sky's insanity. And then she and the Lindquist children would duck over their teaspoons of tomato soup and soda crackers as the town's brooms and scarecrows teetered over them, hooking their green hands on the boy and girl and saying, Tell us about it. She therefore created a heroine's part for herself and tried to keep to it as she floundered through drifts as high as a four-poster bed in a white room of piety and weeping. Hattie pretended gaiety by saying once, See how it swirls! but she saw that the Lindquists were tucking deep inside themselves as they trudged forward and fell and got up again, the wind drawing tears from their squinting eyes, the hard, dry snow hitting their skin like wildly flying pencils. Hours passed as Hattie tipped away from the press of the wind into country that was a puzzle to her, but she kept saying, Just a little farther, until she saw Alma playing Gretel by secretly trailing her right hand along a high wave of snow in order to secretly let go yet another crumb of her rye bread. And then, just ahead of her, she saw some pepper cheese that the girl dropped some time ago. Hissing spindrifts tore away from the snow swells and spiked her face like sharp pins, but then a door seemed to inch ajar and Hattie saw the slight, dark change of a haystack and she cut toward it, announcing that they'd stay there for the night.

She slashed away an access into the haystack and ordered Alma to crawl inside, but the girl hesitated as if she were still thinking of the gingerbread house and the witch's oven, and Hattie acidly whispered, You'll be a dainty mouthful. She meant it as a joke but her green eyes must have seemed crazy, because the little girl was crying when Hattie got inside the haystack next to her, and then Johan was crying, too, and Hattie hugged the Lindquists to her body and tried to shush them with a hymn by Dr. Watts, gently singing, Hush, my dears, lie still and slumber. She couldn't get her feet inside the haystack, but she couldn't feel them anyway just then, and the haystack was making everything else seem right and possible. She talked to the children about hot pastries and taffy and Christmas presents, and that night she made up a story about the horrible storm being a wicked old man whose only thought was to eat them up, but he couldn't find them in the haystack even though he looked and looked. The old man was howling, she said, because he was so hungry.

At daybreak a party of farmers from Neligh rode out on their high plowhorses to the Antelope County schoolhouse in order to get Hattie and the Lindquist children, but the room was empty and the bluetick hound that was with them kept scratching up rye bread until the party walked along behind it on footpaths that wreathed around the schoolyard and into a haystack twenty rods away where the older boys smoked and spit tobacco juice at recess. The Lindquist girl and the boy were killed by the cold, but Hattie Benedict had stayed alive inside the hay, and she wouldn't come out again until the party of men yanked her by the ankles. Even then she kept the girl's body hugged against one side and the boy's body hugged to the other, and when she was put up on one horse, she stared down at them with green eyes that were empty of thought or understanding and inquired if they'd be okay. Yes, one man said. You took good care of them.

Bent Lindquist ripped down his kitchen cupboards and carpentered his own triangular caskets, blacking them with shoe polish, and then swaddled Alma and Johan in black alpaca that was kindly provided by an elder in the Church of Jesus Christ of Latter-Day Saints. And all that night Danish women sat up with the bodies, sopping the Lindquists' skin with vinegar so as to impede putrefaction.

Hattie Benedict woke up in a Lincoln hospital with sweet oil of spermaceti on her hands and lips, and weeks later a Kansas City surgeon amputated her feet with a polished silver hacksaw in the presence of his anatomy class. She was walking again by June, but she was attached to cork-and-iron shoes and she sighed and grunted with every step. Within a year she grew so overweight that she gave up her crutches for a wicker-backed wheelchair and stayed in Antelope County on a pension of forty dollars per month, letting her dark hair grow dirty and leafy, reading one popular romance per day. And yet she complained so much about her helplessness, especially in winter, that the Protestant churches took up a collection and Hattie Benedict was shipped by train to Oakland, California, whence she sent postcards saying she'd married a trolley repairman and she hated Nebraska, hated their horrible weather, hated their petty lives.

■ ■ ■ ■

On Friday the thirteenth some pioneers went to the upper stories of their houses to jack up the windows and crawl out onto snow that was like a jeweled ceiling over their properties. Everything was sloped and planed and capped and whitely furbelowed. One man couldn't get over his boyish delight in tramping about on deer-hide snowshoes at the height of his roof gutters, or that his dogwood tree was forgotten but for twigs sticking out of the snow like a skeleton's fingers. His name was Eldad Alderman, and he jabbed a bamboo fishing pole in four likely spots a couple of feet below his snowshoes before the bamboo finally thumped against the plank roof of his chicken coop. He spent two hours spading down to the coop and then squeezed in through the one window in order to walk among the fowl and count up. Half his sixty hens were alive; the other half were still nesting, their orange beaks lying against their white hackles, sitting there like a dress shop's hats, their pure white eggs not yet cold underneath them. In gratitude to those thirty chickens that withstood the ordeal, Eldad gave them Dutch whey and curds and eventually wrote a letter praising their constitutions in the *American Poultry Yard.*

Anna Shevschenko managed to get oxen inside a shelter sturdily constructed of oak scantling and a high stack of barley straw, but the snow powder was so fine and fiercely penetrating that it sifted through and slowly accumulated on the floor. The oxen tamped it down and inchingly rose toward the oak scantling rafters, where they were stopped as the snow flooded up, and by daybreak were overcome and finally asphyxiated. Widow Shevschenko decided then that an old woman could not keep a Nebraska farm alone, and she left for the East in February.

One man lost three hundred Rhode Island Red chickens; another lost two hundred sixty Hereford cattle and sold their hides for two dollars apiece. Hours after the Hubenka boy permitted twenty-one hogs to get out of the snowstorm and join their forty Holsteins in the upper barn, the planked floor in the cattle lintel collapsed under the extra weight and the livestock perished. Since even coal picks could no more than chip the earth, the iron-hard bodies were hauled aside until they could be put underground in April, and just about then some Pawnee Indians showed up outside David City. Knowing their manner of living, Mr.

Hubenka told them where the carcasses were rotting in the sea wrack of weed tangles and thaw-water jetsam, and the Pawnee rode their ponies onto the property one night and hauled the carrion away.

And there were stories about a Union Pacific train being arrested by snow on a railway siding near Lincoln, and the merchandisers in the smoking car playing euchre, high five, and flinch until sunup; about cowboys staying inside a Hazard bunkhouse for three days and getting bellyaches from eating so many tins of anchovies and saltine crackers; about the Omaha YMCA where shop clerks paged through inspirational pamphlets or played checkers and cribbage or napped in green leather Chesterfield chairs until the great blizzard petered out.

Half a century later, in Atkinson, there was a cranky talker named Bates, who maintained he was the fellow who first thought of attaching the word "blizzard" to the onslaught of high winds and slashing dry snow and ought to be given credit for it. And later, too, a Lincoln woman remembered herself as a little girl peering out through yellowed window paper at a yard and countryside that were as white as the first day of God's creation. And then a great white Brahma bull with street-wide horns trotted up to the house, the night's snow puffing up from his heavy footsteps like soap flakes, gray funnels of air flaring from his nostrils and wisping away in the horrible cold. With a tilt of his head the great bull sought out the hiding girl under a Chesterfield table and, having seen her, sighed and trotted back toward Oklahoma.

Wild turkey were sighted over the next few weeks, their wattled heads and necks just above the snow like dark sticks, some of them petrified that way but others simply waiting for happier times to come. The onslaught also killed prairie dogs, jackrabbits, and crows, and the coyotes that relied upon them for food got so hungry that skulks of them would loiter like juveniles in the yards at night and yearn for scraps and castaways in old songs of agony that were always misunderstood.

Addie Dillingham was seventeen and irresistible that January day of the great blizzard, a beautiful English girl in an hourglass dress and an ankle-length otter-skin coat that was sculpted brazenly to display a womanly bosom and bustle. She had gently agreed to join an upperclassman at the Nebraska School of Medicine on a journey across the green ice of the Missouri River to Iowa, where there was a party at the Masonic Temple in order to celebrate the final linking of Omaha and Council Bluffs. The medical student was Repler Hitchcock of Council Bluffs — a good companion, a Republican, and an Episcopalian — who yearned to practice electro-therapeutics in Cuernavaca, Mexico. He paid for their three-course luncheon at the Paxton Hotel and then the couple strolled down Douglas Street with four hundred other partygoers, who got into cutters and one-horse open sleighs just underneath the iron legs and girders of what would eventually be called the Ak-Sar-Ben Bridge. At a cap-pistol shot the party jerked away from Nebraska and there were champagne toasts and cheers and yahooing, but gradually the party scattered and Addie could only hear the iron shoes of the plowhorse and the racing sleigh hushing across the shaded window glass of river, like those tropical flowers shaped like saucers and cups that slide across the green silk of a pond of their own accord.

At the Masonic Temple there were coconut macaroons and hot syllabub made with cider and brandy, and quadrille dancing on a puncheon floor to songs like "Butterfly Whirl" and "Cheater Swing" and "The Girl

I Left Behind Me." Although the day was getting dark and there was talk about a great snowstorm roistering outside, Addie insisted on staying out on the dance floor until only twenty people remained and the quadrille caller had put away his violin and his sister's cello. Addie smiled and said, Oh what fun! as Repler tidily helped her into her mother's otter-skin coat and then escorted her out into a grand empire of snow that Addie thought was thrilling. And then, although the world by then was wrathfully meaning everything it said, she walked alone to the railroad depot at Ninth and Broadway so she could take the one-stop train called The Dummy across to Omaha.

Addie sipped hot cocoa as she passed sixty minutes up close to the railroad depot's coal stoker oven and some other partygoers sang of Good King Wenceslas over a parlor organ. And then an old yardman who was sheeped in snow trudged through the high drifts by the door and announced that no more trains would be going out until morning.

Half the couples stranded there had family in Council Bluffs and decided to stay overnight, but the idea of traipsing back to Repler's house and sleeping in his sister's trundle bed seemed squalid to Addie, and she decided to walk the iron railway trestle across to Omaha.

Addie was a half hour away from the Iowa railway yard and up on the tracks over the great Missouri before she had second thoughts. White hatchings and tracings of snow flew at her horizontally. Wind had rippled snow up against the southern girders so that the high white skin was pleated and patterned like oyster shell. Every creosote tie was tented with snow that angled down into dark troughs that Addie could fit a leg through. Everything else was night sky and mystery, and the world she knew had disappeared. And yet she walked out onto the trestle, teetering over to a catwalk and sidestepping along it in high-button shoes, forty feet above the ice, her left hand taking the yield from one guy wire as her right hand sought out another. Yelling winds were yanking at her, and the iron trestle was swaying enough to tilt her over into nothingness, as though Addie Dillingham were a playground game it was just inventing. Halfway across, her gray tam-o'-shanter was snagged out just far enough into space that she could follow its spider-drop into the night, but she only stared at the great river that was lying there moon-white with snow and intractable. Wishing for her jump.

Years later Addie thought that she got to Nebraska and did not give up and was not overfrightened because she was seventeen and could do no wrong, and accidents and dying seemed a government you could vote against, a mother you could ignore. She said she panicked at one jolt of wind and sank down to her knees up there and briefly touched her forehead to iron that hurt her skin like teeth, but when she got up again, she could see the ink-black stitching of the woods just east of Omaha and the shanties on timber piers just above the Missouri River's jagged stacks of ice. And she grinned as she thought how she would look to a vagrant down there plying his way along a rope in order to assay his trotlines for gar and catfish and then, perhaps, appraising the night as if he'd heard a crazy woman screaming in a faraway hospital room. And she'd be jauntily up there on the iron trestle like a new star you could wish on, and as joyous as the last high notes of "The Girl I Left Behind Me."

THE GOVERNESS

She come to us at Blythe House oh so pretty and la-di-da, saying she's the new governess like she expected a curtsy from me when she weren't no grander than a scullery maid who handled children instead of dishes. Evelyn, the christening name. A girl of twenty and waiflike she was, though with a bosom and privately tutored, her daft old father a vicar, and she the forgotten youngest of several. Yet she's putting on airs and worldliness, saying she'd bin given "supreme authority" by our gentleman Employer, her face flushing at just the mention of his name. Which naming his name seemed to me overfamiliar from a lass such as she from nothingness in Wiltshire. Well, I had seen what she'd not seen in these surroundings, worlds she'd not but imagined; however, I held my tongue and seemed ever-so-glad as she fawned over little Lily, the niece.

"And the little boy, Mrs. Gross," says she.

"Does he look like her? Is he, too, so very remarkable?"

I was fond of Liam and confessed as much, saying she'd be carried away by the lad.

She said she'd bin carried away already. She were hinting at Him on Regent Street again. The children's uncle. Little wonder in it: handsome gentleman of means and breeding. Was it she noted his gaze traveling her in the interview? The governess before, Miss Lowell, were just the same, fancying a "romantic" when he were next up from London, fancying him so altogether floored by the gift of her beauties that he couldn't help but take her as his wife. She was a scandal, Miss Lowell, so she's here no more. "You're replacing a girl as young and pretty as you," I says by way of fair warning. And I surprised myself by lying. "She's dead."

Was a joy to see the shock.

Our golden little Lily took to the new governess, for that was my sweet darling's way, but I got a trifle jealous on that score. Cook and I would watch them from the kitchen, strolling in the sunshine with Lily naming things, or the both jumping about in nonsense, feeding flowers to the pony, braiding dandelions into each other's hair, playing school games with words that required education.

Evelyn confided in me at our five o'clocks. Whingeing on about she had trouble "adjusting." Couldn't sleep. She heard pacing in the hallway in the gawp of the night. Heard a baby crying though we haven't had wee ones here in ages. But she said, too, it was worst in Wiltshire. That her father was off-kilter. Raging and all. Dodgy. "But all men are like that, aren't they?" she says. "We're attracted to the dangerous."

Electrical her eyes when she said that!

My side of the matter was I left Charity School at eight year old and after I'd done my Yellow Sampler, my mother wanting me to go to a finer school but what her never could afford. Then my father and she was dead, died just a fortnight 'twixt each other, and I was seeking employments. Hard work'd I was by housemaids who was wont to correct me quite sternly in talk, but they teach'd me how to do everything proper and even as a girl I found places. Then I happ'd upon Mr. Joe Gross. He was a postillion for Lady Boughy at Aqualate Hall and good enough looking, but a short little chap, and not steady enough nor worth having. Me being the younger, he only twitter'd and laughed at me, but still I got fond of him against myself and gots married to him in the usual way. With child. But I lost tiny Mary to rheumatic illness and Mr. Gross to accident, and I served at Henham Hall in Suffolk, Wyke Place in Shifnal, Carlton Villas in Kilburn, and in South Street, off Park Lane. At last, ten year ago I found placement in this biggish house in Essex with its splendid halls & gallery & chambers. Earning £16 per annum plus beer money & tea found & half a sovereign at Christmas, with Sundays off and Thursday nights if I ax'd leave. The Master would stop in London for months, kindly leaving us servants our board and wages so we could do as we pleased while he was gone. But we could no keep the house straight that way so it was decided I was the Mistress.

Evelyn took me back to Himself. "And has he got a Lady there?"

"Are you prying?"

She blush'd and gets shylike, but then she confessed that on her hiring he fetched a carriage for her and then rode with her to Charing Cross Station. "I never thought anything of it till he got us to a lonely place and offered to kiss me and said something about me being 'lovely in all my parts.' "

"You hanna let him kiss you, have you? Oh he's fine as a Lord, he is, but he's one of the worst rogues out."

She excused herself by saying, "I felt lonely. And after all, it's not so wicked to have a sweetheart."

"But it fits those like as us to ever recall our limitations."

She was vex'd by that and silent and her face turned stone, then she got up and made me a curtsy and left.

Weeks later, in May, the governess slit open a letter from Highgate School meant for the uncle. And she read aloud to me that Liam, scarce twelve year old, was being "dismissed" for the cause of scampishness, no doubt. Likely something he'd learnt from Peter Quincy. She made it sound worse, though; that Liam was, as she said, "contaminating" his mates, and in proof shook the letter at me as if she didn't know I lacked skill in reading. But I can con out thoughts all right and to the likes of her with no benevolence I was just a stout simple ignorant woman.

With us still in conversation, Lily come in from the schoolroom and of the immediate the governess swoop'd the child up, surprising the tyke with an excess of kisses and tears of regret for speaking billingsgate of her older brother.

A household necessary's life is full of occupations our coddled governess knew not of, and I went off to those chores. Wishing her ill. And Evelyn thinking me a friend and to be quite at one with her on every question.

Soon after, the groom brought our Liam to Blythe House in the hansom and the gardener was first to greet the boy at the north gate, then in the yard it was the dairywoman, scullion, cook, and me, all smiles and heartiness for the lad. But *she* come rushing out the house, full of passion and effort, like Liam was a husband she long thought lost in battle. She confused him with the shrieking distress and tenderness, for they'd never even met, and he gave me a secret look as he surrendered to the undueness.

In the hallway that night she nattered on about Liam and his innocence, of his being "incredibly beautiful" and full of love for all persons and things. She now found the letter from Highgate School "grotesque," if that's a word.

Says I, "You mean the nasty charge against him?"

"It doesn't live an instant! My dear woman, *look* at him!"

She took my hand as she made me vow

that as it was summer now I needn't say nothing of the instant to Him on Regent Street regarding his nephew's removal. Wanting a private talk with Liam, I asked, "Would you mind, Miss, if I used the freedom —"

She jumped to the oddest conclusion: "To kiss me? No!" And there I was in Evelyn's embrace, feeling moist contact on my forehead, my cheek, my late husband's nuzzlespot, and nothing for me to do but wait for the ending of it.

But that was just the start, for a fortnight pass'd and she told me more than once she was "infatuated" with the children, which is fine enough for their teacher, but there were also an excess of sighs and stroppy mooning about. You'd see it as she walked alone in the shades of evening. A girl imagining a lover and what the London ladies call "intimacies." I bin there and call it by franker terms.

We was up at five of each morning and there was a fire to stoke and buckets of hot water to haul upstairs for the children's baths. But she'd slam doors to hide the darlings, or she'd rush at me with wild-looking eyes if I so much as touched Liam's comb. Our Employer suffer'd financial reversals and first gave notice to the groom, then the gardener and scullion — friends I was got used to — so I prayed heartily that he'd change his mind. But go they did and it was up to me to charwoman and clean the kettles & great spits & stew pans. We was only females in the house but for Liam, and that put a few of us on edge. And as for Evelyn, she shew'd her "supreme authority" by acting ever more toffee-nosed and helping in no extra way. She happ'd on me once on my hands and knees sponging the foyer tiles, me drest in my dirt and the governess in a print lilac frock which was the loveliest could be. And as she was in a hurry, she lifted her skirts and stepp'd over me like a sleeping dog.

Yet other times she purposed to join me in front of the hearth fire at night and we'd share some old claret like chums and she joked that she was subject to what some olden poet called "moping, melancholy, and moonstruck madness." She talked about performances at the Crystal Palace, and children singing in Exeter Hall, and a book she read call'd *Adam Bede.* She also tolded me how much she lov'd her dear mother, how when she was sent to the grocer's she'd order things and run home and back again afore the man'd finish'd tying 'em up, so as she sh'dn't be no longer gone from Mama nor she ought. The girl's eyes was Wedgwood blue and dancing as she said there 'twas some of her mother in me, and I felt proud and fond and even something more.

We was chatting in just such a sweet and wholesome manner when Evelyn fancied she saw a face hanging in the fire. I couldn't see nothing but flame, but she smiles frolicsome and describes it as a handsome man with a moustache, and wasn't it an old wife's tale that she was now to meet that face? Evelyn's sisters used to say so.

Well, it just so happened after tea one twilight that Peter Quincy stopp'd by to collect his farrier tools from the shed, for he'd taken a hackney job in Chelmsford. We'd a naughty bit of history together so Quincy could be nagged into going up to the turret near the help's quarters to rake out the pigeon nests, for the cooing was driving us few staff to the brink. And then what do I spy but our governess orphaned in the gloom of the meadow and staring up the cock of the eastern tower? There Quincy was staring down with his hands on the ledge, full of himself and his general designs on the fairer sex.

She seem'd at once afraid and happy. Wondering at first if it was Himself, no doubt. And then all she shew'd was outrage at what she called "his scrutiny."

Peter Quincy had found dire trouble from our Employer before in overstepping his bounds, so he backed off from watching and rumbled down the tower stairs to my awaiting. Expecting a scold, he was surprised that I wanted to put him to use instead, and I allowed him some liberties with my person once he swore he would come back at my fetching.

Like she was ashamed of her feelings, Evelyn said nothing of the encounter at first but late that night made inquiry if there were ghosts on the premises.

"Oh, you hear talk," I told her.

She left that for teasing, but she was hiding nerves, you c'd tell, and she went the other way by prattling on about Lily's rompers and giving me no strict attention at all.

Weeks pass'd and Evelyn's uppityness and slights so got on my nerves that I posted a letter to Quincy saying he was to visit Blythe House that Sunday when staff w'dn't be about and the children w'd be upstairs with friends playing games like "Hide the Slipper" and "Puss in the Corner." All Peter had to do was stand at the dining room window of a wet late afternoon after she'd gone on an errand of mine. Wanted him to frighten Evelyn half out of her skin with his glower and then gallop off like he'd up and vanished. Just to trifle with her. We thought we'd have us a laugh.

Quincy done as told and she gasped in fine startlement. After he hied off, I watched her hike her skirts to scurry outside and onto the terrace to look for him who was gone, and then gape inside through the selfsame window. So I walked into that cold dining room of myself and, chancing to glance to the side, caught sight of her glaring in just as she'd caught sight of Peter doing. And I acted like I should faint at what I seen — the horror of it and all — and hurried away with my face in my hands.

She did not know we's having sport. She did not know she was game.

We met in the hallway and in a fright she said she'd seen an extraordinary man. Looking in. She hadn't the least idea who he was nor where he'd disappeared to.

Like I was afraid to hear it, I asked, "What's he like?"

"Rather like an actor," she said. And she goes on to say other things that could mean *anyone:* no gentleman at all, but handsome, moustached, tall, and "erect" of all things.

Of his clotheses, she described hackney

driver livery and I was all shivers as I exposed that they was most certainly once the Master's.

"You *do* know him, then?"

"Peter Quincy," I cried. "It could be no other!"

"Quincy?"

"Himself's own man, his valet, when he was here in the country."

She asked where he was now and I squared myself to firmly avouch it: "Milady, Mister Quincy is dead."

"A ghost?" she asks, a hand to her throat. She was like to faint. Sitting feeble on the Queen Anne, she crashed thoughts about and fixed on the notion that Quincy weren't seeking a pretty young thing such as she, but our little Liam.

Quincy a nonce? The wild indecency caused me to catch my breath, but liking that she was going mental, I allowed as how that could be so, saying Quincy oft bowled hoops with the boy in the garden, or took Liam with him for a horseback ride, or a fishing, with Liam carrying the creel and stool. The valet altogether forgetting his station.

"Was he too free with my boy, Mrs. Gross?"

"With everyone," I said.

She wanted to know how Peter Quincy had died, which was beyond me of the instant until I recall'd how in fact my own Joe met the Reaper. So I says Peter Quincy got his head stove in after him falling arse over elbow down a steepish slope on his totter from a public house. But that seem'd too tame, so I added that there'd bin wild disorders in his life, secret vices of which I dasn't speak.

Oh grim as winter, she announc'd that she intended to protect her little creatures from such evil.

Was only days later Lily was playing a geography game by the lake and watching over our littlun was the governess on a stone bench. And Evelyn reported that a frail lady walked out from the woods on the far side of the water and just stood there, silent as another tree, her hands lifting some like she was beckoning. Imaginating like even Lily was too old to do, Evelyn was horrified and look'd to the playing child, who she claimed was pretending to see nothing. And then the governess look'd across the lake to the fright-making visitor as she withdraw'd.

Was it a shepherdess she saw? Some farm wife strolling through the woods and, seeing she'd trespass'd, retreating? Howsoever,

Evelyn hurried back to the house and got me alone. She described the gentlewoman to me as "a figure of quite unmistakeable torment and evil." Worse, she felt sure that Lily was aware of the woman but kept that awareness secret. Then Evelyn up and decided it was the ghost of Miss Lowell, the former governess.

Had to remind meself that I'd claimed the flirt gone to the other side. I ax'd Evelyn how she knew it was Miss Lowell, having never seen her. And she said, "She gave me never a glance. She only fixed on the child. With such awful eyes and a determination indescribable. With a kind of fury of intention."

Miss Lowell wanted to get hold of Lily, the governess said. She was dressed for grieving and was almost shabby, but an extraordinary beauty she was, too, and Evelyn could tell from a glance that Miss Lowell was "infamous."

There was a full larder of meanings in that word "infamous." Miss Lowell's own heart's desire was for Himself, but gossip had it she'd also faffed about with Peter Quincy, so I yoked them, saying Miss Lowell tried to be a lady, but were too passionate and erring. Whilst Quincy was without qualities altogether.

She run with that, putting the harshest words against him.

I says, "Sheer menace, he was. He did whatever he wished."

"With *her*?"

"With them all," I says. "Womankind in general."

And she's smiling at that, fascinated.

That Him on Regent Street wished no contact from us was a certainty to all, and I further told staff they was to never discuss Miss Lowell or the former valet with the governess, she being so high-strung. But Evelyn couldn't leave the Mistress and Mister alone. I oughtn't to have let it go on but she was ever getting my dander up. Like saying I could not see all that went on between Miss Lowell and Himself's valet in the olden days because "you haven't my dreadful boldness of mind, and you keep back, out of timidity, the truth of the sinful relations between the children and those fiends."

Soon after that it occurred that the fiend of the masculine persuasion tiptoed up to my quarters upon midnight and whispered his pleadings through the door. I finally sighed and welcomed him into my bed so long as he left unseen before morning. And what should occur next but that herself chances upon him as he's escaping down the hallway? She in nothing but a nightgown and with a flaming candle like some daft heroine in a Gothic. She being a virgin, Evelyn weren't accustomed to ramrods skulking out of a chamber. Easier for her to imagine a ghost. She told me later she "reckoned" with the fiend in silence, him facing her and she him, who was "hideous," she said. And then Peter Quincy turned "as if on receipt of an order" and hurried down the staircase.

Affrighted, the governess rushed straight to the children's chambers to see if they were safe, finding Liam abed but Lily at the casement sill. She'd wak'd at the ruckus and she'd bin staring down at Quincy as he strode away in the moonlight. But Evelyn took to the notion that Miss Lowell was down there and Lily in séance with her.

Oh, I acted I believed every bit of Evelyn's report on the night's events and she rewarded my "simplicity" by saying I was "a monument to the blessing of a want of imagination."

Well, she imagined enough for two. She was blinkered on the idea of those ghosts and wouldn't shake loose of it. She went to

Liam, for example, in the lofty hours one night, in a rainstorm. Again in that night-gown, as if a schoolboy would have no interest in the female properties under the flannel.

She questioned him closely about his schooling, his badness, his past doings in Blythe House. And then, Liam confess'd to me later, he seemed to arouse in the governess such sympathy, if you could call it such, that Evelyn lay her full body upon him in bed and kissed the face of him who was not but twelve. Saying with pity, "Dear little Liam, dear little Liam," and oh so gently arranging his hair. Likely she rankled him greatly.

Then with Lily. It was fall and the weather raw and the hawthorns and oaks were un-leaving. She scared the littlun off, like as not, and she enlisted me in a pursuit. Evelyn took my hand to forthwith me to the lake, for she was sure Lily was there in converse with the ghost of Miss Lowell just as Liam was doing on the sly with Peter Quincy.

"You suppose they really *talk* to them?" I ax, just feeling her out.

Confident as a church door, she said, "They say things that, if we heard them, would simply appall us."

I could tell she feasted on such conjurings. They was her dark mints.

We slogged half the way around the lake and was footsore before we found Lily, all happy and unharmed and candid. Just a wandering child.

But what does the governess ax her? "Where, my pet, is Miss Lowell?" And Evelyn's no sooner said that than she scouts the far side of the lake. Like she was gleeful, Evelyn cried, "She's there, she's there!"

The nothingness weren't worth much more than a frazzled blink from me, but she took that as sign that I at last saw what she was seeing. Lily, though, was as children can be, and she faced the governess with a frown that Evelyn later said seemed "to read and accuse and judge me."

The governess shook the girl while screaming, "She's there, Lily, you little thing — there, there, *there,* and you know it as well as you know me!"

I couldn't let it go on. "*Where* on earth do you see anything?"

Evelyn insisted, "She's big as blazing fire!"

Worried about Lily, I took the tyke to me and said, "She isn't there, little lady. *We* know, don't we, Love? The Mistress is just mistaken. Let's you and me go home now."

And I was tugging the sweet girl away

when she turned to the governess and oh, pitched hot with anger, screamed, "I see nobody. I never *have*. I think you're cruel! I don't like you!"

"Oh now," I said. "Don't vex yourself, Lily." And we left Evelyn there.

Lily shifted her things to my quarters and she taught me funny, taxing children's games all evening. She seem'd none the worse for the afternoon emotions. But when I ax'd Lily what lessons she'd learnt from the governess, she said, "Waltzing. 'Master and Maiden.' How to kiss."

Was it envy I felt? Longing? Rivalry?

Liam heard what went on by lakeside and gallant as Lancelot sought out the governess, finding Evelyn alone in the night of the great room, sulking and shawled in front of a factual fire. In silence, he told me, he shoved over a Regency chair and took a seat beside his aching teacher. She'd excited a hankering in Liam, I'd guess. Stirrings. Enough for him just to be with her in stillness for a few hours.

Lily was fevered with ague in the morning and Evelyn and I settled that I should take the darling & her box & bundle to London and, if Him on Regent Street agreed, to join her uncle in his fancy lodgings until the weather, so to speak, were calmer. But the governess, as she admitted, would be "face-to-face with the elements," meaning the situation was not sorted out concerning Liam. I hesitated over what to do and instead of thithering to London I got Nancy, the dairywoman, to make the journey with Lily in the dray wagon.

Word had got out, and what few staff there was only stared glum at Evelyn now. And how do she react but chuff up and strut about, giving commands to all and sundry? She'd bin a laughingstock if she weren't so fretful for us.

The custom of the schoolroom was canceled and Liam, too, roam'd until half-seven that night when she and him were serv'd a joint of roast mutton. Worried about Evelyn's tendencies, I left the kitchen and slipp'd out to the terrace to stoop next to the dining room window, overhearing Liam imitating his late father in saying something jolly about the meal. And then he asked his governess, "I say, my dear, is Lily really very awfully ill?"

Evelyn told him Blythe House failed to agree with his sister. She'd find herself again in London.

Liam was about to speak when he was interrupted by Cook collecting the leftovers.

Each was silent until Evelyn volunteered in the softest voice, "We're like a couple on a honeymoon, feeling shy in the presence of the waiter."

Cook left, and he said, "We're alone now," and slunk in his chair like a full-grown man all steeped with himself. He'd of lit a cigar if he had one. Still making small talk, he told her he'd had a wonderful day. Walked ever so far in the cold. Round the entire estate. Said he'd never bin so free.

"Well, do you like it?"

"Liberty? Of course."

"I meant *this* freedom, this relaxation of our roles."

"Oh yes," he said, smiling. "It's pipping!"

Evelyn told Liam she, too, enjoyed his company. She seem'd hedging, though, and he wanted more from her. She said then, "Don't you remember how I told you, when I came to you in the night of the rainstorm, that there was nothing in the world I wouldn't do for you?"

Liam's mind looked to be reeling.

She got up and went to him and he got up, too. She fully embraced the boy as she'd never done any chap heretofore, lingering in the hug and holding his face against her bosom, inhaling deeply the scent of his hair.

Liam was wanting just to nestle against

her soft flesh as men do, but she lifted her head and found my face at the window. And like an actress in a penny melodrama, she held out a finger of accusation and scream'd, "There the fiend is! The author of our woe!"

She was yelling other things, but I heard no more. I just walked away.

She'd have to be given warning. She'd have to go. Blythe House failed to agree with her. But I found myself feeling jealous of the family what would have her next. To have the benefit of such frenzy, fear, and excitement.

She'd be, I knew, much loved.

PLAYLAND

After the agricultural exhibit of 1918, some partners in a real-estate development firm purchased the cattle barns, the gymkhana, the experimental alfalfas and sorghums, the paddocks and pear orchards, and converted one thousand acres into an amusement park called Playland. A landscape architect from Sardinia was persuaded to oversee garden construction, and the newspapers made much of his steamship passage and arrival by train in a December snow, wearing a white suit and boater. Upon arrival he'd said, "It is chilly," a sentence he'd practiced for two hundred miles.

He invented gardens as crammed as flower shops, glades that were like dark green parlors, ponds that gently overlipped themselves so that water sheeted down to another pond, and trickle streams that issued from secret pipes sunk in the crannies of rocks. Goldfish with tails like orange scarves hung in the pools fluttering gill fins or rising for crumbs that children sprinkled down. South American and African birds were freighted to Playland, each so shockingly colored that a perceiver's eyes blinked as from a photographer's flash. They screamed and mimicked and battered down onto ladies' hats or the perch of an index finger, while sly yellow canaries performed tricks of arithmetic with green peas and ivory thimbles. Cats were removed from the premises, dogs had to be leashed, policemen were instructed to whistle as they patrolled "so as not to surprise visitors to the park at moments of intimacy."

The corn pavilion was transformed into trinket shops, two clothing stores, a bank, a bakery where large chocolate-chip cookies were sold while still hot from the oven, and a restaurant that served cottage-fried potatoes with catfish that diners could snag out of a galvanized tank. The carnival galleries were made slightly orange with electric arc lights overhead, as was the miniature golf course with its undulating green carpets — each hole a foreign country represented by a fjord, pagoda, minaret, windmill, pyramid, or the like. The Ferris wheels and merry-go-rounds were turned by diesel truck engines that were framed with small barns and insulated lest they allow more than a grandfatherly noise; paddlewheel craft with bicycle pedals chopped down a slow, meandering river. Operas and starlight concerts were staged from April to October, and the exhibition place was redecorated at great cost for weekend dances at which evening gowns and tuxedos were frequently required. A pretty ice-skating star dedicated the ballroom, cutting the ribbon in a hooded white mink coat that was so long it dragged dance wax onto the burgundy carpet. A newspaper claimed she'd been tipsy, that she'd said, "You got a saloon in this place?" But after a week's controversy an editor determined that the word she'd used was "salon," and later the entire incident was denied, the reporter was quietly sent away, and the newspaper grandly apologized to the Playland management.

Lovers strolled on the swept brick sidewalks and roamed on resilient lawns that cushioned their shoes like a mattress, and at night they leaned against the cast-iron lampposts, whispering promises and nicely interlocking their fingers. Pebbled roads led to nooks where couples were roomed by exotic plants and resplendent flowers whose scent was considered an aphrodisiac, so that placards suggesting temperance and restraint were tamped into the pansy beds.

The park speedily rose to preeminence as the one place in America for outings, holidays, company picnics, second honeymoons, but its reputation wasn't truly international until the creation of the giant swimming pool.

Construction took fourteen months. Horse stables were converted to cabanas, steam-powered earth movers sloped the racetrack into a saucer, the shallows and beach were paved, and over twenty thousand railroad cars of Caribbean sand were hauled in on a spur. The pool was nearly one mile long, more than half of that in width, and thirty-six feet deep in its center, where the water was still so pellucid that a swimmer could see a nickel wink sunlight from the bottom. Twelve thousand gallons of water evaporated each summer day and were replaced by six artesian wells feeding six green fountains on which schooling brass fish spouted water from open mouths as they seemed to flop and spawn from a roiling upheaval.

And the beach was a marvel. The sand was as fine as that in hotel ashtrays, so white that lifeguards sometimes became snow-blind, and so deep near the soda-pop stands that a magician could be buried in it standing up, and it took precious minutes for a crew with spades to pull him out when his stunt failed — he gasped, "A roaring noise. A furnace. Suffocation." Gymnasts exercised on silver rings and pommel horses and chalked parallel bars, volleyball tournaments were played there, oiled muscle men pumped dumbbells and posed, and in August girls in saucy bathing suits and high heels walked a gangway to compete for the Miss Playland title. Admission prices increased each season, and yet two million people and more pushed through the turnstiles at Playland during the summers. Playland was considered pleasing and inexpensive entertainment, it represented gracious fellowship, polite surprise, good cheer. The Depression never hurt Playland, cold weather only increased candy sales, rains never seemed to persist for long, and even the periodic scares — typhoid in the water, poisonous snakes in sand burrows, piranha near the diving platform — couldn't shrink the crowds. Nothing closed Playland, not even the war.

Soldiers on furlough or medical release were allowed free entrance, and at USO stations on the beach, happy women volunteers dispensed potato chips and hot dogs on paper plates, sodas without ice, and pink towels just large enough to scrunch up on near the water. Young men would queue up next to the spiked iron fence at six o'clock in the morning when a camp bus dropped them off, and they'd lounge and smoke and squat on the sidewalk reading newspapers, perhaps whistling at pretty girls as the streetcars screeched past. As the golden gates whirred open, the GIs collided and jostled through, a sailor slapped a petty officer's cap off, and little children raced to the teeter-totters and swings as Playland's nursemaids applauded their speed.

The precise date was never recorded, but one morning a corporal named Gordon limped out of the bathhouse and was astonished to see an enormous pelican on the prow of the lifeguard's rowboat. The pelican's eyes were blue beads, and she swung her considerable beak to the right and left to regard Gordon and blink, then she flapped down to the beach and waddled toward him, her wings amorously fanning out to a span of ten feet or more as she struck herself thumpingly on the breast with her beak until a spot of red blood appeared on her feathers. The corporal retreated to the bathhouse door and flung sand at the bird and said, "Shoo!" and the pelican seemed to resign herself and lurched up into eastward flight, her wings loudly swooping the air with a noise like a broom socking dust from a rug on a clothesline.

More guests drifted out of the bathhouse. Children carried tin shovels and sand pails. Married women with bare legs and terry-cloth jackets walked in pairs to the shade trees, sharing the heft of a picnic basket's straw handle. Pregnant women sat on benches in cotton print dresses. Girls emerged into the sun, giggling about silly nothings, their young breasts in the squeeze of crossed arms. On gardened terraces rich people were oiled and massaged by stocky women who spoke no English. Dark waiters in pink jackets carried iced highballs out on trays. A perplexed man in an ascot and navy-blue blazer stood near the overflowing food carts with a dark cigarette, staring down at the pool. Red and yellow hot-air balloons rose up from the apricot orchard and carried in the wind. A rocket ship with zigzag fins and sparking runners and a science-fiction arsenal screamed by on an elevated rail. Children were at the portholes, their noses squashed to the window glass like snails.

A girl of seventeen sat on the beach with her chin in her hands, looking at the mall.

Her name was Bijou. A rubber pillow was bunched under her chest and it made her feel romantic. She watched as her boyfriend, the corporal named Gordon, limped barefoot away from a USO stand in khaki pants belted high at his ribs, a pink towel yoking his neck, a cane in his left hand. He dropped his towel next to Bijou's and squared it with his cane's rubber tip. He huffed as he sat and scratched at the knee of his pants. He'd been a messenger between commanders' posts in Africa and rode a camouflaged motorcycle. A mine explosion ruined his walk. Bijou wondered if she was still in love with him. She guessed that she was.

Bijou knelt on her beach blanket and dribbled baby oil onto her thighs. Her white swimming suit was pleated at her breasts but scooped revealingly under her shoulder blades so that pale men wading near her had paused to memorize her prettiness, and a man with a battleship tattoo on his arm had sloshed up onto the hot sand and sucked in his stomach. But Gordon glowered and flicked his cane in a dispatching manner and the man walked over to a girls' badminton game and those in the water lurched on.

"My nose itches," Bijou said. "That means someone's going to visit me, doesn't it?"

"After that pelican I don't need any more surprises," Gordon replied, and then he saw an impressive shadow fluctuate along the sand, and he looked heavenward to see an airplane dip its wings and turn, then lower its flaps and slowly descend from the west, just over a splashing fountain. His eyes smarted from the silver glare of the steel and porthole windows. The airplane slapped down in a sudden spray of water, wakes rolling outward from canoe floats as it cut back its engines and swung around. The propellers chopped and then idled, and a door flapped open as a skinny young man in a pink double-breasted suit stepped down to a rocking lifeguard's boat.

"Must be some bigwig," said Gordon.

The airplane taxied around, and Bijou could see the pilot check the steering and magnetos and instruments, then plunge the throttle forward, ski across the water, and wobble off. The rowboat with the airplane's passenger rode up on the beach and retreated some before it was hauled up by a gang of boys. The man in the pink suit slipped a dollar to a lifeguard and hopped onto the sand, sinking to his ankles. As he walked toward Bijou he removed a pack of cigarettes and a lighter from his shirt pocket. His pants were wide and pleated and he'd cocked a white Panama hat on his head. He laid a cigarette on his lip and grinned at Bijou, and arrested his stride when he was over her.

"Don't you recognize your cousin?"

She shaded her eyes. "Frankie?"

He clinked his cigarette lighter closed and smiled as smoke issued from his nose. "I wanted to see how little Bijou turned out, how this and that developed."

"I couldn't be more surprised!"

He'd ignored the corporal, so Gordon got up, brushing sand from his khakis, and introduced himself. "My name's Gordon. Bijou's boyfriend."

"Charmed," Frankie said. He removed his hat and wiped his brow with a handkerchief. His wavy hair was black and fragrantly oiled and he had a mustache like William Powell's. He had been a radio actor in New York. He asked if they served drinks on the beach, and Gordon offered to fetch him something, slogging off to a soda-pop stand.

"Sweet guy," Frankie said. "What's he got, polio or something?"

"He was wounded in the war."

"The dope," Frankie said. He unlaced his white shoes and unsnapped his silk socks from calf garters and removed them. He slumped down on Gordon's towel, unbuttoning his coat.

"You're so handsome, Frankie!"

"Ya think so?"

"I can't get over it. How'd you find me at Playland?"

"You're not that hard to pick out," Frankie said, and he gave his cousin the once-over. "You look like Betty Grable in that suit."

"You don't think it's too immodest?"

"You're a feast for the eyes."

The corporal returned with an orange soda and a straw. Frankie accepted it without thanks and dug in his pocket for a folded dollar bill. "Here, here's a simoleon for your trouble."

"Nah," Gordon said. "You can get the next round."

Frankie sighed as if bored and poked the dollar bill into the sand near Gordon's bare left foot. He leaned back on his elbows and winked at someone in the pool. "Somebody wants you, Sarge."

"Say again?"

"Two dames in a boat."

A rowboat had scraped bottom, and two adolescent girls with jammy lipstick, Gordon's sister and her girlfriend, motioned for him to come over. Gordon waded to where the water was warm at his calves and climbed darkly up his pant legs. "What're you doing, Sis?"

"Having fun. Where's Bijou?"

"On the beach, Goofy."

His sister strained to see around him. 'Where?'

He turned. Bijou and Frankie had disappeared.

Frankie strolled the hot white sand with his cousin and sipped orange soda through the straw. Hecklers repeatedly whistled at Bijou and Frankie winked at them. "Hear that? You're the berries, kid. You're driving these wiseacres off their nut."

"Oh, those wolves do that to any female."

"Baloney!" He was about to make a statement but became cautious and revised it. "What am I, nine years older than you?"

"I think so," Bijou said.

"And what about GI Joe?"

Bijou glanced over her shoulder and saw her boyfriend hunting someone on the beach. Gordon squinted at her and she waved, but he seemed to look past her. "He's twenty-one," she said.

"Four years older. What's he doing with a kid like you for his bim?"

"He's mad about me, stupid."

Frankie snickered. He crossed his ankles and settled down in the bathhouse shade.

Bijou sat next to him. Frankie pushed his cigarette down in the sand and lit another, clinking his lighter closed. "Do you and Gordo smooch?"

Bijou prodded sand from between her toes. "Occasionally."

"How shall I put it? You still Daddy's little girl?"

"You're making me uncomfortable, Frankie."

"Nah, I'm just giving you the needle."

The corporal was confused. His nose and shoulders were sunburned and his legs ached and Bijou and Frankie had flat-out evaporated. His sister and her girlfriend stroked the rowboat ahead and Gordon sat on the rim board near a forward oarlock, scouting the immeasurable Playland beach. Soon his sister complained that she was tired and bored and blistered, and Gordon said, "All right already. Cripes — don't think about me. Do what you want to do."

After a while Frankie clammed up and then decided he wanted a little exercise and removed his tie and pink coat as he walked past the USO stand to the gym equipment. He performed two pull-ups on the chalked high bar, biting his cigarette, then amused a

112

nurse in the first-aid station with his impressions of Peter Lorre, Ronald Colman, Lionel Barrymore.

"I love hearing men talk," the nurse said. "That's what I miss most."

"Maybe I could close this door," Frankie said.

"You can't kiss me, if that's what you're thinking. I'm not fast."

"Maybe I should amscray, then."

"No!" the nurse said, and shocked herself with her insistence. "Oh, shoot." She turned her back and walked to the sickbed. "Go ahead and close the door."

Anchored in Playland's twenty-foot waters were five diving platforms fixed as star points radiating out from a giant red diving tower with swooping steel buttresses and three levels, the topmost being a crow's nest that was flagged with snapping red pennants. It reached one hundred feet above the surface and was closed off except for the professionals paid to somersault dangerously from the perch at two and four in the afternoon, nine o'clock at night.

And there Gordon had his sister and her girlfriend row him after he'd wearied of looking for Bijou. The boat banged into a steel brace, and the corporal left his cane and walked off the board seat to a ladder slat. He ascended to the first elevation and saw only shivering children who leaned to see that the bottom was unpopulated, then worked up their courage and leapt, shouting paratrooper jump calls. At the second elevation was a short man with gray hair and a very brief suit and skin nearly chocolate brown. The man paused at the edge, adjusting his toes, and then jackknifed off, and Gordon bent out to see him veer into the water sixty feet down. Gordon wanted to recoup, to do something masculine and reckless and death-defying. He yelled to the platform below him, "Anybody down there?" and there was no answer. Then he saw a woman in a white bathing suit like Bijou's underwater near the tower. Her blond hair eddied as she tarried there below the surface. Gordon grinned.

His sister and her girlfriend were spellbound. They saw Gordon carefully roll up his pant cuffs and yank his belt tight through his brass buckle clasp. They saw him simply walk off the second level into a careening drop that lasted almost two seconds. A geyser shot up twenty feet when he smacked the water, then the surface ironed out and his sister worried; finally he burst up near the boat.

"Something's down there!"

"What is?"

"Don't know!" Gordon swam over, wincing with pain, and when he gripped the boat, blood braided down his fist.

Bijou strapped on a white rubber bathing cap and pushed her hair under it as she tiptoed on the hot sand. She splashed water onto her arms and chest, and then crouched into the pool and swam overhand toward a rocking diving platform. It floated on groaning red drums that lifted and smacked down and lifted again as boys dived from the boards. Bijou climbed a ladder and dangled her legs from a diving platform carpeted with drenched rope. She removed her cap, tossed her blond hair, ignored the oglers who hung near the ladder. Her breasts ached and she wished Gordon could somehow rub them without making her crazy.

The diving platform had sloped because a crowd took up a corner, staring toward the diving tower. Bijou saw that the ferry had stopped and that its passengers had gathered at the rail under the canopy, gaping in the same direction. Four lifeguards hung on a rowboat, struggling with something, as a policeman with a gaff hook stood in the boat and Gordon clinched the anchor lock

115

with a bandaged right hand. Gordon! Two swimmers disappeared underwater, and the policeman hooked the gaff and they heaved up a black snapping turtle as large as a manhole cover and so heavy that the gaff bowed like a fishing rod. The turtle's thorny neck hooked madly about and its beak clicked as it struck at the gaff and its clawed webs snagged at whatever they could, as if they wanted to rake out an eye. Bijou's boyfriend manipulated a canvas mailbag over the turtle's head and nicked it over the turtle's horned shell. The policeman heard a woman shriek, then saw the hubbub and the astonished crowds on the ferry and diving platforms, and he kicked the turtle onto the boat's bottom and said, "Hide it. Hurry up, hide it."

That night the exhibition palace burned so many lightbulbs that signs at the gate warned visitors not to linger too close to the marquee or stare at the electrical dazzle without the green cellophane sunglasses available at the ticket booth. Limousines seeped along an asphalt cul-de-sac that was redolent with honeysuckle, violets, and dahlias, and at least forty taxicabs idled against the curb, the drivers hanging elbows out or sitting against their fenders. Gordon stood on a sidewalk imbedded with gold sparkle and laced his unbandaged fingers with Bijou's as Frankie ostentatiously paid for their admission. Then Bijou left for the powder room with her evening gown in a string-tied box, a pair of white pumps in her hand.

Frankie sauntered inside with Gordon, commenting on the sponge of the burgundy lobby carpet, the vast dance floor's uncommon polish, the vapored fragrances shot overhead from jet instruments tucked into the ceiling's scrolled molding. Bijou's two escorts selected a corner cocktail table and listened to the Butch Seaton Orchestra in sleepy, mopey solitude, without criticism or remark. Then Bijou glided down the ballroom stairs in her glamorous white gown, looking like Playland's last and best creation, Playland's finishing touch, and the men rose up like dukes.

Gordon danced with her and Frankie cut in. Frankie murmured at her ear over sodas, and Gordon asked Bijou to accompany him to the dance floor. The three bandied conversations during breaks, then music would start and they'd detach again. Male hands sought Bijou's hands as she sat; songs were solicited for her from the orchestra; Gordon fanned a napkin near her when it warmed.

By ten o'clock the great ballroom was jammed. Young marines introduced themselves and danced with uneasy strangers, a sergeant danced with a hatcheck girl, some women danced with each other as the Butch Seaton Orchestra played "Undecided," "Boo Hoo," "Tangerine." Bijou stood near the stage, her boyfriend's hand at her back, his thumb independently diddling her zipper as a crooner sang, "I love you, there's nothing to hide. It's better than burning inside. I love you, no use to pretend. There! I've said it again!" Sheet music turned. A man licked his saxophone reed. The crooner retreated from the microphone as woodwinds took over for a measure. A mirrored sunburst globe rotated on the ceiling, wiping light spots across a man's shoulder, a woman's face, a tasseled drape, a chair. The orchestra members wore white tuxedos with red paper roses in their lapels. Gordon's fingers gingered up Bijou's bare back to her neck, where fine blond hairs had come undone from an ivory barrette. Bijou shivered and then gently swiveled into Gordon, not meaning to dance but moving with him when he did. His shoes nudged hers, his khaki uniform smelled of a spicy aftershave that Bijou regretted, his pressure against her body made her feel secure and loving.

The music stopped and Gordon said, "Let's ditch your cousin."

"How mean!"

"The guy gives me the creeps."

"Still."

Gordon thumped his cane on the floor and weighed his hankerings. "How about if you kissed me a big sloppy one right on my ear?"

Bijou giggled. "Not *here.*"

"Maybe later, okay?"

Butch Seaton gripped his baton in both hands and bent into a microphone as a woman in a red evening dress with spangles on it like fish scales crossed to the microphone that the crooner was readjusting lower with a wing nut. The orchestra leader suggested, "And now, Audrey, how about Duke Ellington's soulful tune, 'Mood Indigo'?"

Audrey seemed amenable.

Bijou asked, "I wonder where Frankie is."

"Maybe he was mixing with his kind and somebody flushed him away." The corporal's little joke pleased him, and he was near a guffaw when his nose began to bleed. He spattered drops on his bandaged hand and Bijou's wrist and shoe before he could slump, embarrassed, on a chair with a handkerchief pressed to his nostrils. He remarked, "This day is one for the record books, Bijou. This has been a really weird day."

Bijou complained that she was yukky with Gordon's blood, and she slipped off to the powder room. Gordon watched her disappear among the couples on the dance floor, and then Frankie flopped down on a folding chair next to him.

"How's the schnozzola?" Frankie asked. Gordon removed the handkerchief, and Frankie peered like a vaudeville doctor. "Looks dammed up to me." He slapped Gordon's crippled knee. "I hereby declare you in perfect health. Come on, let's drink to it."

Frankie showed him to a gentleman's saloon, and Gordon paid for a rye whiskey and a Coca-Cola with a simoleon that had grains of sand stuck to it. The Playland glassware was, of course, unblemished with water spots.

Frankie said, "I was a radio actor in New York before the war. I'm coming back from a screen test in Hollywood. Another gangster part. That's about all I do: gunsels, crooks, schlemiels."

"No kidding," the corporal said. He rebandaged his right hand and sulked about his miserable afternoon.

Frankie stared at an eighteenth-century painting of a prissy hunter with two spaniels sniffing at his white leggings, a turkey strangled in his fist. "What a jerk, huh? Here I am, horning in on your girl, and I expect chitchat from you."

"Well, don't expect me to be palsy-walsy. I'll shoot the breeze, okay. But I'm not about to be your pal just because you're Bijou's cousin from Hollywood and radio land."

Frankie scrooched forward on his bar stool. "You oughta see things with my eyes. You take Bijou, for instance. She's a dish, a real hot patootie in anybody's book, but she ain't all she wrote, Gordo, not by a long shot. You and Bijou, you come to Playland, you dance to the music, swallow all this phonus-balonus, and you think you've experienced life to the hilt. Well, I got news for you, GI. You haven't even licked the spoon. You don't know what's out there, what's available." Frankie slid off the bar stool and hitched up his pink pleated pants. "You want a clue, you want a little taste of the hot stuff, you call on Cousin Frankie. I gotta go to the can."

Gordon hunched over his Coca-Cola glass and scowled down into the ice, then swiveled to call to Frankie as he left the saloon, but the schlemiel wasn't there.

Gordon was loitering in the burgundy lobby, slapping his garrison cap in his hand, when Bijou came out of the powder room. He asked, "Do you want to see the moon?"

"Where's Frankie?"

"Who cares?"

A great crush of partygoers were pushing against the lobby's glass doors, yelling to get in, each wearing green cellophane sunglasses. Gordon and Bijou exited and a couple was admitted; screams rose and then subsided as the big door closed.

The two strolled past a penny arcade, a calliope, a gypsy fortune-teller's tent, a lavender emporium where chimpanzees in toddler clothes roller-skated and shambled. At a booth labeled Delights, Bijou observed a man spin apples in hot caramel and place them on cupcake papers to cool, and she seemed so fascinated that the corporal bought her one. Bijou chewed the candied apple as they ambled past the stopped rocket ship, an empty French café, a darkened wedding chapel. They walked near pools where great frogs croaked on green lily pads that were as large as place mats, and gorgeous flowers like white cereal bowls drifted in slow turns. The couple strolled into gardens of petunias, loblolly, blue iris, philodendrons, black orchids. Exciting perfumes craved attention, petals detached and fluttered down, a white carnation shattered at the brush of Bijou's hem and piled in shreds on the walk, the air hummed and hushed and whined. Cat's-eye marbles layered a path that veered off into gardens with lurid green leaves overhead, and this walk they took with nervous stomachs and the near panic of erotic desire. The moon vanished and the night cooled. Creepers overtook lampposts and curled up over benches; the wind made the weeping willows sigh like a child in sleep. Playland was everywhere they looked, insisting on itself.

Then Gordon and Bijou were boxed in by black foliage. The corporal involved himself with Bijou and they kissed as they heard the orchestra playing the last dance. Bijou shivered and moved to the music and her boyfriend woodenly followed, his cane slung from a belt loop, his bandaged right hand on her hip. Her cheek nuzzled into his shoulder. His shoes scruffed the grass in a two-step. The music was clarinets and trombones and the crooner singing about heartache, but under that, as from a cellar, Bijou could pick out chilling noises, so secret that they could barely be noticed: of flesh ripped from bone, claws scratching madly at wood, the clink of a cigarette lighter.

Bijou felt the corporal bridle and cease dancing, and then start up again. He danced her around slowly until she could see what he'd seen, but Bijou closed her eyes and said, "Forget about him. Pretend he's not there."

THE KILLERS

His name is Rex. He says he was fifteen his very first time, and says his boss flew back in his chair like he'd been hit in the chest with a fence post. Rex says he worked in the basement wash rack until he got his chance, then he slapped the chamois twice across the hood and watched the boss close up. The garage door rang down on chain pulleys, then the boss rode the belt lift up to his office. Rex opened the car door and lay across the transmission hump to jerk the shotgun out from under the springs. He zipped up his cracked leather coat and rode the lift up to the parking lot's office. He punched himself out on the time clock, wrapped the shotgun up in coveralls, and slid it under the bench. His boss, who was Art, had his pants unbelted, unzipped, tucking in his shirt. He said good night. This was 1960.

Rex walked up the hill to the lunchroom.

And down by the auditorium, Ron dropped a cigar at his shoe. Ron was the man who got him the job. Rex says the cigar ash blew red across the sidewalk.

At the lunchroom, Rex ate a fried ham on rye. It used to be a trolley, the lunchroom. Green and yellow and too much light. A man at the end of the counter licked egg yolk off his plate. Rex drank milk until the news came on, then paid the cook with two bills and told him thanks for the change. And no tip.

The guy who got him the job was still down the street. He bent over the match in his hand. Cigar smoke sailed up when he lifted his head. Ron gave him the go-ahead.

Rex stood next to the time clock with the shotgun in his hands and the coveralls on his boot tops. The time clock chunked through four minutes, and I guess Rex thought about how some things would stop and some things would just be beginning. He walked to the office in his stocking feet. When he opened the door, Art looked up.

"I thought you were gone," Art said.

Rex swung the shotgun up and dropped it down on the desktop, cracking the glass. He centered the barrel some with his hip. Art grabbed for it quick and then pitched back in a mess while the big noise shook the windows and gray smoke screwed up to the overhead vent. The chair was pushed back three inches. You could see the skid on the tiles. Art sat there like he was worn-out, his glasses cockeyed on his face. Rex turned out the lights. Luckily he saw how his socks picked up the dirt, so he got out a mop and washed the floor, then put on his boots and locked up. He leaned the shotgun next to the drainpipe and walked down the hill, his hands clasped on top of his stocking cap.

Ron dropped the envelope out of his pocket and was gone.

It was in 1940 that Max leaned across the seat and opened the car door. The man at the corner stooped and looked at him, holding his coat flaps together. "You, huh?"

"Get in."

They drove in silence for a while. Al bit a cuticle and looked at his finger. Al got a cigarette out and lit it with the green coil lighter from the dashboard. The smoke rolled up the window glass and out through the opening where it was chopped off by the wind. At a stoplight Al said, "Look at my hands." He held them, shaking, over the dash. "Would you look at that?"

Max said, "To tell you the truth, I'm a little jumpy too."

The man's eyes were glassy. "You know what I've always been scared of ever since I can remember? I was always afraid I'd wet my pants."

Max smiled.

Al looked out the window. "You think it's funny, but it's not."

"I'll let you relieve yourself first. How would that be?"

"That'd be sweet."

They worked in and out of traffic and found a parking place. Al got out and straightened his coat. He pressed his hair in place in the window reflection. Max got out, flattening a gray muffler against his chest, then buttoning his black wool coat. He put his key in the door and turned it. They both wore light-colored homburg hats. Al tied both his shoes on the bumper.

"How far is it?" he asked.

"Three blocks."

They walked in step on the sidewalk. Max held his hat in the wind.

"What are you using?"

"The Smith and Wesson." He put up the collar on his coat. "That okay with you?"

"Oh, that's just swell, Max. You're a real buddy."

Al stopped to light another cigarette. He coughed badly for a long time, leaning with

128

his arms against a building, hacking between his shoes, then wiping his mouth with a handkerchief. Al shoved his hands in his pockets and hunched forward. The cigarette hung from his lip. "Cold, that's all." Smoke steamed over his face. "I feel it in my ticker when I cough."

"You ought to have it looked at," Max said.

"You're a regular funny boy today, aren't ya?"

They turned left at the corner and walked into a lunchroom that used to be a trolley. A bell jingled over their heads. They sat on stools at the counter and ordered coffee and egg salad sandwiches. They were the only customers.

"Do you remember the Swede?"

Max nodded.

The counterman turned over the sign that read CLOSED, then got out a broom and began sweeping the floor. He swept under their feet as they ate. Max turned on his stool.

"Is there a place where a fella could get a newspaper?"

"There's a booth at the corner," the counterman said.

Max handed him a dollar bill that the counterman put in his shirt pocket. "Which one you want?"

"Make it the *Trib.*"

He rested his broom against the counter. "Walk slow."

When the counterman was out the door, Al put down his cup of coffee. "He coulda stayed."

"I know."

"I personally like having people around. Afterward they'll begin to imagine things and get you all wrong in their heads."

Max used a toothpick on all of his teeth. Al put two sticks of chewing gum into his mouth. He crumpled up the wrappers.

"You know how it works," Max said. "You get the call and she says do this, do that. What do you say? She got the wrong number? You do what you have to do. Nothing personal about it." He looked at Al's face in the mirror behind the counter. "What am I telling you this for? You know all the rules." Max got off his stool. "You said you wanted to visit the men's room."

They walked to the back of the place, Max following behind. He stood on a chair to switch on a small radio and turn it up loud. Then he went into the gray lavatory where Al was washing his hands and face. He looked at Max in the spotted mirror. Max was pushing down the fingers of his gloves.

He asked, "What'd you do, anyway?"

Al shrugged. "I started taking it easy." He dried his hands with his handkerchief. "I burned myself out as a kid. I lost my vitality."

Max opened his coat. "Do you want to sit down?"

The man sat down under the sink.

Max crouched close, reaching into his shoulder holster. "Waiting's the worst of it. You don't have to do that now." He felt for the heartbeat under Al's shirt, and Al watched him press the Smith and Wesson's muzzle there. Max fired once and the body jerked dead. The arms and legs started jiggling. They were still doing that when Max walked out and closed the men's room door.

He's short, for one thing, so the cuffs on his jeans are rolled up big and he folds a manila paper up four times to put in the heels of his boots. He chews gum instead of brushing his teeth like he should, and pulls his belt so tight that there're tucks and pleats everywhere. He washes his hair with hard yellow soap, then it's rose oil or Vitalis, and he combs it sometimes three or four times before he gets it right. He keeps aspirin in his locker. He says he falls asleep each night with a washrag on his forehead. He punched a tattoo in himself with a ball-point pen, but it's only a blue star on his wrist and mostly his watch covers it. You can go through school and see his name everywhere: REX on a wall painted over in beige, REX on the men's room door, REX on a desk seat bottom when it's up, REX ADAMS stomped out in the snow. He eats oranges at lunch — even the peel! — and gets Ds in all his subjects, including music and phys ed. If he comes to sock hops, he just stands there like a squirrel, or like he's waiting for lady's choice. He's always giving me the eye. Especially when I wear dresses. He doesn't have a father or listen to records or play sports. He was the first one in school with a motorcycle, which is chrome and black and waxed and which he saved up for with money from the parking lot. His favorite pastime is collecting magazine pictures, but there's only one taped over his bed; it's from the fifties, from *Life,* about a gangster washed up out of Lake Michigan and swelled up yeasty in his clothes. He says the thing he remembers most is the way the blood seeped into the creases of Art's pants and dripped to the floor like out of a tap when it's not tight. He's got a gun. He's the only Rex in school. He's not cute at all. His shirts all smell like potatoes.

■ ■ ■ ■

The Swede? That's an old story.

Max had dressed at the hotel window.
Leaves rattled in the alley. He crossed his
neck with a silk muffler and buttoned a
black overcoat tightly across his chest and
put on gloves and a derby hat. He met the
other man on the street. They both held
their hats as they walked.

"I see you got it," Max said.

The man, whose name was Al, said nothing but kept one hand in his pocket.

"Good," Max said.

This was many years ago. This was 1926.

They sat at the counter of Henry's lunchroom facing the mirror. A streetlight came
on outside the window. There was a counterman and a black cook and a kid in a cracked
leather jacket and cap at the far end of the
bar. He had been talking with the counterman when they came in.

Max read the menu and ordered pork
tenderloin, but they weren't serving that
until six. They were serving sandwiches. He
ordered chicken croquettes but that was
dinner too.

"I'll take ham and eggs," Al said.

"Give me bacon and eggs," said Max.

They ate with their gloves on, then Al got down from his stool and took the cook and the boy back to the kitchen and tied them up with towels. Max stared in the mirror that ran along the back of the counter. Al used a catsup bottle to prop open the slit that dishes passed through into the kitchen.

"Listen, bright boy," Al said to the kid. "Stand a little further along the bar."

Then he said, "You move a little to the left, Max."

For a while Max talked about the Swede. He said they were killing him for a friend.

At six fifteen a streetcar motorman came in, but he went on up the street. Somebody else came in, and the counterman made him a ham and egg sandwich and wrapped it up in oiled paper.

"He can cook and everything," Max said. "You'd make some girl a nice wife."

Max watched the clock. At seven ten, when the Swede still hadn't shown, Max got off his stool. Al came out from the kitchen hiding the shotgun under his coat.

"So long, bright boy," Al said to the counterman. "You got a lot of luck."

"That's the truth," Max said. "You ought to play the races."

They went out the door and crossed the street.

"That was sloppy," Al said.

"What about where he lives?"

"I don't know this town from apples."

They sat down on the stoop of a white frame house. Inside, a man and woman were leaning toward a crystal radio. There were doilies on their chairs, and the man slapped his knee when he laughed. Part of a newspaper blew past Max's shoes. He snatched it and opened it up. Al nudged him when the kid in the leather jacket came out of Henry's. They followed the kid up beside the car tracks, turned at the arc light down a side street, and stood in the yard across from Hirsch's rooming house. The kid pushed the bell and a woman let him in.

"The Swede'll come out looking for us," Al said.

"No he won't," Max said. "He'll just sit there and stew."

Al stared across at the second-story window.

After a while the downstairs door opened again and the woman said good night. The kid walked up the dark street to the corner under the arc lights, and then along the car tracks to Henry's lunchroom.

The two men crossed over to the rooming-house yard. Al stepped over a low fence and

135

went around the back. Max walked up the two steps and opened the door. He stood in the hallway and listened and then he climbed a flight of stairs. He softly walked back to the end of a corridor. Al came up the rear stairs from the kitchen. He unbuttoned his coat and cradled the shotgun.

Max knocked on the door but there wasn't an answer.

He turned the handle and pushed the door with his toe. They walked in and closed the door behind them. The Swede was lying on a bed with all his clothes on, just staring at the wall. He used to be a prizefighter and was too long for the bed. He turned to look at them and Al fired.

Rex got the call on a Thursday. His mom was just home from work at the grocery store and he was in his T-shirt and jeans eating a TV dinner and reading a newspaper spread over the ottoman and not paying me any attention. His mom called him to the phone, said it was some man. Ron, it must've been. He put his finger in his ear and turned with the phone, but he still had to ask the guy to repeat this and that. Rex went ahead and jotted everything down on the calendar from church, then tore off the month and folded it up to fit in his leather-braid wallet. Then he sat down on the couch and belched, he's so uncouth. He looked at his TV dinner with the crumb custard still in the dish. Then he got up to run the sink faucet over it and stuff the tray down in the trash. His mom was cooking at the electric range when he was in there. She moved the teakettle onto another coil and dried her hands on her apron and turned around, kind of smiling. He swung his hand back like he was going to slap her, and she screamed and hid under her arms. When he didn't hit her and just grinned instead, she walked right out of the kitchen, heavy on her heels. She was careful around him the majority of the time. You couldn't help but notice.

So Max was an old man now, with a trimmed white beard and brown eyes and size-eleven shoes and trouble sleeping nights. He combed his thin hair forward to hide his bald spot. His face was baked red from the sun, his shirts were open at the collar, and he could no longer drink wine. When he last met the man in the black suit, they talked about quail hunting and heavy-weight boxing and fishing for marlin off the Keys. Then the man passed a paper to Max, which he signed with a strong cross to the

X and a period at the end of his name. They sent a check twice a year. As he stood up he said, "Let me defend the title against all the good young new ones."

He woke early to stand at his easel and paint still lifes, like Cézanne's. They gave him a lot of trouble. The colors were never right. He stacked them in a closet when they were dry. At noon he left the room and walked the city streets or shopped for his evening meal. Or he would sit in the park with a stale loaf of bread and tear up pieces for the pigeons. At night he sat in the stuffed purple chair and listened to German music. Or he wore his reading glasses and slowly turned the pages of art books about Degas or Braque or Picasso.

But windows he'd closed were opened. Books he'd left open were closed. And he sat in the back of a bus and saw a runty kid on a black motorcycle changing lanes, spurting and braking in traffic. He wore goggles and big-cuffed jeans. The kid saw him staring and gave him the finger. Max read his newspaper.

Then Max saw him again at dinner in the lunchroom downstairs. Max ordered the meat loaf special, and the kid walked his machine to the curb. He sat on it, looking at a map. Every now and then he'd wipe his nose on his sleeve.

The coffee was cold. Max told the waitress and she filled a new cup.

"And give me a piece of whatever pie you've got."

"We've got apple and banana cream."

"Whatever's freshest."

She brought him banana cream.

"That your boyfriend out there?"

"Where?"

He pointed.

"Never seen him before."

"He seems to be waiting for somebody."

"He's reading a map. Maybe he's lost."

"Yeah. And maybe he's waiting for somebody."

He wiped his face with a napkin and threw it down. Then he pulled up his pants and went outside.

"Hey!"

The kid was looking at the letters along the right, then the numbers across the top. He tried to put the two lines together.

"Hey, bright boy. You looking for me?"

"What?"

"Do you want me?"

He squirmed in his seat. "No."

Max slapped the map from his hands. It fluttered, then folded in the wind and was blown against a tire.

139

Max grinned and took a step forward, making fists. The kid hopped off the cycle and into the street. Max put his shoe on the gas tank and pushed. The cycle crashed to the pavement. The back wheel spun free.

The old man was about to tear some wires loose when the kid spit at him. Max straightened slowly and the kid spit again. Max took a few steps back, frowning at the spot on his pant leg, stumbling off balance, and the kid climbed over the cycle, hacking and working his cheeks. Then he spit again, and it struck Max on the cheek.

The old man backed against the building and took out his handkerchief. "Get outa here, huh? Just leave." He slowly sank to the sidewalk and mopped his face. The kid picked up his cycle.

"That's a dirty, filthy thing to do to anybody," Max said.

The kid started his cycle, then smiled and said, "Oh, you're gonna be easy."

Rex poked a jar of turpentine and it smashed to smithereens on the floor. Then he went and ran his arm recklessly along the top of a chest of drawers and everything — hairbrush, scissors, aerosol cans — spilled to the floor in a racket. There was also a mug of pencils and brushes on a drawing table and he shook them out like pickup sticks. He ripped the sheets off the bed and wadded them up. And he dumped out all the drawers.

We came back at dark and saw the roomer in just his undershirt and slacks, wiping the turpentine up with a paper towel. He was big and had a white beard and he used to be good-looking, you could tell. He looked like he might've been a prizefighter or something.

"There was a guy looking for you," Rex says.

Max was gathering the pencils and brushes and tapping them together. He didn't even notice me there.

"He looked pretty dangerous," Rex says.

Max just dropped pieces of glass in a trash can. They clanged on the tin. He struggled to his feet like a workingman with a chunk of pavement in his hands. He looked for just a second at Rex, then he went to the chest of drawers and began picking up clothes.

The kid sat down at the lunchroom counter and unzipped his cracked leather coat. From the other end of the counter Max watched him. He had been talking to the waitress when the door opened. The waitress gave the kid water and a menu. The kid rubbed his knees with his hands as he read. He said, "I'll have a roast pork tenderloin with applesauce and mashed potatoes."

"Is that on the menu?"

"I've changed my mind," the kid said. "Give me chicken croquettes with green peas and cream sauce and mashed potatoes."

The waitress didn't know what to say.

The kid smiled, and then he stopped smiling. He flicked the menu away. "Just give me ham and eggs."

She wrote on her order pad. "How do you want your eggs?"

"Scrambled."

The waitress spoke through the wicket to the cook. The kid put his chin in his hand. He turned his water glass.

Max stared as he drank from his coffee cup and set the cup down in the saucer. The kid jerked his head.

"What are *you* looking at?"

Max put a quarter next to his cup. "Nothing."

Max went to the coat tree. He pulled off a mackinaw jacket and buttoned it on. The kid was swiveled around on his stool. "The hell. You were looking at *me*."

The waitress had gone through the swinging door in the kitchen. Max blew his nose in a handkerchief. He smiled at the kid. "You're not *half* of what I was."

The kid smiled and leaned back on the counter. "But I'm what's around these days."

It will happen this way:

He'll kick at the door and it will fly open, banging against the wall. Max will be at his easel. He'll try to stand. The kid will hold his gun out and fire. Max will slump off his stool. He'll spill his paints. He'll slam to the floor.

Or Max will open the door and the kid will be to his left. He'll ram the pistol in Max's ear. He'll hold his arm out straight and fire twice.

Or he'll rap three times on the door. When it opens, he'll push his shotgun under Max's nose. Max will stumble back, then sit slowly on the bed, where he'll hold his head in his hands. The kid will close the door softly behind him. Max will say, "What are you waiting for?" and the kid will ask, "Where do you want it?" Max will look up, and the kid's gun will buck and the old man will grab his eyes.

Or the kid will let the pistol hang down by his thigh. He'll knock on the door. Max will answer. The kid will step inside, shoving the old man. The pistol will grate against Max's belt buckle until he's backed to the striped bedroom wall. The kid will fire three times, burning the brown flannel shirt. Smoke will crawl up over the collar. The old man will slide to the floor, smearing red on the wall behind him.

Or the door will open a crack. Max will peer out. The kid will shoot, throwing him to the floor. The kid will walk into the room. Max will crawl to a chair, holding his side. He'll sit there in khakis and a blue shirt going black with the blood. He'll say, "I think I'm gonna puke." The kid will say, "Go ahead." He'll say, "I gotta go to the bathroom." He'll pull himself there with the bedposts. Water will run in the sink. He'll come out with a gun. But the kid will fire, and Max's arm will jerk back, his pistol flying. He'll spin and smack his face against a table in his fall.

Or Max will jiggle his keys in one hand while the other clamps groceries tight to his buttoned gray sweater. He'll open the door. The kid will be sitting there in the purple chair by the brushes with a shotgun laid over his legs. The old man will lean against the doorjamb. The groceries will fall. The kid will fire both barrels at the old man's face, hurling him back across the hall.

Apples will roll off the rug.

Rex took a wad of rags from a barrel in the garage while I sat against his mom's car brushing my hair. He unwrapped a gun and wiped it off with his shirttail. He sat against his motorcycle seat and turned the chamber round and round, hearing every click. Then he got cold without a coat and covered the gun again and crammed it down his pants. He gave me a weird look. He said, "Ready?"

Max tried to sleep but couldn't. He got up and put on a robe, then took a double-barrel shotgun from the closet, and two shells from a box in one of the drawers. He sat in a stuffed chair by his brushes, lowered the gun butt to the floor, and leaned forward until his eyebrows touched metal. Then he tripped both triggers.

Rex was just about to climb the stairs when he heard the shotgun noise. He just stood there sort of blue and disappointed until I took his hand and pulled him away and we walked over to the lunchroom. Ron was there in a booth in the back. He'd had the pork tenderloin. We sat in the booth with him and as usual he told me how pretty I looked. Rex just sulked, he was so disappointed.

"You should be happy," Ron said.

"Do I still get the money?"

Ron nodded. He was grinning around a cigar. He pushed an envelope across the table.

Rex just looked at it. "Then I guess I *am* happy."

"You should be."

Rex stuffed the envelope inside his coat pocket. Everybody was quiet until I spoke up and said, "I just can't stand to think about him waiting in the room and knowing he's going to get it. It's too damned awful."

Rex looked at me strangely. Ron knocked the ash off his cigar. "Well," he said, "you better not think about it."

NEBRASKA

The town is Americus, Covenant, Denmark, Grange, Hooray, Jerusalem, Sweetwater — one of the lesser-known moons of the Platte, conceived in sickness and misery by European pioneers who took the path of least resistance and put down roots in an emptiness like the one they kept secret in their youth. In Swedish and Danish and German and Polish, in anxiety and fury and God's providence, they chopped at the Great Plains with spades, creating green sod houses that crumbled and collapsed in the rain and disappeared in the first persuasive snow and were so low the grown-ups stooped to go inside; and yet were places of ownership and a hard kind of happiness, the places their occupants gravely stood before on those plenary occasions when photographs were taken.

And then the Union Pacific stopped by, just a camp of white campaign tents and a boy playing his harpoon at night, and then a supply store, a depot, a pine water tank, stockyards, and the mean prosperity of the twentieth century. The trains strolling into town to shed a boxcar in the depot side-yard, or crying past at sixty miles per hour, possibly interrupting a girl in her high-wire act, her arms looping up when she tips to one side, the railtop as slippery as a silver spoon. And then the yellow and red locomotive rises up from the heat shimmer over a mile away, the August noonday warping the sight of it, but cinders tapping away from the spikes and the iron rails already vibrating up inside the girl's shoes. She steps down to the roadbed and then into high weeds as the Union Pacific pulls Wyoming coal and Georgia-Pacific lumber and snow-plow blades and aslant Japanese pickup trucks through the open countryside and on to Omaha. And when it passes by, a worker she knows is opposite her, like a pedestrian at a stoplight, the sun not letting up, the plainsong of grasshoppers going on and on between them until the worker says, "Hot."

Twice the Union Pacific tracks cross over the sidewinding Democrat, the water slow as an oxcart, green as silage, croplands to the east, yards and houses to the west, a green ceiling of leaves in some places, whirlpools showing up in it like spinning plates that lose speed and disappear. In winter and a week or more of just above zero, high-school couples walk the gray ice, kicking up snow as quiet words are passed between them, opinions are mildly compromised, sorrows are apportioned. And Emil Jedlicka unslings his blue-stocked .22 and slogs through high brown weeds and snow, hunting ring-necked pheasant, sidelong rabbits, and — always suddenly — quail, as his little brother Orin sprints across the Democrat in order to slide like an otter.

July in town is a gray highway and a Ford hay truck spraying by, the hay sailing like a yellow ribbon caught in the mouth of a prancing dog, and Billy Awalt up there on the camel's hump, eighteen years old and sweaty and dirty, peppered and dappled with hay dust, a lump of chew like an extra thumb under his lower lip, his blue eyes happening on a Dairy Queen and a pretty girl licking a pale trickle of ice cream from the cone. And Billy slaps his heart and cries, "Oh! I am pierced!"

And late October is orange on the ground and blue overhead and grain silos stacked up like white poker chips, and a high silver water tower belittled one night by the sloppy tattoo of one year's class at George W. Norris High. And below the silos and water tower are stripped treetops, their gray limbs still lifted up in alleluia, their yellow leaves crowding along yard fences and sheeping along the sidewalks and alleys under the shepherding wind.

Or January and a heavy snow partitioning the landscape, whiting out the highways and woods and cattle lots until there are only open spaces and steamed-up windowpanes, and a Nordstrom boy limping pitifully in the hard plaster of his clothes, the snow as deep as his hips when the boy tips over and cannot get up until a little Schumacher girl sitting by the stoop window, a spoon in her mouth, a bowl of Cheerios in her lap, says in plain voice, "There's a boy," and her mother looks out to the sidewalk.

Houses are big and white and two stories high, each a cousin to the next, with pigeon roosts in the attic gables, green storm windows on the upper floor, and a green screened porch, some as pillowed and couched as parlors or made into sleeping rooms for the boy whose next step will be the Navy and days spent on a ship with his hometown's own population, on gray water that rises up and is allayed like a geography of corn-fields, sugar beets, soybeans, wheat, that stays there and says, in its own way, "Stay." Houses are turned away from the land and toward whatever is not always, sitting across from each other like dressed-up children at a party in daylight, their parents looking on with hopes and fond expectations. Overgrown elm and sycamore trees poach the sunlight from the lawns and keep petticoats of snow around them into April. In the deep lots out back are wire clotheslines with flapping white sheets pinned to them, property lines are hedged with sour green and purple grapes, or with rabbit wire and gardens of peonies, roses, gladiola, irises, marigolds, pansies. Fruit trees are so closely planted that they cannot sway without knitting. The apples and cherries drop and sweetly decompose until they're only slight brown bumps in the yards, but the pears stay up in the wind, drooping under the pecks of birds, withering down like peppers until their sorrow is justly noticed and they one day disappear.

Aligned against an alley of blue shale rock is a garage whose doors slash weeds and scrape up pebbles as an old man pokily swings them open, teetering with his last weak push. And then Victor Johnson rummages inside, being cautious about his gray sweater and high-topped shoes, looking over

paint cans, junked electric motors, grass
rakes and garden rakes and a pitchfork and
sickles, gray doors and ladders piled overhead in the rafters, and an old windup Vic-
trola and heavy platter records from the
twenties, on one of them a soprano singing
"I'm a Lonesome Melody." Under a green
tarpaulin is a wooden movie projector he
painted silver and big cans of tan celluloid,
much of it orange and green with age, but
one strip of it preserved: of an Army pilot
in jodhpurs hopping from one biplane onto
another's upper wing. Country people
who'd paid to see the movie had been
spellbound by the slight dip of the wings at
the pilot's jump, the slap of his leather
jacket, and how his hair strayed wild and
was promptly sleeked back by the wind. But
looking at the strip now, pulling a ribbon of
it up to a windowpane and letting it unspool to the ground, Victor can make out
only twenty frames of the leap, and then
snapshot after snapshot of an Army pilot
clinging to the biplane's wing. And yet
Victor stays with it, as though that scene of
one man staying alive were what he'd paid
his nickel for.

Main Street is just a block away. Pickup
trucks stop in it so their drivers can angle
out over their brown left arms and speak

about crops or praise the weather or make up sentences whose only real point is their lack of complication. And then a cattle truck comes up and they mosey along with a touch of their cap bills or a slap of the door metal. High-school girls in skintight jeans stay in one place on weekends, and jacked-up cars cruise past, rowdy farmboys overlapping inside, pulling over now and then in order to give the girls cigarettes and sips of pop and grief about their lipstick. And when the cars peel out, the girls say how a particular boy measured up or they swap gossip about Donna Moriarity and the scope she permitted Randy when he came back from boot camp.

Everyone is famous in this town. And everyone is necessary. Townspeople go to the Vaughn Grocery Store for the daily news, and to the Home Restaurant for history class, especially at evensong when the old people eat graveled pot roast and lemon meringue pie and calmly sip coffee from cups they tip to their mouths with both hands. The Kiwanis Club meets here on Tuesday nights, and hopes are made public, petty sins are tidily dispatched, the proceeds from the gumball machines are tallied up and poured into the upkeep of a playground. Yutesler's Hardware has picnic items and kitchen appliances in its one window, in the manner of those prosperous men who would prefer to be known for their hobbies. And there is one crisp, white, Protestant church with a steeple, of the sort pictured on calendars; and the Immaculate Conception Catholic Church, grayly holding the town at bay like a Gothic wolfhound. And there is an insurance agency, a county coroner and justice of the peace, a second-hand shop, a handsome chiropractor named Koch who coaches the Pony League baseball team, a post office approached on unpainted wood steps outside of a cheap mobile home, the Nighthawk tavern where there's Falstaff tap beer, a green pool table, a poster recording the Cornhuskers scores, a crazy man patiently tolerated, a gray-haired woman with an unmoored eye, a boy in spectacles thick as paperweights, a carpenter missing one index finger, a plump waitress whose day job is in a basement beauty shop, an old woman who creeps up to the side door at eight in order to purchase one shot glass of whiskey.

And yet passing by, and paying attention, an outsider is only aware of what isn't, that there's no bookshop, no picture show, no pharmacy or dry cleaners, no cocktail parties, extreme opinions, jewelry or piano stores, motels, hotels, hospital, political headquarters, philosophical theories about Being and the soul.

High importance is only attached to practicalities, and so there is the Batchelor Funeral Home, where a proud old gentleman is on display in a dark brown suit, his yellow fingernails finally clean, his smeared eyeglasses in his coat pocket, a grandchild on tiptoes by the casket, peering at the lips that will not move, the sparrow chest that will not rise. And there's Tommy Seymour's for Sinclair gasoline and mechanical repairs, a green balloon dinosaur bobbing from a string over the cash register, old tires piled beneath the cottonwood, FOR SALE in the sideyard a Case tractor, a John Deere reaper, a hay mower, a red manure spreader, and a rusty grain conveyor, green weeds overcoming them, standing up inside them, trying slyly and little by little to inherit machinery for the earth.

And beyond that are woods, a slope of pasture, six empty cattle pens, a driveway made of limestone pebbles, and the house where Alice Sorensen pages through a child's World Book Encyclopedia, stopping at the descriptions of California, Capetown, Ceylon, Colorado, Copenhagen, Corpus Christi, Costa Rica, Cyprus.

Widow Dworak has been watering the lawn in an open raincoat and apron, but at nine she walks the green hose around to the spigot and screws down the nozzle so that the spray is a misty crystal bowl softly baptizing the ivy. She says, "How about some camomile tea?" And she says, "Yum. Oh, boy. That hits the spot." And bends to shut the water off.

The Union Pacific night train rolls through town just after ten o'clock when a sixty-year-old man named Adolf Schooley is a boy again in bed, and when the huge weight of forty or fifty cars jostles his upstairs room like a motor he'd put a quarter in. And over the sighing industry of the train, he can hear the train saying *Nebraska, Nebraska, Nebraska, Nebraska.* And he cannot sleep.

Mrs. Antoinette Heft is at the Home Restaurant, placing frozen meat patties on waxed paper, pausing at times to clamp her fingers under her arms and press the sting from them. She stops when the Union Pacific passes, then picks a cigarette out of a pack of Kools and smokes it on the back porch, smelling air as crisp as Oxydol, looking up at stars the Pawnee Indians looked at, hearing the low harmonica of big rigs on the highway, in the town she knows like the palm of her hand, in the country she knows by heart.

THE SPARROW

She'd been flying a Cessna, shooting practice takeoffs and landings with a flight instructor at an Omaha airstrip that was just a wind sock and one lane of unnumbered concrete runway veined with tar repairs. Richard Nixon was president, the month was September, the temperature was sixty degrees, and she was Karen Manion, mother of two. The flying lessons were a gift from her husband for her fortieth birthday. The flight instructor was a gruff, retired warrant officer named Billy who claimed he'd flown everything the Army had, from fixed wings to Chinooks. Within a week Karen would take the flight test to get her private pilot's license, and she'd told her husband a night earlier that Billy was trying to prepare her for it by pulling stunts that some examiners were known to do, hiding flight plans and cross-country maps, or forcing the plane too steep in its climb so that the horn warned of a stall. Yesterday Billy had watched Karen's face with a confident smile as she recovered from a hammerhead spin. And now as she ran the Cessna up to sixty-five miles per hour, eased back on the yoke, and felt the plane lift up from the runway, the front window would have filled with skies that were the blue of old jeans, nothing more, and she probably glanced at the vertical speed and turn-and-bank indicators before she noticed that Billy's hand was on the plunger throttle and suddenly jerking it back, cutting the power. Karen was supposed to immediately push down the nose to maintain air speed, but she may have glared with shock and insult at Billy or screamed a question about what he thought he was *doing,* and in that hesitation the Cessna fell forty or fifty feet. The stall horn would have blared and Billy would have lunged for the control yoke as he hurriedly said, "I've got it," giving the plane full throttle as he tilted the nose down. But they'd fallen too far and they would have seen skid marks on concrete rushing up into the front window fast as the Cessna crashed into the runway, very hard.

Karen's son, Aidan, was twelve years old and he was at home hitting a shag bag of golf balls into a peach basket with his father's chrome-bright sand wedge when he heard the kitchen telephone and ran inside to answer it. "Oh, Aidan," Kelli, their neighbor, said, not sounding right. She paused and with some strain asked, "Is Lucy there?"

Lucy was fifteen, his older sister, so he first thought his mother's friend was hunting a babysitter. "She's at a friend's house," he said.

Kelli seemed to be crying. A hand seemed to clench her throat. "Would you go get her, honey? And then I'll come get you both."

"Why?"

She told him there had been an accident and his mother was at Immanuel, nothing more.

Aidan found Lucy four houses down the street. She and Molly were lying on the floor of the yellow living room, Lucy's head pillowed by Molly's stomach as she read aloud from Dylan Thomas's *Adventures in the Skin Trade.* Wildly giggling at the prose, Lucy tried to go on, but Molly's stomach bulged with laughter too and Lucy yelled in pretend anger, "You're jiggling the pages!" Molly guffawed, rolling away and holding her waist with both crossed arms, and Lucy caught sight of Aidan in his loneliness of grief. She got up on an elbow and she quieted as she stared. "What's happened?"

"Mom's hurt," Aidan said.

Kelli drove them to Immanuel Hospital. She told them their father had been contacted at work and that he was already there when he phoned her. The flight instructor had been killed in the accident.

"His name was Billy," Aidan said.

Kelli looked at him in the rearview mirror and said, "Billy. Thank you." She tried to give them further information, but she ran out quickly; there was too much she'd only be guessing at, and so she just held on to the steering wheel tightly as she raced through yellow lights. Aidan sat in the backseat, mutely watching as tears trickled down Kelli's cheek and she wiped them with her palm. She blurted an embarrassed laugh as she said, "I'm such a rock."

Lucy reached across and gave a sisterly touch to her hand. "That's okay."

Kelli was driving them through a cathedral of shade made by stately elm trees. Aidan looked outside at a boy half his age wobbling down the sidewalk on a bicycle too big for him. And there on a porch a mother was watching too, a hand to her mouth,

161

imprisoning her warnings. But still the boy did not fall.

At Immanuel, a nurse told Aidan and Lucy that their father had gotten there in time to accompany the gurney as their mother was rushed upstairs into surgery. Mrs. Manion was in a coma. The head and chest wounds were "traumatic." Kelli went down the hallway to the banks of telephones and Aidan and Lucy sat next to each other on hard plastic chairs in the uncoziness of the waiting area, saying nothing, staring at the floor. Aidan's thoughts were discontinuous, furious, forlorn, like a child's Crayola scribble on the wall, and when he heard Lucy whisper, "Are you praying?" he felt convicted.

"Uh-huh," he said.

"Me too," Lucy said, and she surprised him by holding his hand in hers. "She'll live," Lucy said. "She's got to."

He was shocked that he hadn't yet considered the fact that his mother could die from the injuries. With great urgency, Aidan silently recited the prayers he'd memorized in religion class, prayers he'd say hurriedly, his heart hammering, whenever he woke up from a nightmare. But he was convinced more was expected now, some plea, some contract, a way of prevailing against the grim odds with earnest promises that he'd be good, say a rosary every day, even become a priest, if only God would let his mother live. *Please, God,* he prayed, *don't let my mom die. I need her.*

And then they saw their father at the far end of the hallway, walking toward them in hospital scrubs with a friend who was an orthopedic surgeon. Aidan got up from his chair just as his sister did, but when he saw Lucy freeze and fail to run forward, he stayed as he was too. He took it as a good sign that there were no bloodstains on either of the men, but he noticed their solemnity. Dr. Welter's stare drifted from Aidan's to the floor. When their father was a few feet away, he quietly said, "Hi, kids." Lucy forgot her pretense of calm and flung herself into him, her face in his chest as she screeched her misery. Worn-out, red-eyed, seemingly lost, Emmett Manion held her and kissed her head as she wept, then petted her hair and said, "Shh now. Shh."

Lucy screamed, "I don't want to shh! I'm *sad!*"

Their father looked at Aidan and held out his left arm. Aidan fitted himself under it and his father kissed his head too. The hospital scrubs smelled of medicines, like a bathroom cabinet. The wing tip of his father's left shoe shone with a coin of moisture. His strong chest swelled as he forced himself to inhale. "She's gone, kids," he told them.

Lucy fell to her knees on the floor and wailed. And Aidan felt childish and empty and impossibly stupid, for he'd at first thought his father meant she'd gotten well and left the hospital. But he hadn't said "dead," he'd said "gone." Wouldn't he have said "dead" if she was dead? She wasn't, maybe.

Kelli had found cold cans of Coca-Cola for them and was strolling toward them in the hallway. But Aidan saw her halt when she saw his father. His face must have communicated with a great deal of accuracy, for she sank into a chair and folded over and cried.

The funeral was hard, but harder were the sentiments afterward as swarming people tried to console them. Either it was a touch of assurance and a sighed confession of mystery, as in "His ways are not our ways," as if with fathomless ulterior motives God coldly intended the crash; or they'd pat Lucy's or Aidan's hands while confiding in faith that much good would come from this, as if their mother's death were a lesson they would not have learned otherwise.

Classmates stood far away from them, hollowed and ill at ease, as if death were contagious. Even lofty, fearsome Monsignor Florio fell out of character, his soft handshake holding fast to Emmett Manion's as he instructed, "Saint Augustine wrote, '*Non enim fecit atque abiit*,' meaning, God did not just make us and go away. We have a personal relationship with Him. Whatever happens to us, good or bad, it is equally as important to God."

Aidan's father shamed his son by weakly answering, "Thank you, Monsignor," seeming no older than twelve himself.

But hours later he found Aidan in his room and a football in the crook of his arm. Emmett worked up a smile as he asked, "How about throwing the oblate spheroid around?"

There was a competition over their father for a while. Kelli kept showing up with her little children and a casserole, a pan of fudge, a lasagna, and Lucy fumed, wordlessly ate, and afterward referred to Kelli as "The Divorcée." Even in her embarrassment at vying for their father's attentions, Kelli would find a reason to stay around

165

until Emmett got home, and then they would drink chardonnay in coats on the patio as Aidan whacked his Wiffle ball against the garage door and Lucy played desultory games of Candy Land inside with the children.

But then there must have been an earnest nighttime conversation that Lucy and Aidan didn't hear, for with fall's unleaving Kelli stopped stopping by.

Still his sister cried for hours on end. Wherever she could in her room, Lucy hung old photographs of Karen from high-school yearbooks, from the scrapbook *Our Wedding,* from the obituary in the *Omaha World-Herald.* She researched her mother's injuries and hung up a framed poster on "The Anatomy of the Brain." She reread her mother's handwritten sentiments in the birthday cards she'd collected over the years and constructed a kind of shrine around a snapshot from her mother's fortieth birthday party: the one where Karen Manion smiled as she held up a small plastic Cessna airplane in her right hand, and in her left a gift certificate for flying lessons. Wedged in a corner of the photograph was a slip of paper on which Lucy had written: "I will not leave you orphaned . . . John 14:18."

Lucy lost weight. She forgot tests and

homework. Wouldn't answer Molly's phone calls. She confided in her father, shared errands with him, and flew into his embrace when he got home from work, as if she'd been storing up those tears. She said she often dreamed about her mother and gladly reported the dreams at breakfast, but neither Aidan nor her father could invent the correct reply. Out of the blue she told Aidan once, "She wants you to sign up for sixth-grade basketball. She says you'll be good at it." And then she wept and fell into him and Aidan held her as his father did, patting her jerking back awkwardly, but not saying "There, there."

Their father was stoic about it. Strong for them. Each Sunday evening Emmett wrote out the week's schedules and chores. Listed grocery store items, his obligations at work, things that still needed to be done. Everybody was very careful with each other and avoided any harsh words. They were responsible for their own laundry now, shared the dishwashing chores, and once there was a rigorous inspection of their rooms, but he forgot to continue most of the other programs he established.

Aidan once wandered into the bedroom he still thought of as his mother's, though only his father slept there now. Nothing had changed since September. His mother's clothing still hung in the closet — a faint hint of her sweat in her gardening shirt, a faint trace of Chanel in a cocktail dress. And hair was still in her hairbrush; her creams, conditioners, and cleansing lotions were like a cityscape on the mirrored counter in the master bathroom.

Was that healthy, having her present like that? Lucy was continually emotional, but Aidan noticed his father's grief only once, when he woke up in the middle of the night and saw him out in the late November cold of the backyard, coatless, facing nothing at all, and weeping so like a child that Aidan himself wept with him.

Some friends from Emmett's office visited the house in December to toast his promotion. Each was introduced to the children, but Aidan remembered only the pretty secretary's name: Gayl, with a *y.* His jealousy confused him. His father cooked ribeye steaks on the outdoor grill as fat snowflakes fluttered down and decomposed on the patio bricks. Everyone seemed too loud. Homework took Lucy and Aidan up to their rooms after dinner, but Aidan came out after an hour and crouched on the landing, his knees in a hug, to listen in on the conversation. Only Gayl had stayed and she was contrasting their father with her ex, lavishing praise on Emmett, telling him how crucial he was to the company, what a pleasure it was to watch him succeed, and how much his friendship meant to her. Could he see how lonely she'd been?

Aidan's father said nothing.

And then she asked, "Are you aware I love you . . . passionately?"

Sheez, who talks like that? Aidan thought.

Emmett flatly told her, "Yes, I know how you feel."

Aidan held his hands over his ears as he got up to go back to his room. But then he saw his sister standing there behind him, listening too, and far more interested than Aidan in whatever happened next. She chose to defend her father in advance, whispering to Aidan, "He's human, you know."

Aidan entered his room, shut the door, and, just in case, tuned his radio between stations so he couldn't hear anything but a hissing, crackling noise, like tires on their cinder alley. A half hour later, however, he rose above the white forest of frost on his window to see Gayl hurrying to her Volvo with her face in her hands, as if she were holding it on, and he wasn't sure how he felt about that.

The assistant pastor in their parish was Father Jim Schwartz. He was handsome, humorous, in his late twenties, and all the schoolgirls got desperate and dreamy looks whenever he was around. Aidan's father said of his preaching that "he really gets you thinking," but the tone was that of a criticism. And Aidan's mother once joked that he was "Father What-a-Waste." Aidan misunderstood until she told him she meant it was a shame Father Schwartz could never marry. "The good husbands," she said, "are always taken."

Aidan had never visited the old rectory, no one his age ever did. It was like tempting the porch of a haunted house. He was an altar boy and one morning had to go to the kitchen door to get a cruet of wine from the old Belgian cook, and he'd seen the wide back of Monsignor Florio at the kitchen table, his black suit coat off and his trousers held up by crossed suspenders as he smeared jam on a slice of toast. Aidan was shocked by that secret look, his violation of the fathers' hard-won privacy, and the cook shooed him away as soon as she'd poured the red Cribari wine.

And yet one afternoon after sixth-grade basketball practice, his hair still wet and stiffening in the cold, Aidan went to the front door of the rectory and Father Schwartz himself answered the four-toned bell. Without his Roman collar and in his sneakers and jeans and Creighton sweatshirt, Schwartz could have been the high-school senior who coached them. Smiling as if he'd just heard a joke, Schwartz said, "Hi."

With hesitation Aidan asked, "Could I talk to you?"

"Is this confessional matter?"

Aidan wasn't sure and said no.

"It's my day off," the assistant pastor said, but he invited him in. "I'm trying to remember your name."

"Aidan Manion."

"Oh, right. Let's go to the parlor."

Schwartz strode jauntily to a hot, musty front room that was wallpapered in shades of lavender and was congested with ornate furniture that seemed at least a century old. He fell nonchalantly into an overstuffed chair and Aidan put his gym bag on the floor as he sat on the edge of a plush sofa cushion. Schwartz crossed his ankle-high black sneakers on an ottoman. "You're a fifth grader, right?"

"Sixth."

"Sister Josefina?"

Aidan nodded.

"So what's up?"

"You knew my mom died?"

"Oh gosh, I forgot. I'm so, so sorry, Aidan. I was racking my brain."

"That's okay."

"Is that what this is about?"

"She was really nice," Aidan said. "She never did anything wrong."

Sins of Aidan's own started vagrantly populating his thoughts.

"And you're wondering why she died?"

"Sort of."

The priest's right elbow was on the arm of the chair and his right cheek was against his knuckles, as in a book jacket photograph illustrating wise consideration. "The psalmists asked it long ago," he said. "Why do the evil prosper? Why do the innocent suffer? Why, when a loved one is dying, doesn't God intercede? Those are philosophical questions and they fall under a category called theodicy."

"I'm just twelve," Aidan said.

Even in winter there, sunlight hurled itself through the southern windows and formed hatchings of shadow on the floor. Aidan's right shoe was untied but he didn't fix it.

Schwartz linked his fingers on top of his head. His hair was Christ-long, the fashion then, and Aidan had heard older parishioners joke about it. Schwartz gazed outside at huddling girls scuttling against the wind as he told the boy, "There was an eighteenth-century Scottish philosopher named David Hume who said that our experience of the world contradicted our conception of God, because if God allowed evil to exist, He was not all good; or if evil was loose in the world and God was unable to counteract it, He was not omnipotent. Evil, for Hume, demolished God, and he became an atheist. But he raises good questions. Because sometimes it does seem God has lost interest in us. Children starve. Wars rage on. Illness goes the wrong way too often. I get a phone call and a lady says she's gotten a death sentence from her doctor and she cries, 'Why me?' I just look at Jesus hanging there on the crucifix and want to say, 'Why *not* you?' Are you following me?"

"Sort of," Aidan said, even though he was lost. Each sentence seemed less like a window and more like a shutting door.

"We have to let God be God," the priest said.

The conclusion felt overly routine. *It's my day off,* he'd said. "But my sister and my dad and me. We ache."

Schwartz's head jerked as if he'd been insulted, but his frown gradually soothed. "Hey, I'm sorry, Aidan. I was off in systematic theology and you're there with a cosmic knee in your gut. I'm no help at all, am I?"

"You helped."

"Really? How?"

His question felt intentionally difficult and unfair, but his face was sincere. "I guess just talking," Aidan said. "Hearing about other people."

"So you don't feel so alone," Schwartz said.

"Uh-huh."

"Are you feeling responsible — that she died?"

Aidan felt accused. "Why?"

"Sometimes people do."

Aidan gripped his gym bag and stood up. "Is your mom still alive?"

"Yes." Schwartz stood too, seeming puzzled. "Are we finished?"

"I have a long walk home. And it's getting cold."

Classes started again in January. Each week that year the sixth graders had been visited by parents in differing occupations for their "What I Want to Be" project, and now Emmett Manion was there to explain accounting while Sister Josefina hunched at a back desk correcting their English homework.

The clanging radiators in the old brick grade school were generally too hot in winter, and on that near-zero afternoon there was a kind of sauna in their second-story classroom. Sister Josefina noticed aloud that the children were becoming dull, and Aidan's father opened the upper half of the four tall windows with a long, hooked pole. Waterfalls of cold air poured in.

Aidan's father returned to the accounting lesson, chalking a ledger page on the blackboard and printing in capitals "DEBITS" and "CREDITS." But then a sparrow flew in through one upper window opening, wildly looping around overhead like a frantic bat so that Aidan's classmates ducked down and covered their hair with their hands. One girl squealed, and Sister Josefina held her textbook overhead and swatted at the bird, trying to shoo it toward the window opening. But still the sparrow insanely circled and veered and swooped, hunting a way out, bashing into window-panes, increasingly harassed and scared by every screech and waving arm.

At last, Emmett Manion told the class, "Let's try this, kids. Why don't we all quietly leave the room?" And staring over their heads at the thrashing bird, he held the door open in an official way as the class and Sister Josefina filed out. When the thirty of them were in the school hallway, Aidan's father let him and a few others look through the window in the classroom door.

Aidan watched the sparrow flapping its wings in a panicky swirl, but as quiet took over the room, the sparrow calmed and cruised the four corners of the classroom until it felt the chill from the foot-high opening in an upper window and with a sudden swerve was flying into the immensity of outdoors.

Emmett Manion said nothing as he softly stared out at nothing at all, but Sister Josefina smiled and said, "Let us resume."

Aidan filed back inside with the others. His father never mentioned it, and Aidan didn't tell Lucy because he wanted it for himself: that feeling of friendship with the silence he had been hearing but had not understood.

RED-LETTER DAYS

JAN 25. Etta still poorly but up and around. Hard winds all day. Hawk was talking. Helped with kitchen cleanup then shop work on Squeegee's fairway woods. Still playing the Haigs I talked him into in 1963. Worth plenty now. Walked up to post office for Etta's stamps. $11.00! Went to library for William Rhenquist's book on Court and Ben Hogan's *Five Lessons*. Finest golf instructions ever written. Will go over with Wild Bill, one lesson per week. Weary upon return. Skin raw. Etta said to put some cream on. Didn't. We sat in the parlor until nine, Etta with her crossword puzzles, me with snapshots of Wild Bill at junior invitational. Will point out his shoe plant and slot at the top.

FEB 2. Will be an early spring, according to the groundhog. Went ice fishing on Niobrara with Henry. Weren't close as boys but everybody else dying off. Extreme cold. Snaggle hooks and stink bait. Felix W on heart and lung machines and going downhill in a handcart. Dwight's boy DWI in Lincoln. Sam Cornish handling trial. Would've been my choice too. Aches and pains discussed. Agriculture and commodities market and Senior Pro/Am in August. Toughed it out till noon — no luck with catfish — then hot coffee at Why Not? Upbraided for my snide comments about *The People's Court.* Everyone talking about Judge Wapner the way they used to gush about FDR. Wild Bill's poppa slipped into the booth and hemmed and hawed before asking had *William* said anything to me about colleges. You know how boys are. Won't talk to the old man. Writing to Ohio State coach soon re: sixth place in Midwestern Junior following runner-up in Nebraska championship. And still a sophomore! Etta tried for the umpteenth time to feed me haddock this evening. Went where it usually does.

FEB 9. Hardly twenty degrees last night. Felix W's funeral today. Walked to Holy Sepulchre for the Mass, then to cemetery; taking a second to look at our plots. Hate to think about it, but I'll have my three score and ten soon. Felix two years younger.

Estate papers now with Donlan & Upshaw. (?!) Widow will have to count her fingers after the settlement. Etta stacked her pennies in wrappers while watching soaps on television. Annoying to hear that pap, but happy for her company. And just when I was wishing that kids and grandkids would have been part of the bargain, Wild Bill showed up! And with his poppa's company car, so he took us out to the golf club and we practiced his one and two irons from the Sandhills patio, hitting water balls I raked up from the hazards in September. Wild Bill in golf shoes and quarterback sweats and Colorado ski sweaters, me in my gray parka and rubber overboots. You talking *cold*? Wow! Wild Bill getting more and more like Jack Nicklaus at sixteen. Lankier but just as long. His one irons reaching the green at #2! And with a good tight pattern in the snow, like shotgun pellets puncturing white paper. Homer and Crisp stopped by to hoot and golly, saw how amazing the kid is, but I wouldn't let 'em open their traps. The goofs. W. B.'s hands got to stinging — like hitting rocks, he said — so we quit. Have spent the night perusing *Reader's Digest.* Our president making the right decisions. Feet still aching. Hope it's not frostbite.

FEB 20. Helped Etta with laundry. Hung up sheets by myself. Brrr! Heard Etta yelling "Cecil!" over and over again, nagging me with instructions. Would not look back to house. We're on the outs today. Walked the six blocks to Main for the groceries ($34.17!) and got caught out in the snow right next to liquor store. Woman I knew from a Chapter Eleven took me home. Embarrassing because I couldn't get her name right. Verna? Vivian? Another widow. Says she still misses husband, night and day. Has the screaming meemies now and again. Was going to invite her inside but thought better of it. In mailbox the *Creighton Law Review* and *Golf Digest,* plus a jolly letter from Vance and Dorothy in Yuma, saying the Winnebago was increasing their "togetherness." A chilling prospect for most couples I know. Worked in shop putting new handgrips on Henry's irons. Eighteen-year-old MacGregors. Wrong club for a guy his age, but Henry's too proud to play Lites. Work will pay for groceries, just about. Half pint of whiskey behind paint cans. Looked and looked and looked at it; took it up to Etta. Ate tuna-fish casserole — we appear to be shying away from red meat — and sat in parlor with magazines. Tom Watson's instructions good as always but plays too recklessly. Heard he's a Democrat. Shows. Etta's been watching her programs since seven. Will turn set off soon and put out our water glasses as the night is on the wane and we are getting tired.

MAR 4. Four inches last night and another batch during the day. Old Man Winter back with a vengeance. Woke up to harsh scrape of county snowplows. Worried the mail would not get through, but right on the button, including Social Security checks! Helped Etta put her Notary Sojack on, then trudged up to the Farmer's National. Whew! Kept a sawbuck for the week's pocket money. Hamburger and coffee at the Why Not? Happy to see Tish so chipper after all her ordeals. Checked out Phil Rodger's instruction book from library — great short game for Wild Bill to look at, although Lew Worsham and Paul Runyan still tops in that category. Helped Etta tidy up. Wearing my Turnberry sweater inside with it so cold, but Etta likes the windows open a crack. Shoes need polishing. Will do tomorrow or next day. Early to bed.

MAR 12. Etta has been scheming with Henry's wife about retirement communities in Arizona. And where would our friends be? Nebraska. We put a halt to that litigation in September, I thought. Expect it will be annual thing now. Dishes. Vacuumed. Emptied trash. Hint of spring in the air but no robins yet. Wild Bill lying low, sad to say. Girlfriend? Took a straw broom into rooms and swatted down cobwebs. Etta looking at me the whole time without saying a word. Haircut, just to pass the time. Dwight snipping the air these days, just to keep me in his chair. We avoided talk of his boy and jail. Seniors potluck meeting in Sandhills clubhouse at six. Shots of me with Dow Finsterwald, Mike Souchak, Jerry Barber still up in the pro shop. Worried new management would change things. (Pete Torrance still my idea of a great club professional.) And speaking of, a good deal of talk about our own Harlan "Butch" Polivka skunking out at Doral Ryder Open and the Honda Classic. Enjoyed saying I told you so. We'll plant spruce trees on right side of #11 teebox, hoping to make it a true par five. Alas, greens fees to go to six dollars (up from 50¢

in 1940) and Senior Pro/Am will have to go by the way this year. Hours of donnybrook and hurt feelings on that score, but Eugene late in getting commitments. Everybody regretting August vote now. Would likes of Bob Toski or Orville Moody say no soap to a $1,000 appearance fee? We'll never know. Betsy said it best at Xmas party. Eugene looks very bad, by the by. Chemotherapy took his hair, and a yellow cast to his eyes now. Wearing sunglasses even indoors. Zack much improved after operation. Wilma just not all there anymore. Etta tried to make coherent conversation but got nowhere. Sigh. Upon getting home, wrote out checks to water and sewer and Nebraska power and so on, but couldn't get checkbook to zero out with latest Farmer's National statement. Frustrating. Sign of old age, I guess. Will try again tomorrow.

MAR 17. Looked up Wild Bill's high-school transcript. Would appear he's been getting plenty of sleep. We'll have to forget about Stanford and the Eastern schools and plug away at the Big Eight and Big Ten. Etta wearing green all day in honor of old Eire. Was surprised when I pointed out that Saint Patrick was English. Told her that *Erin go bragh* joke. She immediately telephoned

Betsy. Late in the day I got on the horn to Wild Bill, but Cal said he was at some party. Kept me on the line in order to explore my opinions on whether Wild Bill ought to get some coaching from the Butcher, acquire some college-player techniques. Well, I counted to ten and took a deep breath and then patiently, patiently told old Cal that golf techniques have changed not one iota in sixty years and that Harlan "Butch" Polivka is a "handsy" player. Lanny Wadkins type. Hits at the golf ball like he was playing squash. Whereas I've taught Wild Bill like Jack Grout taught Nicklaus. Hands hardly there. And did Cal really want his boy around a guy known to have worn knickers? Well, old Cal soothed my pin feathers some by saying it was only a stray notion off the top of his head, and it was Cecil says this and Cecil says that since his son was ten years old. Told *him* that *Erin go bragh* joke. Heard it, he said. From Marie.

MAR 20. Took a morning telephone call for Etta, one of those magazine-subscription people. Enjoyed the conversation. Signed up for *Good Housekeeping*. Weather warming up at last, so went out for constitutional. Wrangled some at the Why Not? Squeegee getting heart pains but don't you dare talk to him about his cigarettes! Lucky thing Tish got between us. She says Squeegee still doesn't know what to do with his time; just hand-washes his Rambler every day and looks out at the yard. Encouraged her talk about a birthday party for Etta with the girls from the Altar Sodality and the old "Roman Hruska for Senator" campaign. Ate grilled cheese sandwich in Etta's room. Did not blow it and broach party subject. Etta's hair in disarray. We sang "The Bells of St. Mary's" and "Sweet Adeline" while I gave it a hundred strokes. Etta still beautiful in spite of illness. Expressed my sentiments.

MAR 25. Worked out compromise with insurance company. Have been feeling rotten the past few days. Weak, achy, sort of tipsy when I stand up. Hope no one stops by. Especially Wild Bill. Sandhills' one and only PGA golf professional is again favoring us with his presence in the clubhouse. Will play dumb and ask *Harlan* about his sickly day at the Hertz Bay Hill Classic. Etta's temperature gauge says it's fifty-two degrees outside; March again going out like a lamb. Ike biography petered out toward the end. Haven't been able to sleep, so I took a putter from the closet and have been hitting balls across the parlor carpet and into my upended water glass. *Tock, rum, rum, plonk.*

APR 1. Hard rains but mail came like clockwork. Nice chat with carrier. (Woman!) Quick on the uptake. April Fool's jokes, etc. Letters to occupant, assorted bills, and then, lo and behold, government checks. Wadded up junk mail and dropped it in circular file, then Etta walked with me to Farmer's. Enjoys rain as much as ever, but arthritis acting up some. Hefty balance in savings account thanx to Uncle Sam, but no pup anymore. One hospital stay could wipe us out. Have that to think about every day now as 70 looms on the horizon. Will be playing nine tomorrow with Zack, Mel, and Dr. Gerald S. Bergstrom, PC. Hoping for another Nassau with old PC. Lousy when "pressed," and the simoleons will come in handy. Evening supper with *Reader's Digest* open under milk glass and salad bowl. National Defense called to task. Entire Navy sitting ducks. Worrisome.

APR 4. Have put new spikes in six pairs of shoes now; at $15 a crack. Wrist is sore but easy money. Dull day otherwise. Walked over to Eugene's and played cribbage until five. Eugene is painting his house again. Etta and I have been counting and think this is the sixth time since Eugene put the kibosh on his housepainting business. You know he's retired because he will *not* do anyone else's house. Have given up trying to figure Eugene. Walked past Ben's Bar & Grill on the way home. Just waved.

APR 10. Wonderful golf day. Timothy grass getting high in the roughs, but songbirds out, womanly shapes to the sandhills up north, cattails swaying under the zephyrs, great white clouds arranging themselves in the sky like sofas in the Montgomery Ward. Homer and Crisp played nine with me and zigzagged along in their putt-putt. Hijinks, of course. Exploding golf ball, Mulligans, naughty tees. (Hate to see cowboy hats on the links. We ought to have a rule.) Even par after six, then the 153-yard par three. Hit it fat! Chopped up a divot the size of Sinatra's toupee and squirted the pill all of twenty yards. Sheesh! Examined position. Easy lie and uphill approach. Eight iron would have got me there ten years ago, but I have given in to my age. Went over my five swing keys and thought "Oily," just like Sam Snead. Hard seven iron with just enough cut to tail right and quit. Kicked backward on the green and then trickled down the swale to wind up two feet from the cup.

Homer and Crisp three-putted as per usual — paid no attention to my teaching — and I took my sweet time tapping in. *Quod erat demonstrandum.* Crisp says Butch has been claiming he shot a 62 here last July but, conveniently, with some Wake Forest pals who were visiting. Funny he never gets up a game with me. Tax returns in. Have overpaid $212, according to my pencil. Early supper, then helped Etta strip paint from door-jambs. Hard job but getting to be duck soup with practice. Will be sore tomorrow.

APR 15. Squeegee passed away just about sunup. Heart attack. Etta with Mildred as I write this. The guy had been complaining of soreness in his back but no other signs of ill health other than his hacking and coughing. Looking at yesterday's diary entry, I spot my comment on his "hitching," and it peeves me that I could not have written down some remarks about how much his friendship meant to me over these past sixty-five years. Honest, hardworking, proud, letter-of-the-law sort of guy. Teetotaler. Excellent putter under pressure. Would not give up the cigarettes. Will keep pleasant memories of him from yesterday, say a few words at the service. Weather nippy. Wanted booze all day.

■ ■ ■ ■

APR 17. S. Quentin German consigned to his grave. Especially liked the reading from Isaiah: "Justice shall be the band around his waist, and faithfulness a belt upon his hips. Then the wolf shall be a guest of the lamb, and the leopard shall lie down with the kid; the calf and the young lion shall browse together, with a little child to guide them." And then something about a lion eating hay like the ox. Excellent applications to old age/ erosion of powers/nature's winnowing process. Following, there was a nice reception at the Why Not? Haven't seen Greta since she had her little girl. Mildred wisely giving Squeegee's Haigs to the golf team at William Jennings Bryan. Etta and I took short constitutional at nightfall. Warm. Heather and sagebrush in the air. Have begun Herbert Hoover biography. Iowa boy. Engineer. History will judge him more kindly than contemporaries did. Low today; no pep.

APR 20. Etta sixty-seven. Took a lovely little breakfast to her in bed, with one yellow rose in the vase. Nightgown and slippers just perfect, she says. Foursome with Sam Cornish, Henry, and Zack. Shot pitiful.

Kept getting the Katzenjammers up on the teebox. Hooked into the Arkwright rangeland on #3. Angus cattle just stared at me: Who's the nitwit? And then skulled a nine iron approach on #17 and my brand-spanking-new Titleist skipped into the water hazard. *Kerplunk.* Hate the expense more than the penalty stroke. And to top it off, Cornish approached me in pro shop with a problem on the Waikowski codicil. Hadn't the slightest idea what he was talking about. Sam has always loved those *ipse dixits* and *sic passims,* but that wasn't the problem. The problem is me. I just can't listen fast enough. Everything gets scrambled. I say to him, "What's your opinion?" And when he tells me, I pretend complete agreement, Sam pretends I helped out. Humiliating. Roosevelt at Yalta. Etta had her party today. She hadn't predicted it, so apparently I managed to keep the cat in the bag for once. Had a real nice time; plenty of chat and canasta. She needed the pick-me-up.

APR 25. Walked a slow nine with Henry and Eugene. No birdies, two bogeys, holed out once from a sand trap. Eugene and Henry getting straighter from the tees. Haven't pointed out to them that their mechanics haven't improved — they're just too weak to put spin on the golf ball these days. Lunched at Sandhills and shot the breeze until four, then walked by the practice range. Wild Bill out there with you know who. And Wild Bill slicing! shanking! Everything going right. Lunging at the ball like Walter Hagen. Butch dumbfounded. Addled. Looked at hands, stance, angle of club face, completely overlooking the problem. Head. Yours truly walked up without a word, put a golf ball on the tee, took a hard hold of Wild Bill's girl-killer locks and said, "You go ahead and swing." Hurt him like crazy. About twenty hairs yanked out in my hand. I said, "You keep that head in place and you won't get so onion-eyed." I just kept holding on and pretty soon those little white pills were riding along the telegraph wire, and rising up for extra yardage just when you thought they'd hang on the wind and drop. Walked away with Wild Bill winking his thanx and our kid pro at last working up the gumption to say, "Good lesson." Will sleep happy tonight.

APR 30. I puttered around the house until ten when Wild Bill invited me to a round with Wilbur Gustafson's middle boy, Keith. We've let bygones be bygones. Keith also on golf team. Ugly swing — hodgepodge of

Lee Trevino and Charlie Owens — but gets it out okay. Keith says he hasn't got *William*'s (!) touch from forty yards and in, but scored some great sand saves. Was surprised to hear I lawyered. And Wild Bill says, "What? You think he was a *caddy*?" Was asked how come I gave up my practice, but pretended I didn't hear. Was asked again and replied that a perfectionist cannot put up with mistakes. Especially his own. Hit every green in regulation on the front nine, but the back jumped up and bit me. Old Sol nice and bright until one p.m., and then a mackerel sky got things sort of fuzzy. (Cataracts? Hope not.) Well: on #12, Wild Bill couldn't get the yardage right, so without thinking I told him, "Just get out your mashie." You guessed it: "What's a mashie?" And then we were going through the whole bag from brassie to niblick. Kids got a big kick out of it. Hung around and ate a hot dog with Etta, Roberta, and Betsy, then jawed with Crisp on the putting green. Watched as a greenskeeper strolled from the machine shed, tucking his shirt in his pants. Woman walked out about two minutes later. Won't mention any names.

MAY 6. Weather getting hotter. Will pay Wild Bill to mow yard. ($5 enough?) Endorsed government check and sent to Farmer's with deposit slip. Helped Etta wash and tidy up. Have been bumping into things. Match play with Zack, a one-stroke handicap per hole. Halved the par threes, but his game fell apart otherwise. Would have taken $14 bucks from him but urged Zack to go double or nothing on a six-footer at #18 and yanked it just enough. Zack's scraping by just like we all are. AA meeting, then Etta's noodles and meat sauce for dinner. (According to dictionary, P. Stroganoff a 19th-century Russian count and diplomat. Must be a good story there.) Early sleep.

MAY 15. Nice day. Shot a 76. Every fairway and fourteen greens in regulation. Four three-putts spelled the difference. Took four Andrew Jacksons from Dr. Bergstrom, but ol PC probably makes that in twenty minutes. Will stop playing me for cash pretty soon. Tish got a hole-in-one at the 125-yard par three! Have telephoned the *Press-Citizen.* Her snapshot now in pro shop. Oozy rain in the afternoon. Worked on Pete Upshaw's irons until four p.m. His temper hasn't improved. Went to Concord Inn — Etta driving — for the prime-rib special. Half price before six. And then out to Sandhills for Seniors meeting. We *finally* gave out prizes for achievements at Amelia Island tournament. (Marie sorry for tardiness, but no excuse.) Joke gifts and reach-me-downs, but some great things too. Expected our "golf professional" to give me a chipper or yardage finder, something fuddy-duddy and rank amateur, but the guy came through with a seven wood, one of those nifty presents you don't know you want until you actually get it. We have no agreement, only a truce. Zack got a funny Norman Rockwell print of some skinny kids with hickory sticks arguing golf rules on a green. Looked exactly like Zack and Felix and Squeegee and me way back in the twenties. Talked about old times. We're thinking Pinehurst for next winter trip. Have suggested we open it up to get some *mannerly* high-school golfers to join us. (Would be a nice graduation present for Wild Bill.) Everybody home by nine.

MAY 22. Early Mass and then put in an hour mixing up flapjack batter at the Men's Club pancake breakfast. Heard Wilma has Alzheimer's. Earl Yonnert having thyroid out. Whole town getting old. Went out to links at noon. Wild Bill there by the green with his shag bag, chipping range balls into a snug group that looked just like a honeycomb. Etta asked him to join us. Have to shut my eyes when she gets up to the ball, but she skitters it along the fairway okay. Wild Bill patient, as always. Has been getting great feelers from Ohio State, thanx to my aggressive letter campaign and his Nebraska state championship. Everything may depend upon his ranking on the Rolex All-American team. Says he hopes I'll visit him in Ohio, maybe play Muirfield Village, look at videotapes of his swing now and then. Has also politely let me know that he now prefers the name William. Wonder what Frank Urban "Fuzzy" Zoeller would have to say about that? But of course the kid never heard of Wild Bill Mehlhorn and his cowboy hat at the 1925 PGA. Well: Went nine with him and got skinned. His drives now a sand wedge longer than mine, so I'm hitting my seven wood versus his nine iron or my sixty-yard pitch versus his putt. Waited on the teebox at #7 while some guys in Osh Kosh overalls and seed-company caps yipped their way across the green. Etta laughed and said she just had a recollection of Squeegee saying, Even a really bad day of golf is better than a good day of work. We all grinned like fools. Especially Wild Bill. Hit me that my lame old jokes have always seemed funny and fresh to him. One facet of youth's attractiveness for tiresome gaffers like me. Tried a knock-down five iron to the green, but it whunked into the sand trap. Easy out to within four feet, and then a one-putt for par. Wild Bill missed an opportunity. Etta got lost in the rough with her spoon and scored what the Pro/Am caddies used to say was a "newspaper 8." Walked to the next tee in a garden stroll under an enormous blue sky, just taking everything in, Wild Bill up ahead and my wife next to me and golf the only thing on my mind. And I was everywhere I have ever been: on the public course at age nine with Dad's sawed-down midiron, and again when I was thirteen and parred three in a row, and on my practice round with Tommy Armour and Byron Nelson in 1947, or playing St. Andrews, Oakmont, Winged Foot, Pebble Beach, or here at Sandhills years ago, just hacking around with the guys. Every one was a red-letter day. Etta said, "You're smiling." "Second childhood," said I. Wild Bill played scratch golf after that and then went over to the practice range. Has the passion now. Etta and I went out to the Ponderosa for steak and potatoes on their senior-citizen discount. Have been reading up on Columbus, Ohio, since then. Home of the university, capital of the state, population of 540,000 in 1970, the year that her own Jack Nicklaus won his second British Open.

MAY 30. Went to Holy Sepulchre Cemetery with Etta and put peonies out for the many people we know now interred there. Etta drove me to the course — getting license back Wednesday. Eugene was there, trying out putters, stinking like turpentine, getting cranky. Went eighteen with me, but only half-decent shot he could manage was a four-wood rouser that Gene Sarazen would have envied. Were joined by a spiffy sales rep from Wilson Sports and Eugene just kept needling him. And a lot of that raunchy talk I don't like. Then hot coffee in the clubhouse. Was asked how long I have been playing the game and said sixty years. Eugene worked out the arithmetic on a paper napkin and the comeuppance was I have spent at least five years of my life on a golf course. "Five years, Cecil! You can't have 'em back. You could've accomplished something important. Ever feel guilty about that?" I sipped from my cup and said, "We're put here for pleasure too." And then we were quiet. Eugene crumpled up the napkin and pitched it across the room. Looking for a topic, I asked how his chemotherapy was playing out, and Eugene said he'd stopped going. Enjoyed my surprise. Said, "What's the point? Huh? You gotta die of somethin'." And I had a picture of Eugene at forty, painting my window sashes, and headstrong and ornery and brimming with vim and vigor. Saddening. Hitched a ride home with him, and Eugene just sat behind the wheel in the driveway, his big hands in his lap, looking at the yard and house paint. "We have all this technology," he said. "Education. High-speed travel. Medical advances. And the twentieth century is still unacceptable." "Well," I said, "at least you've had yourself an adventure." Eugene laughed. Went inside and repaired the hosel on Butch's Cleveland Classic. ($15.) Watched TV. Looked at Nebraska Bar Association mailing about judges under consideration. Have no opinion on the matter. Etta sleeping as I write this. Hope to play nine tomorrow.

CAN I JUST SIT HERE FOR A WHILE?

He was called a traveler, and that was another thing he loved about the job. If you wanted the hairy truth, Rick Bozack couldn't put his finger on any one thing that made his job such a clincher. It might have been his expense account or the showroom smell of his leased Oldsmobile or the motel rooms — God, the motel rooms: twin double beds, a stainless-steel Kleenex dispenser, and a bolted-down color TV topped with cellophane-wrapped peppermints that the maid left after she cleaned. He loved the coffee thermos the waitress banged down on his table at breakfast, he loved the sweat on his ice-water glass, he loved the spill stains blotting through the turned-over check, and he loved leaving tips of twenty percent even when the girl was slow and sullen and splashed coffee on his newspaper. His sales, his work, his vocation, that was all bonus. The waiting, the handshakes, the lunches, the Close, jeepers, that was just icing.

If you asked Rick Bozack what he did for a living, he wouldn't come out with a song and dance about selling expensive incubators and heart and kidney machines for Doctor's Service Supply Company, Indianapolis. Not off the top of his head he wouldn't. Instead he'd flash on a motel lobby with all the salesmen in their sharp, tailored suits, chewing sugarless gum, while the sweet thing behind the counter rammed a roller over a plastic credit card and aftershaves mixed in the air. It was goofy when he thought about it, but walking out through those fingerprinted glass doors, throwing his briefcase onto the red bucket seat, scraping the ice off the windshield, and seeing all those other guys out there in the parking lot with him, scowling, chipping away at their wipers, blowing on their fingers, sliding their heater control to defrost, Rick felt like a team player again, like he was part of a fighter squadron.

What was this *Death of a Salesman* crap? he'd say. What were they feeding everybody about the hard life on the road? You'd have to be zonkers not to love it.

Then Rick had a real turnaround. A college buddy said something that really clobbered him. Rick and his wife, Jane, had returned to South Bend, his home, for the Notre Dame alumni picnic, where they collided with people they hadn't even thought of in years. They sat all night at a green picnic table with baked beans and hot dogs and beer, laughing so much that their sides hurt, having a whale of a time. They swapped pictures of their kids, and Rick drew a diagram of an invention he might go ahead and get patented, a device that would rinse out messy diapers for daddies right there in the toilet bowl. He told all comers that he was thirty-four years old and happily married, the father of two girls, and he woke up every morning with a sapsucker grin on his face. Then Mickey Hogan, this terrific buddy in advertising who had just started up his own firm, said you don't know the thrill of business until it's your own, until every sale you make goes directly into your pocket and not to some slob back in the home office.

This guy Hogan wasn't speaking de profundis or anything, but Rick was really blown away by what he said. It was one of those fuzzy notions you carry with you for years, and then it's suddenly there, it's got shape and bulk and annoying little edges that give you a twinge whenever you sit down. That's how it was. He and Jane talked about it all the way back to their three-bedroom apartment on Rue Monet in Indianapolis. "How much of what I earn actually makes my wallet any fatter? What do I have besides a measly income? When am I going to get off my duff and get something going on my own?"

Jane was great about it. She said she loved him and she'd go along with whatever his choice was, but she had watched him waste himself at Doctor's Service Supply Company. She knew he was a great salesman, but he had all the earmarks of being a fantastic manager too. She had been hoping he'd come up with something like this but didn't want to influence Rick one way or the other. "I don't want to push" were her words.

Jane's enthusiasm put a fire under Rick, and he began checking things out on the sly: inventory costs, car leases and office-space rentals, government withholding tax and Social Security regulations, and though it seemed dopey and juvenile, the couple decided that they'd both stop smoking, watch their caloric intake, avoid between-meal treats, and exercise regularly. Sure, they were mainly concerned with hashing out this new business venture, but how far afield was it to take stock of yourself, your physical condition, to discipline yourself and set goals? That was Rick's thinking, and Jane thought he was "right on the money."

The two of them let a half gallon of ice cream melt down in the sink, got out the scale and measuring tape, bought matching running outfits, and they took turns with Tracy and Connor at breakfast while one of them jogged around the block.

And Rick was no slouch when he was out on the road. He jogged in cold cities and on gravel county roads and in parking lots of Holiday Inns. Other salesmen would run toward him in wristbands and heavy sweat-shirts, and Rick would say, "How's it going?"

"How's it going?" they'd reply.

Rick imagined millions of joggers saying the same thing to each other. It felt as good as the days of the Latin Mass, when you knew it was just as incomprehensible in Dusseldorf, West Germany, as it was in Ichikawa, Japan.

On one of his business trips to South Bend, Rick jogged on the cinder track of Notre Dame's great football stadium, where who should he see but Walter Herdzina, a terrific buddy of his! Rick was flabbergasted. The guy had aged — who hadn't? — but he remembered Rick like it was only yesterday, even recited some wild dorm incidents that Rick had put the eraser to. The two men ran an eight-minute mile together and leaned on their knees and wiped their faces on their sweatshirts, and after they had discussed pulse rates, refined sugar, and junk foods, Walter said, "You ought to move back to South Bend."

Jane, bless her heart, kept bringing up South Bend too. It was smack in the middle of his territory and a natural home base, but he had never really thought about South Bend much before the alumni picnic. When the company hired Rick, they had assumed he'd want to settle in a giant metropolis like Indianapolis so he could have some jam-packed leisure time, and he had never mentioned his roots farther north. And it wasn't unusual for Rick to spend two or three days in South Bend and not give anyone except his mom a call. But now there seemed to be a come-as-you-are feeling, a real hometown warmth he hadn't noticed before.

In September he closed a deal with a gynecological clinic that would earn him six thousand dollars, what salesmen called "the Cookies." But instead of immediately driving home for a winging celebration, Rick decided to make some business phone contacts — thank-yous, actually — and ride out his hot streak, see what fell in his lap. He stopped in the lobby of a downtown bank building to use its plush telephone booths, then, on an impulse, he asked to see someone in the business-loan department. A receptionist said a loan vice president could see him and Rick walked into his office and — how's this for a coincidence? — the vice president was Walter Herdzina! You could've knocked Rick over with a feather. "Boy," he said, "you're really going places."

Walter smirked. "They'll probably wise up and have me sweeping the floors before my pen's out of ink."

Rick spoke off the top of his head. He had been with Doctor's Service Supply Company, Indianapolis, for six years, after three years with Johnson & Johnson. He'd built up a pretty good reputation in Indiana and southern Michigan, and now and then got offers from industries in Minnesota and California to switch over to a district manager's job and a cozy boost in salary. What he wanted to know was, could a banker like Walter, with years of experience and a shrewd eye for markets and money potential, give him a good solid reason why he shouldn't go into business for himself? Crank up his own distributorship?

Walter Herdzina glanced at his watch and suggested they go out for lunch.

Rick figured that meant *You gotta be kidding.* "This is pretty off-the-wall," he said. "I really haven't had time to analyze the pros and cons or work up any kind of prospectus."

Walter put a heavy hand on his shoulder. "How about us talking about it at lunch?"

Mostly they talked about rugby. It had been a maiden sport at Notre Dame when they played it, but now it was taking the college by storm. Why? Because when you got right down to it, men liked seeing what they were made of, what sort of guts they had.

"Lessons like that stick," Walter said. "I get guys coming to me with all kinds of schemes, packages, brilliant ideas. And I can tell right away if they were ever athletes. If they never really hurt themselves to win at something, well, I'm a little skeptical."

Walter ordered the protein-rich halibut; Rick had the dieter's salad.

Rick told the banker traveler stories. He told him anecdotes about salesmanship. He had sold insurance and mutual funds in the past and, for one summer, automobiles, and he had discovered a gimmick — well, not that, a *tool* — that hadn't failed him yet. It was called the Benjamin Franklin Close.

"Say you get a couple who're wavering over the purchase of a car. You take them into your office and close the door and say, 'Do you know what Benjamin Franklin would do in a case like this?' That's a toughie for them so you let them off the hook. You take out a tablet and draw a line down the center of the page, top to bottom. 'Benjamin Franklin,' you say, 'would list all the points in favor of buying this car, and then he'd list whatever he could against it. Then he'd total everything up.' You're the salesman, you handle the benefits. You begin by saying, 'So okay, you've said your old car needs an overhaul. That's point one. You've said you want a station wagon for the kids; that's point two. You've told me that particular shade of brown is your favorite.' And so on. Once you've written down your pitches, you flip the tablet around and hand across the pen. 'Okay,' you tell them. 'Now Benjamin Franklin would write down whatever he had *against* buying that car.' And you're silent. As noiseless as you can be. You don't say boo to them. They stare at that blank side of the paper and they get flustered. They weren't expecting this at all. Maybe the wife will say, 'We can't afford the payments,' and the husband will hurry up and scribble that down. Maybe he'll say, 'It's really more car than we need for city driving.' He'll glance at you for approval, but you won't even nod your head. You've suddenly turned to stone. Now they're really struggling. They see two reasons against and twelve reasons for. You decide to help them out. You say, 'Was it the color you didn't like?' Of course not, you dope. You put that down as point three in favor. But the wife will say, 'Oh, no, I like that shade of brown a lot.' You sit back in your chair and wait. You wait four or five minutes if you have to, until they're really uncomfortable, until you've got them feeling like bozos. Then you take the tablet from them and make a big show of making the tally. They think you're an idiot, anyway; counting out loud won't surprise them. And when you've told them they have twelve points in favor, two points against, you sit back in your chair and let that sink in. You say, 'What do you think Benjamin Franklin would do in this situation?' You've got them cornered and they know it and they can't think of a way out because there's only one way and they rarely consider it. Pressed against the wall like that the only solution is for the man or woman to say, 'I — just — don't — *feel* — like — it — now.' All the salesman can do then is recapitulate. If they want to wait, if the vibes don't feel right, if they don't sense it's the appropriate thing to do, they've got him. 'I just don't feel like it now.' There's no way to sell against that."

Walter grinned. He thought Rick might have something. Even in outline his distributorship had real sex appeal.

So that afternoon Rick drove south to Indianapolis with his CB radio turned down so he wouldn't have all the chatter, and he picked up a sitter for his two little roses and took Jane out for prime rib, claiming he wanted to celebrate the six-thousand-dollar commission. But after they had toasted the Cookies, he sprang the deal on her, explained everything about the lunch and Walter's positive reaction, how it all fit together, fell into place, shot off like a rocket. And what it all boiled down to was, they could move up to South Bend, buy a house, and in two months, three months, a year, maybe he'd have his very own medical instruments and supplies company.

Jane was ecstatic. Jane was a dynamo. While Rick did the dog-and-pony show for his boss and got him to pick up the tab for a move to the heart of Rick's territory, Jane did the real work of selecting their two-story home and supervising the movers. Then Rick walked Tracy and little Connor from house to house down the new block in South Bend, introducing himself and his daughters to their new neighbors. There were five kids the same age on just one side of the street! Rick imagined Tracy and Connor as gorgeous teenagers at a backyard party with hanging lanterns and some of Rick's famous punch, and maybe two thousand four hundred boys trying to get a crack at his girls.

He drank iced tea with a stockbroker who crossed his legs and gazed out the window as Tracy tried to feed earthworms to his spaniel.

"Plenty of playmates," said Rick.

"This place is a population bomb."

"Yeah, but I love kids, don't you? I get home from a week on the road and there's nothing I like better than to roll on the floor a few hours with them."

The man spit ice cubes back into his glass. "But your kids are girls!" the man said.

Rick shrugged. "I figure my wife will tell me when I should stop it."

What'd he think, that Rick would be copping feels, pawing them through their training bras? Maybe South Bend had its creepy side, after all. Maybe a few of these daddies could bear some scrutiny.

Rick gave a full report to his wife, Jane, as they sat down with beers on the newly carpeted floor of the living room, telling her about all the fascinating people he had met in just a casual swing down the block. Jane said, "I don't know how you can just go knocking on doors and introducing yourself. I can't think of a single thing to say when I'm with strangers."

Rick said, "That's one of the things that comes with being a traveler. You just assume you're welcome until someone tells you otherwise."

But how did that square with the uneasiness Rick Bozack felt with his old chum Mickey Hogan? A year ago Mickey had been a high-priced copywriter, but then he had gone out on a limb to take over a smaller house that had been strictly an art and layout jobber, and the gamble had paid off in spades. Mickey turned the firm into a real comer in South Bend, what they call in the trade a "hot shop."

Of course, Mickey had always been a brain. They had been rugby buddies at Notre Dame, and they used to shoot snooker together and swap tennis shoes and generally pal around like they were in a rowdy television commercial for some brand of light beer. Now Mickey was almost skinny and as handsome as Sergio Franchi, and taking full advantage of it, don't let anybody kid you. They had doubled to the Notre Dame/Army game last season, and Mickey brought along a knockout who kept sneaking her hand under Mickey's blue leg warmer. Rick couldn't keep his eyes off her. Even Jane noticed it. "Boy, I bet she put lead in your pencil," she said.

So Rick was delighted but amazed when in February Mickey said he'd make the third for a terrific bunch of seats at the Notre Dame/Marquette basketball game. Mickey was even sitting on the snow-shoveled steps of his condominium, like some company president on the skids, when Rick pulled up along the curb. And now Mickey was smoking a black cigarillo as Rick told him how astonished he was these days to see that everyone he met was about his age; they had all risen to positions of authority, and he was finding they could do him some good. You always thought it was just your father who could throw a name around. Now Rick was doing it himself, and getting results! "I'm really enjoying my thirties," Rick said, and then smiled. "I've got twenty credit cards in my wallet, and I don't get acne anymore."

Mickey just looked at him, bored.

"Okay, maybe not twenty credit cards, but my complexion's all cleared up."

Mickey sighed and looked out the window. Rick had forgotten how much of a jerk Mickey could be.

Rick kept the engine running and shoved the Captain and Tenille in his tape deck so Mickey could nestle in with some good tunes, then he pressed the door chimes to a house the Herdzinas had just bought: eighty thousand smackers, minimum. A small girl in pink underpants opened the door.

"Hi," said Rick in his Nice Man voice.

The girl shoved a finger up her nose.

Karen Herdzina hugged him hello. The hugging was a phenomenon that was totally new to South Bend and Rick never felt he handled it well. He lingered a bit too long with women, and with men he was on the lookout for a quick takedown and two points on the scoreboard.

"I'll put some hustle into Walt," she said. "Tell him to get it in gear."

Walter came out of the bedroom with a new shirt he was ripping the plastic off of. "Mickey in the car?"

Rick nodded. "But it really belts out the heat."

Walter unpinned the sleeves and the cardboards and shoved the trash into a paper sack that had the cellophane wrappers of record albums in it.

"Look at that," he said. "My wife. She goes out spending my hard-earned money on records. The Carpenters. John Denver. I don't know what gets into her sometimes."

"I kind of enjoy John Denver," said Rick.

"See?" Karen called.

As they walked to the thrumming Oldsmobile, Walter leaned into Rick, fanning three tickets out like a heart-stopping poker hand. "How about these beauties, Richard?"

"Wow! What do I owe ya?"

He frowned and pushed the tickets back into his wallet. *"De nada,"* said Walter. "Buy me a beer."

As Rick drove, he and Walter talked about their budding families. You could see it was driving Mickey bananas. Here he was a bachelor, giving up a night when he could've probably had some make-out artist in the sack, and all he was hearing was talk about drooling and potties and cutting new teeth. So as he climbed up onto the highway Rick introduced the topic of college basketball, and Walter scrunched forward to talk about the Marquette scoring threat, but Mickey interrupted to ask Walter if he knew that

Rick was considering his own distributor-ship.

"Hell," the banker said, "I'm the one who put the gleam in his eye." He settled into the backseat and crossed his kid leather gloves in his lap. "I think that's a tremendous opportunity, Rick. Where've you gone with it lately?"

"He's been testing the waters," said Mickey.

"I've sort've put it on the back burner until Jane and the kids get a better lay of the land," said Rick. "I think it might be a pretty good setup, though. Almost no time on the road and very little selling. I'll see what it's like to stay around the house and carry those canvas money bags up to the teller's window."

Walter grew thoughtful. "I read somewhere that every person who starts a new business makes at least one horrible mistake. Something really staggering. If you get through that and you don't get kayoed, I guess you got it made."

They were quiet then for several minutes, as if in mourning for all those bankrupts who had been walloped in the past. The tape player clicked onto the second side. Mickey tapped one of his black cigarillos on his wrist.

"You really like those things?" Rick asked.

Mickey lit it with the car lighter. "Yep," Mickey said. "I like them a lot."

Rick turned into the Notre Dame parking lot. "Since I gave up smoking, I notice it all the time. This health kick's really made a difference. I'm down two notches on my belt, my clothes don't fit, and I want to screw all the time now." He switched off the ignition. "How's that for a side benefit?"

Mickey said, "You smile a lot, you know that?"

It was just an okay game, nothing spectacular as far as Rick was concerned. In fact, if you conked him on the head, he might even have said it was boring. Where was the teamwork? Where was the give-and-take? A couple of black guys were out there throwing up junk shots, making the white guys look like clowns, propelling themselves up toward the hoop like they were taking stairs three at a time. It went back and forth like that all night, and except for the spine-tingling Notre Dame songs, except for the perky cheerleaders and the silver flask of brandy Mickey passed up and down the row, Rick caught himself wishing he was in a motel room somewhere eating cheese slices on crackers.

At the final buzzer the three guys filed out

with the crowd, giving the nod to other old buddies and asking them how tricks were. The Oldsmobile engine turned slowly with cold before it caught, and as Rick eyed the oil pressure gauge Mickey removed the Captain and Tenille from the tape deck. Mr. Sophisticated.

Rick took the crosstown and shoved in a tape of Tony Orlando. Walter was paging through one of the catalogs for Doctor's Service Supply Company, Indianapolis, when he noticed a pizza parlor was still open, how did that sound? Rick admitted it didn't blow the top of his head off, but he guessed he could give it a whirl. Mickey just sat there like wax.

Rick swerved in next to a souped-up Ford with big rear wheels and an air scoop on the hood. SECRET STORM was printed in maroon on the fender. As the three walked up to the pizza parlor's entrance, Rick saw them mirrored by the big windows, in blue shirts and rep ties and cashmere topcoats, with scowls in their eyes and gray threads in their hair and gruesome mortgages on their houses, and not one of them yet living up to his full potential.

Walter stood with Rick at the counter as he ordered a twelve-inch combination pizza. An overhead blower gave them pompadours.

"Hey," said Rick, "that was fun."

Walter showed three fingers to a girl at the beer taps. He said, "My wife encourages me to go out with you boys. She thinks it'll keep me from chasing tail."

Rick wished he had been somewhere else when Walter said that. It said everything about the guy.

Mickey walked to the cigarette machine and pressed every button, then, deep in his private Weltschmerz, he wandered past a sign that read, THIS SECTION CLOSED. Rick backed away from the counter with the beers, sloshing some on his coat, and made his way to the dark and forbidden tables where Mickey was moodily sitting.

Mickey frowned. "How long are we going to dawdle here?"

"You got something you wanted to do?"

"There's *always* something to do, Rick."

A girl in a chef's hat seated an elderly couple in the adjoining area. She had pizza menus that she crushed to her breast as she sidestepped around benches toward the drinking buddies, bumping the sign that read THIS SECTION CLOSED, schoolmarm disapproval in her eyes.

Mickey rocked back in his chair. "Can I just sit here for a while? Would it ruin your day if I just sat here?"

The girl stopped and threw everything she had into the question and then shrugged and walked back to the cash register.

Rick almost smacked his forehead, he was that impressed. Mickey could get away with stuff that would land Rick in jail or small-claims court.

Soon he and Walter tore into a combination pizza, achieving at once a glossy burn on the roofs of their mouths. Mickey must not have wanted any. He seemed to have lost the power of speech. After a while Walter asked if either of them had read a magazine article about a recent psychological study of stress.

Rick asked, "How do you find time to *read*?"

"I can't," Walter said. "Karen gets piles of magazines in the mail, though, and she gives me digests of them at dinner."

Mickey looked elsewhere as Walter explained that this particular study showed that whenever a person shifted the furniture of his life in any significant way at all, he or she was increasing the chances of serious illness. Change for the better? Change for the worse? Doesn't matter. If your spouse dies, you get a hundred points against you. You get fired, that's fifty. You accomplish something outstanding, really excellent, still you get something in the neighborhood of thirty points tacked on to your score. The list went on and on. Mortgages counted, salary bonuses, shifts in eating habits. "You collect more than three hundred of these puppies in a year," Walter said, "and it's time to consult a shrink."

Neither Walter nor Rick could finish the pizza, so Rick asked the kitchen help for a sack to take the remains home in. Then the three men walked out into the night, gripping their collars at their necks, their ears crimped by the cold. It was getting close to zero. Rick could hear it in the snow.

There were three boys in Secret Storm, each dangling pizza over his mouth and getting cheese on his chin.

Rick opened the car door on his side and bumped the trim on the souped-up Ford. He smiled and shrugged his shoulders at the kid on the passenger's side.

The kid called him a son of a bitch.

Mickey immediately walked around the car. "What'd he call you?"

"Nothing, Mickey. He was kidding."

But Mickey was already thumping the kid's car door with his knee. "I want to hear what you called him!"

The door bolted open against Mickey's cashmere coat, soiling it, and a kid bent out, unsnapping a Catholic high-school letterman's jacket. Before he had the last snap undone, Mickey punched him in the neck. The kid grabbed his throat and coughed. Mickey held his fists like cocktail glasses.

Walter stood in the cold with his gloved hands over his ears as Rick tried to pull Mickey away from the fracas. The kid hooked a fist into Rick's ear and knocked him against the car. Mickey tackled the kid and smacked him against the pavement. Dry snow fluffed up and blew. Rick covered his sore ear and Mickey tried to pin the kid's arms with his knees, but the other boys were out of the Ford by then and urging their friend to give Mickey a shellacking. And at once it was obvious to Rick that the boys weren't aware they were dealing with three strapping men in the prime of their lives, men who had played rugby at Notre Dame when it was just a maiden sport.

Rick and Walter managed to untangle Mickey and grapple him inside the car. Rick spun his wheels on the ice as he gunned the Oldsmobile out of the parking lot. One of the kids kicked his bumper, and another pitched a snowball that *whumped* into the trunk.

Rick said, "I don't believe you, Mickey."

Mickey was just getting his wind back.

"You don't believe what?" Mickey said.

"You're thirty-five years old, Mick! You don't go banging high-school kids around."

Walter wiped the rear window with his glove. "Oh, no," he groaned.

Mickey turned around. "Are they following us?"

"Maybe their home's in the same direction," said Rick.

Mickey jerked open the door. Cold air flapped through the catalogs of Doctor's Service Supply Company, Indianapolis. "Let me out," Mickey said.

"Are you kidding?" Rick gave him a look that spoke of his resolute position on the question while communicating his willingness to compromise on issues of lesser gravity.

And yet Mickey repeated, "Let me out."

"What are you going to do?"

"Shut up and let me out of this car."

Walter said, "I think those are *Catholic* kids, Michael."

Rick made a right-hand turn, and so did the souped-up Ford. They were on a pot-holed residential street of ivied brick homes and one-car garages.

Mickey pushed the door open and scraped off the top of a snow pile. He leaned out toward the curb like a sick drunk about to lose it until Rick skidded slantwise on the ice pack and stopped. Then Mickey hopped out and slipped on the ice and sprawled against the right front door of the Ford.

The boy who'd called Rick a son of a bitch cracked his skull on the door frame trying to get out, and he sat back down pretty hard, with pain in his eyes and both hands rubbing his stocking cap.

"All right, you bastard," the driver, a big bruiser, said, and lurched out, tearing off *his* letterman's jacket. The kid in the backseat squeezed out through the passenger door as if they were only stopping for gas. He stripped a stick of gum and folded it into his mouth, then put his hands in his jeans pockets. Rick walked over to him and the kid's eyes slid. "Bob's going to make mincemeat out of your friend, man."

Mickey and the kid named Bob stepped over a yard hedge and Mickey was hanging his coat on a clothesline pole. Walter was on the sidewalk, stamping snow off his wing tips, apparently hoping he couldn't be seen.

Rick sought a pacifying conversational gambit. "How about this weather?" Rick asked the kid. "My nose is like an ice cube."

The kid smiled. "Colder than a witch's tit, ain't it?"

The kid was in Rick's pocket. Rick still

had the goods, all right; spells he hadn't tapped yet.

Mickey and the boy named Bob were closing together in the night-blue snow, like boxers about to touch gloves, when Mickey swung his right fist into the kid's stomach and the kid collapsed like a folding chair. "Ow! *Ow!*" he yelled. "Oh, man, where'd you hit me? Jeez, that hurts!"

A light went on in an upstairs bedroom.

The passenger got out of the souped-up car, still holding his stocking cap, and the kid next to Rick tripped through deep snow to help Bob limp back to the Ford. "Get me to a hospital quick!"

One of them said, "Oh, you're okay, Bob."

"You don't know, man! I think the dude might've burst my appendix or something! I think he was wearing a ring!"

Mickey carefully put on his coat and sucked the knuckles of his right hand when he sat down inside the Oldsmobile. As Rick drove to Mickey's condominium, Mickey pressed a bump on his forehead and put on his gloves again.

"What made you want to do that, Mick?"

Mickey was red-eyed. "Are you going to let some punk call you a son of a bitch?"

Rick slapped the steering wheel. "Of course! I do it all the *time*! Is that supposed

224

to destroy you or something?"

Mickey just looked at the floor mats or out the window. He jumped out when Rick parked in front of his place, the sack of cold pizza clamped under his arm. He didn't say good-bye.

Walter Herdzina moved up to the front seat and brought the seat belt over to its catch. "Whew! What an evening, huh?"

"I feel like I've run twenty miles."

Walter crossed his legs and jiggled his shoe until Rick drove onto Walter's driveway, where he shook Rick's hand and suggested they do this again sometime, and also wished him good luck in getting his business out of the starting gate.

The light was on in the upstairs bedroom of the Bozacks' blue Colonial home. Jane had switched the lights off downstairs. Rick let himself in with the milk-box key and hung up his coat. He opened the refrigerator door and peered in for a long time, and then Rick found himself patting his pockets for cigarettes. He went to the dining room breakfront and found an old carton of Salems next to the Halloween cocktail napkins.

He got a yellow ruled tablet and a pen from the desk and sat down in the living room with a lit cigarette. He printed VENTURE at the top. He drew a line down the center of the paper and numbered the right-hand side from one to twelve. After a few minutes there, Jane came down the stairs in her robe.

"Rick?"

"What?"

"I wanted to know if it was you."

"Who else would it be?"

"Why don't you come up? I'm only reading magazines."

"I think I'd like to just sit here for a while."

"In the *dark*?"

He didn't speak.

"Are you smoking?"

"Yep. I was feeling especially naughty."

She was silent. She stood with both feet on the same step. "You're being awfully mysterious."

"I just want to sit here for a while. Can I do that? Can I just sit here for a while?"

Jane climbed back up the stairs to their bedroom.

Rick stared at the numbered page. Why quit the team? Why risk the stress? Why give up all those Cookies?

If pressed against the wall, he'd say, "I just don't feel like it now."

MY COMMUNIST

I am conscious of the lacks at my English, which is my least language, so you will please correct my errors. My story is happening in California during 1982. But it is beginning far, far away in my country of Poland, where I was born and growing up in Kraków and where I matriculated in philosophy at famous, six-hundred-year-old Jagiellonian University. In fall 1975, I have begun four years of theology studies at Rome's Pontifical University of Saint Thomas Aquinas, which is called "the Angelicum," and in 1979 I was ordained a priest for the diocese of Kraków by its former archbishop, Karol Wojtyla, who is then just a few months Pope John Paul II. We have much in common, such as homeland and schoolings, and as friends it is day of great happiness for us, my ordination.

My first parish is in difficult times. We are oppressed country and hardworking people

227

who cannot afford government price increases of sometimes one hundred percent on meats, and waves of strikes for social justice and freedom from Soviet Union have begun at shipyards, railways, bakeries, diary farms. Many priests such as me join the strikers and preside at outdoor Masses for many thousands of workers. A revolution which is called *Solidarnosc* is under way, and there is nearly a military invasion by Warsaw Pact countries to "save socialist Poland," but it is halted by interventions from the Pope and warnings from the United States. Even so, priests are kidnapped and murdered to scare and make sad the strikers. In fall 1981, General Wojciech Jaruzelski becamed first secretary of Polish Communist Party and it is December when he declares state of war in my country. Martial law there is put on us, and many thousands of Solidarity activists without warnings they are being arrested like with Nazis in Occupation.

I can hear the question, "Why this histories?" I will answer the asking in a small while, and you will find out why is necessary.

Also in December it was a bad news that my cardinal archbishop finds out the name of Stefan Nowak, me, is on a list of party enemies, and I am invited to his excellency's residence. There I hear a communication from His Holiness himself that his young friend, Stefan, not even yet three years from his ordination, is to go to California as a missionary. A big surprise, belief me!

I disliked to leave home so soon after joining my first parish, and if I open my heart to you I will confess I was thinking my friends would consider me coward. To die like Christ for my faith is a dear wish since childhood when I am reading about old-time martyrs, so I am prepared to stay. But also ever since seminary I have dreamed to work in countries where Catholics suffer without the sacraments. Initially my thinking is Africa, Latin America, or Russia, but California is also still missionary country. And obedience to the Pope is no question.

With one week spending in Chicago city, giving lectures about my country in parishes and visiting beautiful churches and museums, I board an aeroplane for its fly to San Francisco, first time to visit in my life, though I have seen it, naturally, in the cinema. I am met at San Francisco International by the wonderful old pastor of All Souls parish, whose family name when I first heard in Kraków was sounding very homely for a man from Poland. Smolarski

is very typical name there. Monsignor Smolarski asks I address him Joseph and admits
he does not know Polish language. A disappointment. I promise to teach him some
sentences, and songs too, and Joseph promises to correct my broken English. My
much-in-pieces English.

All Souls is not old, old parish like in
Kraków or Warsaw, but from beginning of
twenty century. Forty kilometers south of
San Francisco, and in the number of two
thousand people, maybe less, the church
has only fourteen parishioners from Eastern
Europe, and none who speak my dear-to-
my-heart Polish. Immediately upon learning, my soul cries out, *Why have I come to
this far place?* The first nights there are long
for me. Hours and hours I pray. I write
hundreds letters home. But I feel silenced
and not as much useful. I have looked up
the word: I am "forlorn."

California, so big a state and rich in different beauties, I like very much with its
weather always in a good mood and its
people friendly because not cold or perse-
cuted. The Mass is familiar even in English,
though I am embarrassed by my "charming" accent and I am frustrated to be sounding unintelligent with homilies too like a
child. At first many humiliations, as in Italy

and first-year theology.

And such wealth here is horrifying, really. I have a day off and all afternoon I walk through a gigantic proportion supermarket. I have arrived in America with one luggage. With how many shall I leave? The both sides of the building seem a distance of a kilometer as up and down the aisles I am wandering, seeing fruits and vegetables even in winter, so much different foods to be sold, such plenty, but not wanting to buy even a chocolate piece for thinking of how much people in my homeland must do without.

And that is when I first see him. In a gray trench coat, no kidding, and gray Homburg hat, holding a shopping basket in the vegetable aisle but watching me, for sure, the face maybe from cousin to Leonid Brezhnev, the pig eyes, the slicked-back hair. Weighty. You would not think: *A Californian!* This is herring man, a favorite to vodka. He is like to have hammer and sickle tattooed on his chest. Here for what is this spy? A friend of mine was found in a northern forest with a bullet in his brains. Has this fellow gun in pocket? Little hidden camera? Wanting confrontation, I walk forward but he is too fast away. On a bin for green cabbage that is being rained on he has left behind his plastic basket and inside it are kielbasa, piroshki, and from delicatessen a carton of *kutia,* which is Polish Christmas pudding. My father would buy such for the holy days.

Is fat man waiting for me outside? I do not wish to be surprised in lonesome place, so I rush opposite to his going and push through a steel door. I find myself in storing house where a garage door is lifting high overhead as outside a fruits truck backs up, a horn beeping. I hurry out and jump from the dock, and I do not stop hurrying until he for sure cannot be behind me. I say nothing to Monsignor, for he is old man with conditions of heart.

On Sunday again I notice my spy, looking hard at Stefan in my long white alb and green stole and chasuble after the ten o'clock Mass, and the not-yet-thirty priest is smiling because a sweet girl of sixteen has taught herself enough Polish to say, "Good morning, Father Nowak," and it is not so bad, her accent. Of mine, she says I mispronounce the word "love" like "laugh." I glance across the street and my Communist is standing in a wide circle of shade, for the sun is miraculous even in March, and he is in many clothings and Homburg hat, his hands behind his back, just watching me. I am certainly not an amusement to him. I am some garbages, some striker's wreckage that must to be removed. I lift my right hand high. Half a hello is it, and half a salute. My spy holds on to his expression, like his face is inflexible, and then he strolls away.

I find less and less I am afraid as weeks go by and he is around now and then only. I have no idea his thoughts, if he wants me dead, if he is KGB and I am only his idle hours, his hobby, and his main jobs is military secrets. But I have decided for sure he is Polish, and it pleases that whenever he is watching me he is thinking of me in the same language that I am thinking of him. I do not care the words he uses.

We are now last week of March, and he sends in mailing four photographs of me and back of each he is labeled in Polish handwriting: "Nowak at local bookstore," "Nowak in front of All Soul's rectory," "Nowak at funeral on 20 March," "Nowak, home of Mrs. Kaniecki." Was this to harass me? Was he just getting rid of? The photos are nice of me. One I send to parents. Others I hang them in my office.

But I am thinking: I like my pastoral job very much. I have a fine rectory to live in, my first car ever, friendly priests who join us for drinks or nights at the cinema, invitations to dinners with families, the joy and honor of my vocation. And how much could my Communist have? A flat maybe with small television, food he cooks for himself and eats lonely, a hundred worries and secrets, and no god to pray to? Was I a priest to have luxuries while another has so little?

With April, quite suddenly he is not spying on me anymore. I find myself looking and looking, but he is like I invented him. Poland is still in a "state of war" and my mailings from homeland tell of jailings and intimidations, but I seem to be no longer of interest. I am surprised by the loss I experience. To "stew and fret" is good slang for my feelings. I miss him, this Pole. Has he been recalled to Europe, or is he ill with no one to help him? I pray it is not so.

On first day off, I decide to investigate. I have habit of visiting a fine bookstore in Palo Alto where I read for free — please to excuse me, lovely store owners — their French, German, and Italian newspapers so to find out more about Poland, which is not so well covered in America. Many Europeans must do the same, for sure. I go to very nice woman at bookstore counter and describe, "My old friend whom I have lost touches with." Smiling, she remembers a man also with my charming accent who fits exactly my describing. Oskar, his name. She thinks he lives not far, since he drinks espresso in next-doors café as he reads journals each mornings. She has not seen this Oskar lately.

Let me tell you, are fourteen apartment buildings within few blocks of bookstore. It is quite a job for me until I figure to go to cheapest apartments first, for this is Soviet system, not CIA. The Spirit is leading me, for in third place I look I read his handwriting on the mailbox: "O. Sienkiewicz." In Poland a very typical name. Weird that I am so happy, as if I have forgotten evil and murderous regime.

Up an outside flight of stairs to Apartment C, with no signs of life inside. I ring the doorbell many time and shade my eyes to peek through kitchen window, seeing nothing but a heap of dishes. Oskar's bathroom window is frosted glass and like Venetian blinds, each cranked open an inch for California air. I look in through slit and find his foot in pajamas as he sits on the bathroom floor, and when I stand taller there are his hands in his lap, and then just a slice of his square head can I make out, tilted toward his right shoulder, some trickles of sickness around his mouth.

"Oskar Sienkiewicz!" I shout, and there is

a flutter like he wants to waken. "Are you ill?" I ask in Polish.

He a little nods and answers in Polish, "I'm resting," and just the one sentence in mother's tongue puts me in happiest mood. I walk to the flat's front door, try the handle, and find it is unlocked, no problem. His flat inside is torn furnitures that Monsignor would call "shoddy." Loud on small television is noontime sex opera. On food tray beside a stuffed chair is feast for a hundred flies and a half-full bottle of famous Wyborowa vodka, its blade of grass still floating in it.

Oskar is on hands and knees on the bathroom floor when I get there. His stink is hard to take, for sure, but I help him stand and he lets me, then my hands he hits away. We speak in Polish from now on. With sarcasm, he asks, "Why aren't you praying?"

"Are you so certain I'm not?"

He falls into the bathroom wall and just there he stays for a while, like he is drunk. But he recites: " 'But I say unto you which hear, Love your enemies, do good to them which hate you.' " With satisfaction he smiles. "I have the quote right, no?"

"If you meant the Sermon on the Mount."

His forehead he taps. "I'm smart." And then he slides a foot or so until I catch his hot-with-fever weight and heave him to the hallway and onto his bed, its sheets in riot and still wet with night sweatings. He sits there, his head down, his hands useless beside him. "We are not friends," he says, "but I am glad to see you."

"I have missed speaking Polish."

"A hard language for outsiders," he says. Oskar squints at me. "I am from Wambierzyce. Have you heard of it?"

"Naturally. It's in Lower Silesia. A shrine to Mary is there."

Oskar falls to his left. "I have to lie down," he says.

Lifting up his white feet, I ask, "Is there anything can I do for you?"

His left forearm covers his eyes as he sighs and gives it some thought. And then he says, "Die."

"I could find a doctor for you. And medicines. Wash your clothes and dishes."

"Were you to die," he says, "that would make me happiest; that would be quite enough."

And that is when I tell him how even in such a terrible times it was to me pleasing to have him around. We shared thousand-year history. Wawel Castle meant to him. Rynek Główny, he knew, is a marketplace. Mariacki church. The scent of the Vistula

River. Hiking in the Carpathians. We are feeling nostalgia for identical things, and for these reasons he could never be my enemy.

With irritation he stares at me. "I was a Catholic once," Oskar says. "But I grew up."

Why this is hilarious to me is not clear, but he is infected by my laughter. I find a spot on the foot of his bed for sitting and he glances at me from under his forearm before shifting his legs to give me more room. "I found the kielbasa you left behind. And the delicatessen carton of *kutia*," I say. "And I was sure you were a real Polander."

"Oh, say nothing of Christmas pudding! My belly aches for it even now."

"And roasted walnuts?"

Oskar groans.

"And the pastries from that shop by the Jagiellonian?"

"Stop it, Stefan, or I shall weep!"

And so I go on naming foods until we both are crying.

CRAZY

Critics have said that Shakespeare's Macbeth is a man who fell in love with his wife's madness. I have seen a crazy woman's hands knitting the air in her sleep, as if she were darning what was torn in her mind. There are so many wanderers, all pleasantness lost, claiming microchips have been installed in their heads, having hot arguments with enemies who are no longer present. "Who are you yelling at?" I yelled, and his insanity stared through me as if *I* wasn't there. I heard a Marine ask the girl, "Then why did you invite me here?" and she said, "Because I wanted you to beat me." Kierkegaard called Abraham a knight of faith because he was willing to give up everything, even his son, in obedience to the instructions he'd heard. Confident he would get it all back. And there was a fascinating student who wanted me to read her fiction. But she handed me a scrapbook of stories written in

Crayola and in glossy words razored from magazines and glued onto the page. She thought writing was a ransom note. The child was not returned.

TRUE ROMANCE

It was still night out and my husband was shaving at the kitchen sink so he could hear the morning farm report and I was peeling bacon into the skillet. I hardly slept a wink with Gina acting up, and that croupy cough of hers. I must've walked five miles. Half of Ivan's face was hanging in the circle mirror, the razor was scraping the soap from his cheek, and pigs weren't dollaring like they ought to. And that was when the phone rang and it was Annette, my very best friend, giving me the woeful news.

Ivan squeaked his thumb on the glass to spy the temperature — still cold — then wiped his face with a paper towel, staring at me with puzzlement as I made known my shock and surprise. I took the phone away from my ear and said, "Honey? Something's killed one of the cows!"

He rushed over to the phone and got to talking to Annette's husband, Slick. Slick saw it coming from work — Slick's mainly on night shift; the Caterpillar plant. Our section of the county is on a party line: the snoops were getting their usual earful. I turned out the fire under the skillet. His appetite would be spoiled. Ivan and Slick went over the same ground again; I poured coffee and sugar and stirred a spoon around in a cup, just as blue as I could be, and when Ivan hung up, I handed the cup to him.

He said, "I could almost understand it if they took the meat, but Slick says it looks like it was just plain ripped apart."

I walked the telephone back to the living room and switched on every single light. Ivan wasn't saying anything. I opened my robe and gave Gina the left nipple, which wasn't so standing-out and sore, and I sat in the big chair under a shawl. I got the feeling that eyes were on me.

Ivan stood in the doorway in his underpants and Nebraska sweatshirt, looking just like he did in high-school. I said, "I'm just sick about the cow."

He said, "You pay your bills, you try and live simple, you pray to the Lord for guidance, but Satan can still find a loophole, can't he? He'll trip you up every time."

"Just the idea of it is giving me the willies," I said.

Ivan put his coffee cup on the floor and snapped on his gray coveralls. He sat against the high chair. "I guess I'll give the sheriff a call and then go look at the damage."

"I want to go with you, okay?"

The man from the rendering plant swerved a winch truck up the pasture until the swinging chain cradle was over the cow. His tires skidded green swipes on grass that was otherwise white with frost. I scrunched up in the pickup with the heater going to beat the band and Gina asleep on the seat. Ivan slumped in the sheriff's car and swore out a complaint. The man from the rendering plant threw some hydraulic levers and the engine revved to unspool some cable, making the cradle clang against the bumper.

I'd never seen the fields so pretty in March. Every acre was green winter wheat or plowed earth or sandhills the color of camels. The lagoon was as black and sleek as a grand piano.

Gina squinched her face up and then discovered a knuckle to chew as the truck engine raced again; and when the renderer hoisted the cow up, a whole stream of stuff poured out of her and dumped on the ground like boots. I slaughtered one or two in my time. I could tell which organs were missing.

Ivan made his weary way up the hill on grass that was greasy with blood, then squatted to look at footprints that were all walked over by cattle. The man from the plant said something and Ivan said something back, calling him Dale, and then Ivan slammed the pickup door behind him. He wiped the fog from inside the windshield with his softball cap. "You didn't bring coffee, did you?"

I shook my head as he blew on his fingers. He asked, "What good are ya, then?" but he was smiling. He said, "I'm glad our insurance is paid up."

"I'm just sick about it," I said.

Ivan put the truck in gear and drove it past the feeding cattle, giving them a lookover. "I gotta get my sugar beets in."

I thought: the cow's heart, and the female things.

Around noon Annette came over in Slick's Trans Am and we ate pecan rolls hot from the oven as she got the romance magazines out of her grocery bag and began reading me the really good stories. Gina played on the carpet next to my chair. You have to watch the little booger every second because she'll put in her mouth what most people wouldn't step on. Annette was four months pregnant but it hardly showed — just the top snap of her jeans was undone — and I was full of uncertainty about the outcome. Our daytime visits give us the opportunity to speak candidly about things like miscarriages or the ways in which we are ironing out our problems with our husbands, but on this occasion Annette was giggling about some goofy woman who couldn't figure out why marriage turned good men into monsters, and I got the ugly feeling that I was being looked at by a Peeping Tom.

Annette put the magazine in her lap and rapidly flipped pages to get to the part where the story was continued, and I gingerly picked Gina up and, without saying a peep to Annette, walked across the carpet and spun around. Annette giggled again and said, "Do you suppose this actually happened?" and I said yes, pulling my little girl tight against me. Annette said, "Doesn't she just crack you *up*?" and I just kept peering out the window. I couldn't stop myself.

That night I took another stroll around the property and then poured diet cola into a glass at the kitchen sink, satisfying my thirst. I could see the light of the sixty-watt bulb in the barn, and the cows standing up to the fence and rubbing their throats and chins. The wire gets shaggy with the stuff; looks just like orange doll hair. Ivan got on the intercom and his voice was puny, like it was trapped in a paper cup. "Come on out and help me, will you, Riva?"

"Right out," is what I said.

I tucked another blanket around Gina in the baby crib and clomped outside in Ivan's rubber boots. They jingled as I crossed the barnyard. The cattle stared at me. One of the steers got up on a lady and triumphed for a while, but she walked away and he dropped. My flashlight speared whenever I bumped it.

Ivan was kneeling on straw, shoving his arm in a rubber glove. An alarm clock was on the sill. His softball cap was off, and his long brown hair was flying wild as he squatted beside the side-laying cow. Her tail whisked a board, so he tied it to her leg with twine. She was swollen wide with the calf. My husband reached up inside her and the cow lifted her head indignantly, then settled down and chewed her tongue. Ivan said, "P.U., cow! You stink!" He was in her up to his biceps, seemed like.

"You going to cut her?"

He shook his head as he snagged the glove off and plunked it down in a water bucket.

"Dang calf's kaput!" He glared at his medicine box and said, "How many is that? Four out of eight? I might as well give it up."

I swayed the flashlight beam along the barn. Window. Apron. Pitchfork. Rope. Lug wrench. Sickle. Baling wire. And another four-paned window that was so streaked with pigeon goop it might as well've been slats. But it was there that the light caught a glint of an eye and my heart stopped. I stepped closer to persuade myself it wasn't just an apparition, and what I saw abruptly disappeared.

Ivan ground the tractor ignition and got the thing going, then raced it backward into the barn, not shutting the engine down but slapping it out of gear and hopping down to the ground. He said, "Swing that flashlight down on this cow's contraption, will ya, Riva?" and there was some messy tugging and wrestling as he yanked the calf's legs out and attached them to the tractor hitch with wire. He jumped up to the spring seat and jerked into granny, creeping forward with his gaze on the cow. She groaned with agony and more leg appeared and then the shut-eyed calf head. My husband crawled the tractor forward more and the calf came out in a surge. I suctioned gunk out of its throat with a bulb syringe and squirted it into the straw but the calf didn't quiver or pant; she was patient as meat and her tongue spilled onto the paint tarp.

Ivan scowled and sank to his knees by the calf. The mother cow struggled up and sniffed the calf and began licking off its nose in the way she'd been taught, but even she gave up in a second or two and hung her head low with grief.

"Do you know what killed it?"

Ivan just gaped and said, "You explain it." He got up and plunged his arms into the water bucket. He smeared water on his face.

I crouched down and saw that the calf was somehow split open and all her insides were pulled out.

After the sheriff and the man from the rendering plant paid their visits, the night was just about shot. Ivan completed his cold-weather chores, upsetting the cattle with his earliness, and I pored over Annette's romance magazines, gaining support from each disappointment.

Ivan and I got some sleep and even Gina cooperated by being good as can be. Ivan arose at noon but he was cranky and understandably depressed about our calamities, so I switched off *All My Children* and suggested we go over to Slick's place and wake him up and party.

Annette saw I was out of sorts right away, and she generously agreed to make our supper. She could see through me like glass. At two we watched *General Hospital,* which was getting crazier by the week according to Annette — she thought they'd be off in outer space next, but I said they were just keeping up with this wild and woolly world we live in. Once our story was over, we made a pork roast and boiled potatoes with chives and garlic butter, which proved to be a big hit. Our husbands worked through the remaining light of day, crawling over Slick's farm machinery, each with wrenches in his pockets and grease on his skin like war paint.

Annette said, "You're doing all right for yourself, aren't you, Riva."

"I could say the same for you, you know."

Here I ought to explain that Annette went steady with Ivan in our sophomore year, and I suspect she's always regretted giving him to me. If I'm any judge of character, her thoughts were on that subject as we stood at the counter and Slick and Ivan came in for supper and cleaned up in the washroom that's off the kitchen. Annette then had the gall to say, "Slick and me are going through what you and Ivan were a couple of months ago."

Oh no you're not! I wanted to say, but I didn't even give her the courtesy of a reply.

"You got everything straightened out, though, didn't you?"

I said, "Our problems were a blessing in disguise."

"I know exactly what you mean," she said.

"Our marriage is as full of love and vitality as any girl could wish for."

Her eyes were even a little misty. "I'm so happy for you, Riva!"

And she was; you could tell she wasn't pretending like she was during some of our rocky spots in the past.

Slick dipped his tongue in a spoon that he lifted from a saucepan and went out of his way to compliment Annette — unlike at least one husband I could mention. Ivan pushed down the spring gizmo on the toaster and got the feeling back in his fingers by working them over the toaster slots. My husband said in that put-down way of his, "Slick was saying it could be UFOs."

"I got an open mind on the subject," said Slick, and Ivan did his snickering thing.

I asked if we could please change the topic of conversation to something a little more pleasant.

Ivan gave me his angry smile. "Such as what? Relationships?"

Slick and Annette were in rare form that night, but Ivan was pretty much a poop until Slick gave him a number. Ivan bogarted the joint and Slick rolled up another, and by the time Annette and I got the dishes into the sink, the men were swapping a roach on the living-room floor and tooling Gina's playthings around. Annette opened the newspaper to the place that showed which dopey program was on the TV that evening. Slick asked if Ivan planted the marijuana seeds he gave us and Ivan shrugged. Which meant no. Slick commenced tickling Annette. She scooched back against the sofa and fought him off, slapping at his paws and pleading for help. She screamed, "Slick! You're gonna make me pee on myself!"

Ivan clicked through the channels but he was so stoned all he could say was, "What is that?"

Annette giggled but got out, *Creature from the Black Lagoon!*

I plopped Gina on top of her daddy's stomach and passed around a roach that was pinched with a hairpin. I asked Ivan, "Are you really ripped?" and Ivan shrugged.

Which meant yes.

The movie was a real shot in the arm for our crew. My husband rested his pestered head in my lap and I rearranged his long hair. There was a close-up of the creature and I got such a case of the stares from looking at it you'd think I was making a photograph.

Ivan shifted to frown at me. "How come you're not saying anything?"

And I could only reply, "I'm just really ripped."

Days passed without event, and I could persuade myself that the creature had gone off to greener pastures. However, one evening when Ivan was attending a meeting of the parish council, my consternation only grew stronger. Gina and I got home from the grocery store and I parked the pickup close by the feed lot so I could hear if she squalled as I was forking out silage. Hunger was making the cattle ornery. They straggled over and jostled each other, resting their long jaws on each other's shoulders, bawling *mom* in the night. The calves lurched and stared as I closed the gate behind me. I collared my face from the cold and as I was getting into the truck, a cry like you hear at a slaughterhouse flew up from the lagoon.

I thought, I ought to ignore it, or I ought to go to the phone, but I figured what I really ought to do is make certain that I was seeing everything right, that I wasn't making things up.

Famous last words!

I snuggled Gina in the baby crib and went out along the pasture road, looking at the eight-o'clock night that was closing in all around me. I glided down over a hill and a stray calf flung its tail in my headlights as its tiny mind chugged through its options. A yard away its mother was on her side and swollen up big as two hay bales. I got out into the spring cold and inspected the cow even though I knew she was a goner, and then I looked at the woods and the moonlit lagoon and I could make out just enough of a blacker image to put two and two together and see that it was the creature dragging cow guts through the grass.

The gun rack only carried fishing rods on it, but there was an angel-food-cake knife wedged behind the pickup's toolbox, and that was what I took with me on my quest, my scalp prickling with fright and goose-bumps on every inch of me. The chill was mean, like you'd slapped your hand against gravel. The wind seemed to gnaw at the trees. You're making it up, I kept praying, and when I approached the lagoon and saw nothing, I was pleased and full of hope.

The phone rang many times the next day, but I wouldn't get up to answer it. I stayed in the room upstairs, hugging a pillow like a body, aching for the beginning of some other life, like a girl in a Rosemary Rogers book. Once again Annette provided an escape from my doldrums by speeding over in the orange Trans Am — her concern for me and her eternal spunk are always a great boost for my spirits.

I washed up and went outside with Gina, and Annette said, "What on earth is wrong with your phone?"

I only said, "I was hoping you'd come over," and Annette slammed the car door. She hugged me like a girlfriend and the plastic over the porch screens popped. The wind was making mincemeat of the open garbage can. And yet we sat outside on the porch steps with some of Slick's dope rolled in Zig-Zag papers. I zipped Gina into a parka with the wind so blustery. She was trying to walk. She'd throw her arms out and buck ahead a step or two and then plump down hard on her butt. The marijuana wasn't rolled tight enough and the paper was sticking all the time to my lip. I

looked at the barn, the silo, the road, seeing
nothing of the creature, seeing only my
husband urging the tractor up out of a ditch
with Slick straddling the gangplow's hook-
ups and hoses. Slick's a master at hydraulics.
The plow swung wide and banged as Ivan
established his right to the road, then he
shifted the throttle up and mud flew from
the tires. One gloved hand rested on a
fender lamp and he looked past me to our
daughter, scowling and acting put out, then
they turned into the yard and Annette
waved. Ivan lifted his right index finger just
a tad, his greeting, then turned the steering
wheel hand over hand, bouncing high in the
spring seat as Slick clung on for dear life.

Annette said, "My baby isn't Ivan's, you
know."

I guess I sighed with the remembering of
those painful times.

Annette said, "I'm glad we were able to
stay friends."

"Me too," I said, and I scooched out to
see my little girl with an angel-food-cake
knife in her hands, waddling over to me.
"Gina!" I yelled. "You little snot! Where'd
you get that?"

She gave it to me and wiped her hands on
her coat. "Dut," Gina said, and though my
husband would probably have reprimanded

her, I knelt down and told her how she mustn't play with knives and what a good girl she was to bring it right to me. She didn't listen for very long, and I put the knife in my sweater pocket for the time being.

Annette was looking peculiar, and I could tell she wanted an explanation, but then there was a commotion in the cattle pen and we looked to where Ivan and Slick were pushing cow rumps aside in order to get close to the trough. They glared at something on the ground out there, and I glanced at the cake knife again, seeing the unmistakable signs of blood.

"I'm going out to the cattle pen," I imparted. "You keep Gina with you."

Annette said, "I hope your stock is okay."

The day was on the wane as I proceeded across the yard and onto the cow path inside the pen, the cake knife gripped in my right hand within my sweater pocket. The cattle were rubbing against the fence and ignorantly surging toward the silage in the feed trough. Slick was saying, "You oughta get a photograph, Ivan." My husband kept his eyes on one spot, his gloved hands on his hips, his left boot experimenting by moving something I couldn't see.

I got the cattle to part by tilting against

them with all my weight. They were heavy as Cadillacs. And I made my toilsome way to my husband's side only to be greeted with a look of ill tidings and with an inquiry that was to justify all my grim forebodings. He asked, "Do you know how it happened, Riva?"

I regarded ground that was soggy with blood and saw the green creature that I'd so fervently prayed was long gone. He was lying on his scaly back and his yellow eyes were glowering as if the being were still enraged over the many stabbings into his heart. Death had been good for his general attractiveness, glossing over his many physical flaws and giving him a childlike quality that tugged at my sympathy.

Again Ivan nudged the being with his boot, acting like it was no more than a cow, and asking me with great dismay, "How'd the dang thing get killed, do ya think?"

And I said, "Love. Love killed it. Love as sharp as a knife."

Slick gazed upon me strangely, and my husband looked at me with grief as I sank to the earth among the cattle, feeling the warmth of their breathing. I knew then that the anguish I'd experienced over those past many months was going to disappear, and that my life, over which I'd despaired for so long, was going to keep changing and improving with each minute of the day.

WILDERNESS

On a green lake in the Adirondacks a tanned old man was rowing. It was six a.m. and the lake was glass, and fog lingered under the juniper trees. Milos swung the oars up and the rowboat glided. His right hand wiped his bald head and the gray hair on his chest. He looked at the sweat on his palm. His blue sweater was on the other seat and water drops from the oars darkly spotted it. A gray wolf slinked out of the fog through high, poking grass and stepped onto the painted white dock. His tongue hung long as he panted. Milos adjusted his direction and pulled toward the wolf. The bray of his oarlocks was the only sound.

Her name was Sylvia and she wrote poetry at a cottage table that thumped when she punched the typewriter keys. She was dark, rather pretty, and forty-two, a full professor of English at Williams, one of the foremost experts on the Romantic Age. She was Axel's second wife, the woman they said was too good for him. She drank iced tea from a jelly glass and slept in an extra-large gray sweatshirt with WILLIAMS lettered in purple on it. She smoked clove cigarettes and used the lid of a jelly jar for an ashtray. She stood on the porch of the island cottage and watched yellow-raincoated fishermen cast their lines into the green Atlantic as seagulls looped and dropped and climbed heavily out of the water with scraps. She read each day's product at night with a soft calico cat on her lap, a cat that she guessed belonged to a neighbor.

Her husband, Axel, was in Mexico with a second-year graduate student, Arietta, who meant more to him than his marriage now. He was a heavy man, fifty-five years old, with a gray crew cut and a white beard, a professor in the field of art restoration at Williams. He was gingerly excavating the ruins of what might have been a cooking room five hundred years ago, and if he looked up he could see gorgeous, sexy, too-admiring Arietta tenderly scraping intricate pottery with a fine sculptor's tool, the shade of a Panama hat around her pale neck like a scarf. Axel pried a root from the ground and without looking up inquired, "Tell me, do you know any opera, Arietta?"

Arietta held up a hand to shade her eyes and asked, "I beg your pardon?"

Axel said, "I find it funny that we've been together for so long, and yet I haven't asked you about —" He did not complete his thought, for as he picked up a spade he saw a white cat with gray patches carefully licking its forepaw.

Milos poured honey from a jar onto a bowl of oatmeal and milk and centered the bowl on a place setting in the dining room. The teapot whistled and Milos made Earl Grey tea and sat in a green leather chair in his study. His soft white calico cat pounced up onto his lap. Milos petted it soothingly and spoke a foreign language into its ear. The cat thumped down to the carpet and oozily disappeared outside. Milos frowned into space.

Sylvia shut up the cottage and packed into a foreign car a typewriter, teapot, paperbacks, and string-tied boxes heaped with camping clothes, poems, and one hundred pages of scholarship that she could read only with great displeasure. She drove west with her wrist on the steering wheel, her mind preoccupied, uncoupled, even as she repeated the Spanish phrases spoken on the language tapes she listened to on a Walkman. And she was crossing the Adirondacks, past Lake Pleasant, when she pulled over to the roadside in order to unpack her husband's red wool hiking coat and walk among the junipers, eating one of the green apples she kept in a picnic basket. She heard on the Walkman, "I'm just passing through," and she said, *Estoy solo de paso.*" And she was listening hard to find out if she was right when she turned at a weird roadside noise and saw what may have been a wolfhound tearing at groceries in the front of her car.

She yelled, "Hey! How'd you get in there? Shoo!"

The wolfhound regarded her insultingly before retreating a little through the wide-open door and trotting off with a half-filled grocery sack in his jaws.

Sylvia yelled again and the wolfhound simply regripped his loot before loping down a woodcutter's road, stopping after fifty yards or so to get a new purchase on the grocery sack and to gaze back at the hurrying woman as if he were letting her catch up. She flung a stick that the hound dodged in a way she found sarcastic, and she looked back to her car on the highway and watched wild pages flap out the front window, looping high as seagulls into the air.

The cat approached Milos again upstairs as the man was slipping into a nightshirt. The cat roped between the old man's tanned legs and Milos moved a window curtain aside to peer out.

Arietta stood with one hand in a pocket of her khaki shorts while the other picked skin tissue off her upper arm. She was golden-haired and painfully sunburnt and she regretted every choice she'd made in the past six months. Axel was deep in a cellar he'd happened upon and she could only see his brown calves and ankle-high boots as he cleaned a room painting with a camel-hair brush. The white cat whined and whiled its way between her legs, and she gathered it up. She asked, "Do you see anything written?"

Axel paused before saying, "The script is unfamiliar." He looked up at Arietta, shading his eyes. "So our cat has reappeared."

"Do you want me to get the camera?"

"Please," said Axel. "And with a new roll of film, please."

She walked to the Jeep, petting the cat, and squatted down in the shade of the car in order to reload the camera. She smelled candle wax. She snapped on the flash attachment and heard the clinking of glasses. She stood in surprise but could see nothing except sunlight and pink foothills over a beige Mexican landscape. A man's voice said, "Do you think I would poison you?" and she let the cat fall out of her arms. She experienced a pressure against her breasts as if she were being petted. "Axel!" she screamed, but kisses smeared against her lips and cheek and she was being whispered to in a language foreign to her. She struggled away and got to the cellar, crying, "Oh, Axel help me!" But when she looked down into the room, she saw only a gray hound that was large as a wolf, growling up at her.

Axel was strolling back from the Jeep as slow as a dawdler in a park. He grinned and dangled the camera down to her. "So!" he said. "Just as you ordered."

She combed her gold hair away from her eyes. The wolf, of course, was gone. Axel stooped to peer into the cellar, saying, "And now perhaps you'll let me see this marvelous painting?"

Sylvia was lost, by then, in wilderness. Her

only thought was that the wolfhound would be going back to a cottage and she could get directions there. So she followed a path through the dark green foliage that was swiped awry with the animal's passing, and she had gone miles in a darkness that made midday seem night when she began to see sunlight dappling the upper leaves of the trees and then the path and then she emerged into a clearing of sponge grass where the hound was standing, swinging his tail, as seagulls dipped into the grocery sack and carried scraps to the porch of a large yellow house.

Sylvia called, "Hello? Is anybody home?" and instantly felt girlish and ignorant. She stamped away the seagulls and picked up the grocery sack as the wolfhound panted and looked to a porch swing that was rocking as though somebody had just gotten up.

The yellow house was a strange anthology of designs, with gables and spires and parapets, scalloped cornices, intricate porch posts, and red chimneys of miscellaneous heights. Sylvia looked through a window and saw a library of books that climbed so high that the owner used a stepladder on wheels. She called again and looked through an oval glass at a dining table with a teapot and a place setting and one lighted candle.

A phonograph was playing Bach, the Gold-berg Variations. She rapped on the entryway door three separate times and then permit-ted herself to trespass, certain that she could explain the lapse in etiquette once the oc-cupants returned.

Axel peered at contact prints under the shade of a flapping tent canopy. Arietta sat across from him, her chin in her hand, see-ing now how old he was, how parental, how caught up in his project and incurious about her. He'd said, in the rigid English of a foreigner, "You have been getting too much sun, maybe." He'd said, "If there are guilty parties, there are always voices." Axel moved his magnifying glass over a photograph and said, "Such a disappointment, Arietta. Not Spanish, not Aztec, perhaps no more than a century old. The gods help a peasant girl to go to the court of the sun king. She makes love to a prince but then — I cannot tell why — flees the place, and the prince must spend many years looking for this girl. They meet and there is great happiness." Axel pushed the contact prints away and sat back in his fold-up chair. "Cinderella," Axel said. "Some children were playing a little joke, perhaps. I hope you are not too sorry."

Arietta budged forward and squinted at

the photographs. "Do these diagonal lines mean anything?"

"They mean I made a particularly stupid mistake. I ought to punish myself so and so." He lightly slapped his cheeks and grinned as he got up to crouch over his graduate student. "Look you: a face appears here; next, a car, could it be a Mazda? And here, a yellow house, a gable, a gray-haired man — who it could be, I don't know. The roll is being used once before."

"And the woman is Sylvia," Arietta said.

Axel shrugged. "Naturally." He pulled Arietta up and chaperoned her over to the tent they'd pitched next to the Jeep. He said, "It is very comical, really. The prince is one time superimposed on me. And my dear wife is the golden-haired girl I am seeking."

"How silly," Arietta said.

Sylvia took off her red wool hiking coat and stood alone in every room in the house. She ate the oatmeal on the dining room table without knowing why and though she emptied the teapot she grew so sleepy that she went upstairs to one of the many beds and collapsed on top of the covers. She kept thinking, Why are you so unhappy? And she slept deeply until nightfall.

She could recall the clicking of the dog's

claws on the glossy floorboards, the rapid gasps of the dog's respiration, the change in the mattress as the dog jumped up and flung his weight down next to hers, but Sylvia could do nothing but grant the dog his right to the room, and she only thought about his coming when she felt a change in the mattress again and got up on an elbow to see a man of some age in a wingback chair angrily glaring at her. "I'm sorry," she said, and the man's expression became one of pleasure.

"Don't be," Milos said. "You look so pretty sleeping."

"You must think me terribly impolite. I just couldn't help myself."

"Yes, but you must speak no more apologies, please. I get so little company up here. I will pretend you are one of my grandchildren having her nap before supper."

Axel was sitting outside, smoking a pipe, when Arietta came out of the tent in blue jeans and a wool pullover. "So many stars," she said.

"Do you hear the wolves?"

She looked to the darker inch of night where she knew the foothills were but she could only make out the sounds of the flapping canopy, plaintive insects, wind. "Do you think they'll come for our food?"

Axel shrugged. "If they're hungry." He got up, lighting his pipe again. "I'll go for my axe."

The soft calico cat meowed and Arietta crouched to encourage it to come forward, patting her thighs and calling "Kitty." The cat stepped closer and posed like a sculpture, peeking at Arietta without recognition as though its eyes were no more than gold marbles. Axel rummaged through the Jeep, singing opera phrases, and Arietta approached the cat, pretending it knew what she meant when she spoke about happiness, missing it, milk. The cat simply licked a gray patch on its chest and, as she knelt to scoop it up, hopped aslant of her, pausing just beyond her grasp and opening its mouth in an unvoiced reply. Arietta walked to it and the cat walked away; Arietta swooped it and stepped into the pit that Axel had happened upon, dropping into nothing at all and spinning like paper on air.

Milos sat opposite Sylvia and pinged his champagne glass against hers. "To my companion," he said, "who is writing such good poetry."

"To Milos," Sylvia said.

Milos said, "You will find me interesting."

He peered at her as he sipped his champagne and she looked away at the many candles, the expensive red plates, the gold trays heaped with enough food for eight. "You are not eating," he said. He put his champagne glass down and ripped off a scrap of fish, pushing it into his mouth. "See? Do you think I would poison you?"

"I'd really prefer to get back to my car," Sylvia said, and without really knowing why she added, "People are expecting me."

"You are being particularly stupid."

The cat with the gray patches paid no attention to Axel as the man walked the perimeter of the camp yelling, "Arietta!" over and over again. The cat paid no attention even when the man approached with an axe, it simply gave itself pleasure in any way it could and was so preoccupied that it didn't jump aside when Axel shouted his rage or even when the axe chopped into it.

Axel gaped in surprise, for the axe was splitting a sheet of paper and the cat had disappeared. He ripped the paper from the axe and moved a match light over it, seeing Sylvia's handwriting on a typewritten poem. More pages were looping up from the pit so Axel jumped down into it, getting up from his hands and knees on sponge grass at the edge of a lake. A rowboat nodded at a painted white dock and water slapped and a dog that was as large as a wolf growled only briefly before it lunged.

Milos was wooing Sylvia by complimenting himself, saying his green eyes were meant for worshipping her, his ears were meant to indulge her, his arms were big even in his old age in order to gather her close to his heart, which was redder than her wool coat. He got up from his chair to put an opera on the phonograph and Sylvia attempted to push away from the dining room table and politely make an exit. Milos stopped over her, however, nuzzling his whiskered chin into her pale neck, crushing her breasts in his palms, smearing kisses over her lips and cheeks even as she slapped at him, whispering persistently, *"Warum bist Du so ungluck-lich?"*

The dog yelped once and Milos stalled, looking toward the painted dock and the lake as a cat might. He then yanked Sylvia into a side kitchen and put a match to the oven. The candlelight was extinguished.

Having slaughtered the dog, Axel crept to the porch of the large yellow house. The Mazda was parked on the sponge grass and seagulls were roosting inside it like teapots. He pulled open a porch door and crept inside and the floorboards made a speech about each step he took as if he wore spades for shoes. He stopped by a study and saw the white cat with gray patches sitting on a green leather chair, its gold eyes peering at him, and he heard a knife clatter in a porcelain sink — not as if it slipped off a plate, but as if a hand had simply let it go to provide him with information. Axel wiped the dog's blood off the axe and onto the carpet and then he passed through a room that smelled of candle wax and champagne and passion, on into a room with a porcelain sink and a pool of Sylvia's blood on the floor. His wife had been chopped into little pieces and Milos was eating the last scrap of her.

"So it's you, old sinner!" Axel said, as if he were greeting a man he recognized. And he swung the woodcutter's axe through the man's yielding neck, cleaving Milos from his body like a fish head from a fish so that he was gasping and attempting to speak as he rolled along the floor. Axel then split open the belly as quickly as one might unzip a bag and Sylvia reappeared in one piece just as the girls do a magic show. She and Axel stuffed Milos with poetry before they sewed him up and they dropped him over the side of the rowboat into the accepting green lake, where Milos sank like an iron spike.

The cat with gray patches Sylvia kept and it paws at the typewriter from her lap as she taps a cigarette into a jar lid. Axel stamps his hip waders on the porch steps and opens the cottage door, saying, "Look what I caught," and he lifts aloft not a fish but a seagull, the fishhook poking out of its neck.

"Did you enjoy Mexico?" Sylvia asks, and Axel frowns at her. "Mexico?" For she's made him forget everything, as if it never happened.

MECHANICS

Each of them was good with his hands. Earl, Kim, Lamar, and Mike wore green shirts and generally pretended to hate their jobs though they got there early and hung around late. Ian was handsome and serious and twenty-eight, already the White Shirt at Speedway Chevrolet-Oldsmobile-Pontiac and a night school student at Metro Tech Community College. His long blond-brown hair was tied back in a ponytail and soon he'd put on his sunglasses. The five mechanics hunched out of the cold holding their hot coffees in the half-darkness of sunrise, watching commuters jam up the six lanes out front.

Mike liked the looks of that Pontiac Grand Prix, no not that one, the other one, and Ian informed him it had a 3.4-liter DOHC 24-valve V6. Mike frowned at him like he did when Ian called car manuals "literature." He asked, "If you know so much, what's in that Subaru Legacy?"

"If it's the turbo, it's a flat-four," Ian said. "Hundred thirty-five cubic inches."

"What's the suspension?" Lamar asked, just to play it out.

Ian shut his eyes tight like he does. You'd have thought this was *The 39 Steps.* "Mac-Pherson struts in front, of course," and he hesitated before adding, "and I'm pretty sure Chapman struts in back."

Each of them was looking for the other guy to contradict him.

"What kind of links?" Old Earl asked.

"Trailing. And dual lower lateral." Child's play, his smile said.

"See that Cadillac?" Mike asked.

"The Eldorado?"

"What kind of engine?"

Ian gave it hard thought. "V-eight, sequential port, four point nine liter. Electronic fuel injection."

"Well hell, tell me something new," Mike said.

"And variable-assist steering."

"You gonna tell me it's got four wheels next?"

Ian half smiled and finished his coffee. "It's a gray car, Mike."

"Don't get me started."

"You just have to read the literature."

"Hold me back, somebody," Mike said.

Young Kim was in awe; he asked Earl, "*You* know all that stuff?"

"Engine's under the hood," Earl said. "You give it gas and it goes."

"It's a miracle," Lamar said.

Whining motors hoisted the four bay doors just before seven and the general manager was there in his hand-painted tie and gray Armani suit to gloomily watch as his five mechanics punched in. "Roc" O'Connell was on his name cards but the mechanics all called him Richard.

She was thirty or so and thought of herself as pretty. She pouted at Ian in that frustrated way and said she didn't *know* what she needed done. She felt so helpless. She hated it.

"Okay. What's it sound like?" Ian asked.

"Whirring."

"Whirring noise. Where?"

She pointed, wrinkling her nose, playing the innocent. "You know, the wheel thingie."

"The axle," he said.

She smiled.

"High-pitched or low?"

"Maybe it's more like a growl."

"Is it fairly constant?"

"Yes."

"And you're getting this even when you go slow?"

"Yep," she said, "sure enough."

"Worn pinion bearing," Ian said.

She posed, and he went to his paperwork.

Lamar held his hands out like boobs and gave Ian his "Ho-ho!" look.

Children, Ian thought.

While Ian sorted the service orders, Roc bummed a Camel from Old Earl and told him to have one himself. Earl obeyed; he'd retire in October and lately found himself uttering "No muss, no fuss" or "Whatever you say" like he was leaking pints of testosterone wherever he parked himself.

"I'll get an Up on the floor," Roc told Earl. "An Up is an unattended person."

"Thanks. You have to spell things out for me most times."

Roc's Obsession for Men cologne was finding every corner of the office. Roc continued. "The first thing I try to do is get his keys in my pocket. I'll say, 'You thinking about trading your car in?' And I'll get his keys to give it a road test. And if he isn't trading I'll make up a fib about needing that space he's parked in and that I'll just have to hold on to his keys. Either way, I have power over him. We talk about sticker prices, markups, and options, and whether the Up knows it or not he's thinking that I have his keys in my pocket and he'll have to ask me for them."

"Oh, Richard! You got the hammer then," Earl said. "You got all the bullets."

"Exactly. You get the right kind of guy and he's going to try to please you just to get his nuts back. Another kind'll hate my guts, but hey, I'm in *car* sales."

"If you can't stand the heat . . ."

". . . the buck stops here."

Ian walked from his office with a job order that he handed Earl, and Earl ambled out to the hoists. Ian went over the pre-noon schedule with the general manager. "We got a shotgunned transmission, a worn pinion bearing, four oil and lubes, a handful of tune-ups, a hard pedal on a shoe job we did last week, and a guy whose tires are crowning. His tire pressure's too high is the problem, but he's one of our guys and he paid full-boat so I'll put it through the machine."

"No paint and body?"

"We're getting killed there, Roc. We have people getting estimates, but that's just for insurance scams. Otherwise they tootle off to Ultrabrite. Crazy way we're doing it, we'll never even underbid Bondo Bob's."

Roc looked out at Kim hosing the dust off the fifty-four new Chevrolets, Oldsmobiles, Pontiacs, and GMC trucks in his lot. Eight hundred dollars a day just in interest. "We need more paint and body," the general manager said. "Estimate 'em like Ultrabrite for a while. We'll see how it factors."

"You're going to like the numbers, Roc."

Roc sneered. "You figured out which guy you'll fire?"

"Not yet."

"Hop to it."

The guys were at half speed on the floor and the first thing Ian saw was Mike and that gun-in-the-toolbox look of his. Lamar was six foot six and headless under the Pontiac Grand Prix in the fourth bay, Walkman headphones on so he could hear his Bob Seger. And Earl had a Caprice on the hoist, green smoke feathering from the engine and a red fire extinguisher still in his hands.

"Oh, oh, guys," Earl said. "It's the White Shirt."

Mike made a huffing noise through his nose, but then had to use his handkerchief.

Ian looked underneath the Caprice and asked Earl, "You got flame?"

"Oh, a little," Earl said. "She put in too much oil. I guess she was checking the wrong dipstick."

"She's got the right one now," Mike said.

Earl squinched up his face in his ouch expression and shot his flashlight up into the manifold. "Watch out, Mike. You hurt my feelings again and I may just have to retire."

Ian walked over to the lunchroom where MECHANICS was painted on frosted glass on the door. Yesterday's newspaper was in holy terror on the lunchroom table and Kim was tilting back on a wooden chair's hind legs, frowning at Sally Jessy Raphael on the television like he had no idea what he was looking at. Kim was a friendly, pretty-boy father of two and hardly more than a kid himself, a failure-at-all-things kind of guy whom Mike and Earl protected. When he saw Ian, Kim proudly announced, "Coffee's made," as if he'd not just brewed but invented it.

"Early break?"

"Mike said it was okay. I hosed down the cars and no one needed the shuttle so . . ."

Sally Jessy's guests were female impersonators who looked pretty much like Dolly Parton, Cher, and Madonna. Wild laughter from the audience at their winking innuendos. Talk here would be about pansies, though. Mike would trot out his worst jokes.

"Why aren't you watching *Speedweek*?"

Kim looked at Ian in panic, like that was another deal that he'd piddled away. "I don't know," he said. "I guess I forgot it was on."

Ian changed the channel. Engines shrieked and howled in the pits and mechanics huddled to talk about the problems they heard. Heat waves wrinkled the race cars as they prowled the turns.

"You know what race this is?" Kim asked.

A. J. Foyt flashed by in a Copenhagen Lola-Chevy and that was followed by a tracking shot of Al Unser Jr. with his hands hard on the wheel as the *Speedweek* announcer excitedly said his 228 miles per hour was a practice-day record.

"Old show," Ian said. "Indy five hundred."

"Huh," Kim said.

Lamar and Earl joined them. A half-wet, paint-by-number, palomino horse head was hung up next to the paint-by-number foals in a forest that Earl had presented them with last week. Earl got his coffee before sidling over to the horse head and just standing there with his "Look what I did!" face on. Ian sought to ignore him by washing out four coffee cups and upending them on the plastic strainer. Earl finally said, "You see my horse?"

Ian pretended he hadn't heard; he dried out the sink with paper towels.

"Oh hey, I forgot to mention it," Kim said. "You've got a lot of talent, Earl!"

"Nah."

"You do!"

"Well, it's patience mostly."

"My kids have those paint-by-number kits and there's just no comparison."

Earl lost half a foot in height. "Well, maybe when they get to be nine or ten."

And Mike was there. "Don't they have any paint-by-number women?"

"I looked and looked," Earl said. He seemed to be peering at his handiwork from a fresh perspective.

Mike straddled a chair and opened up his lunchbox. Word was he dyed his hair to have it that black. Like Dean Martin, whom he favored, he said. He'd taken to hiding his prison tattoos. "You watching *cars*?" he asked.

"Indy five hundred," Kim said.

"You have something else in mind?" Ian asked Mike.

Mike focused fiercely on him. "Sally Jessy Raphael!"

"We'd rather watch Emerson Fittipaldi."

Mike relaxed. "Emmo! Who's he racing for?"

"Penske."

Lamar ducked under the door casing, took off his headphones, and popped a can of Coke. Lamar and Mike followed the race for a while. Kim seemed to find out for the first time that Mike was a full foot shorter than Lamar, and he smiled to Earl about it, but Earl was facing his horse head.

"Hell, that's not a fast car," Mike said.

"Arie Luyendyk wins," Lamar said.

"Who?" Mike asked.

"Dutch guy. Another Lola-Chevy."

"Even so, that ain't the fastest race car."

You can say the sun's out and Mike will say, not in China.

Ian asked, "What *is* the fastest race car, Mike?"

"A Cobra."

"A Cobra," Ian said.

"Yes, a Cobra!"

Earl opened his lunchbox, and Mike tried to work on him, too. "You get that Caprice fixed yet?"

"Too hot to touch," Earl said.

Mike guffawed and slapped his thigh. "If God loved liars, he'd hug you to death, Earl."

Earl unfolded some waxed paper, took out a peanut butter cookie as if his Mrs. surprised him with it, and gaped up at the television screen for a full minute. "Who's ahead?"

"Fittipaldi and Rahal," Ian said.

"Still?"

"Hell, it's *taped,* you idiot!" Mike screamed. "Indy happens on Memorial Day! You could watch that program forty times and the goddamn winner'd never change!"

Lamar frowned. "You're running a little hot yourself, Mike."

Mike seemed to hunt the right words for a while, and then he got up and went out. Earl finished his cookie. Kim filled his coffee cup. After a while Lamar asked, "Whose kid painted the horse?"

Roc and Mike were talking when Roc saw Ian and waved him over to explain his horsepower formula to Mike. Ian got out his pen and folded over a yellow job order. "You have a fast car but you don't know its horsepower. We'll call the car a Cobra. You *do* know your Cobra's weight and its quarter-mile speed. The formula for speed is two hundred twenty-one times the cube root of the gross horsepower divided by the weight."

Mike frowned at the general manager. *Where's this guy come up with this stuff?* Roc shrugged.

Ian formed letters and told Mike, "We're solving for H."

"H," Mike said. Worry twisted his face.

"Horsepower. And S is speed."

"And W is weight. I get it; go on."

"Well, it's all arithmetic from that point on."

"You see, it's that cube-root business, has me kinda . . ."

Ian jotted it down. "S to the third power, times W . . ."

"Weight," the general manager said.

"Which is divided by one point zero eight, times ten million, which I have here as ten to the seventh power."

"You pulling these numbers outta your hat?"

"Trust me on this, Mike. *Equals* H."

"Horsepower."

"We're talking gross horsepower, not net. Which is standard."

Mike took the formula from him and held it like he'd want to wash his hands pretty soon.

"And the beauty of it is you can solve for any function — speed, weight, horsepower."

Mike handed back the formula. "We oughta just give up having races. We oughta just fax our numbers to our handiest White Shirt and have *him* tell us who won."

"Won't sell as much beer that way," Roc said. "Hellcats won't get to wear helmets and reckless grins and drink their milk right from the bottle."

Lamar got a screwdriver from his red tool cabinet just as Earl was getting a radiator fan belt. "You know that thing I was talking about?"

"What thing?" Earl asked.

"You know, that *thing,*" Lamar said.

"Oh, yeah," Earl said. "Your ultra secret."

"Here," Lamar said, and handed him a sketch of his two-stroke engine design. Lamar unscrewed a fouled plastic distributor cap and the rotor beneath it.

Earl seemed puzzled by his sketch.

"What?" Lamar asked. Without looking, he took the two wiring terminals from the retainer.

"You got some fancy gizmo here looks like a chess piece."

Lamar crooked his neck and Earl helpfully pointed. "Oh. That's the hydraulic injector," Lamar said.

"And what's this? Your intake valve?"

"You got it." Lamar lifted out the condenser.

"And exhaust valve here?"

"Exhaust is on the right."

Earl got the point set from the skirt on the fender and handed it to him. Lamar installed it on the breaker plate. "Trouble was," Lamar said, "I didn't have an eraser for the drawing. Kids used it up on their homework."

Earl tapped the sketch of a jar shape. "Wet sump, I s'pose."

"Uh-huh."

"Like the way you shaded it. Excellent technique."

Lamar hooked up the wires. "Whole secret of the engine is the poppet valves," Lamar said. "Each one opens and closes independent."

"What's that do for ya?"

"Extra external scavenging." Lamar checked the cam lubricator and adjusted it so that it just touched the cam lobes.

Earl shut his eyes and tried to feature the functioning on his lawn mower's two-stroke. "Don't know about this, Lamar." Earl peered at the sketch in his hands. "You got a lotta parts in there," Earl said. His tone was too fatherly, and he heard a hurt silence from his friend. "Don't mean to put a damper on things."

"Well, yes; that's the biggest drawback, silly parts. You get too much to go wrong and it will. We see that day in and day out."

Lamar took his sketch and tried to find a hiding place for it in his floor toolbox.

Earl held out his own eight-inch Allen wrench, but Lamar got one from the toolbox. "I'll tell you what, though," Earl said. "Engineers in Japan are staying awake nights trying to get a power stroke like that."

"Ho-ho," Lamar said. "You better believe it!"

Earl saw Ian staring and strolled to his hoist. Lamar scowled at the high side of the cam and measured the gap in the points.

At lunch, Earl tore open a sack of potato chips and ate one. Lamar flicked the pickle slices from his cheeseburger bun. "I forgot to have it my way," he said.

Cigarette smoke grayed the air. Camels, Chesterfields, Marlboros, Kools.

Kim asked, "How's your wife, Mike?"

Mike didn't look up. "She's still in the hospital," he said. And then in Mike-theater added, "She probably ain't coming out."

Kim looked surprised. "You know what it is?"

"Doctors think it might be cancer." Mike took the lid off his pudding. "Damn bitch probably gave me cancer, too. I just signed divorce papers yesterday."

All the mechanics stared at him.

"You're *divorcing* her?" Lamar asked.

"Hell yes! She gives me cancer, she deserves it." Mike put his spoon in the chocolate pudding but didn't lift it up. "I *knew* I shouldn't a married that bitch. Something told me. I just knew it."

No one said anything for a while.

Mike said, "I feel *fine,* but I've been eating normal and I'm still losing weight."

"You can't catch cancer that way," Lamar said.

Mike scowled at him. "You know, if you was half a foot shorter you wouldn't have so many opinions."

A floor salesman hurried in and the mechanics focused on him so hard he hunched. The floor salesman found Ian and told him he had a guy upside down on his Corvette loan who hoped to get unburied by trading it in on a Camaro Z28. Trouble was, when the salesman gave it a run the Vette kind of hesitated when he put his foot down. "She'll go *uh-uh-uh* and then she'll catch up."

"I forgot your name."

"George."

"You getting rubber changing gears, George?"

The floor salesman was surprised. "Why, yes!"

"It probably isn't the engine," Ian said.

"Sounds like the clutch is slipping."

"Clutch," George said. "That's what I was thinking. Expensive?"

"Well, we'd have to pull the block," Ian said. "About six hundred dollars, minimum."

"That's what I was thinking," George said, and jotted $1000 in his pocket tablet. "Another thing. You know that Ferrari Mondial we got to lure in the tire kickers? What's it mean to have that transverse gearbox layout?"

"Eliminates axle tramp under hard acceleration."

Earl winked at the floor salesman and said, "You love it when he talks dirty, don't ya."

George walked out and Mike told the mechanics, "I'll kill that floor-whore someday, he tries knuckling my head about cars. You'll find him flat under the truck hoist. Won't be nothing there but a stain. Waltzing in here, talking chassis and what all. The golf pants industry'll go bust."

Kim found Ian in his office before three. "Would you mind if I went out? I was kind of thinking of getting a chocolate shake."

"Are you done with your jobs?"

"All you said to do."

"Go ahead then."

"I was kind of hoping you'd like to go with me."

Ian peered up at Kim's pained and half-scared face and got up from his desk.

Kim kept trying to speak on his half-mile drive to the Burger King, and finally got out, "You know that guy that used to be here? Denny?"

"Sure; he used to have your job."

"Well, he's in jail now."

"And that's why he's not with us," Ian said.

"We weren't really that close. Mr. O'Connell though, he thinks since Denny got me hired here and our wives are friends, we're good buddies, and with him in jail I'm probably that way, too."

"Uh-huh."

"What I'm saying is, I'm not. You know? I've been trying real hard, but it seems like the littlest thing, Mr. O'Connell counts it against me and I can't get ahead."

"You're looking for a promotion?"

"Well, yeah. What I'd like is to work the fourth bay instead of just handling the shuttle and detailing cars."

"You haven't been to the factory school."

"Earl didn't go," Kim protested.

"Earl was grandfathered," Ian said. "Earl's

been here twenty-nine years."

"Well, I still think I could do little things. And then if I proved myself, you could have them send me to the factory. Won't ever be as good a mechanic as you are, but I'm pretty handy. My father-in-law and me rebuilt the transmission on my wife's Escort, and she's happy with it."

Kim overran the sign with the food choices on it and had to back his truck up to hear the intercom voice. Kim ordered a Whopper and a chocolate shake; Ian ordered a Coke or Pepsi, he didn't care which. Kim gunned them forward to the pickup window, where a hefty woman with a headset on smiled at Kim as she pushed the food toward the truck. She said, "You don't have to be so gloomy!"

Kim blushed and said, "I'm sorry." He handed her the money and put the food sack beside him on the seat. He put the truck in gear and he rolled out to the street. "My wife's always saying that to me, too. 'You're always frowning!' she says. I guess I just forget to smile."

"She and the kids okay?"

"Well, we never go out anymore. You'd like to take the kids out somewhere, just to the movies or camping, but it's cheaper to stay home in front of the television. It's got so having a telephone seems like a luxury. And we *never* call long distance."

"You know how to do paint and bondo work?"

Kim said he did but in a way that said, *How hard could it be?* "What? You need a body guy?"

"We might pretty soon. I'll put in a good word for you."

Kim looked at him solemnly. "Even seven dollars an hour would be a help." And then he remembered to smile.

Earl was working on a Cutlass Supreme when Kim and Ian got back. "We got a problem, boss," Earl said, and talked with him under the hoist. Kim sipped his chocolate shake through a straw as he took it all in.

"We have the parts?" Ian asked.

"Chappy says no."

Ian sent Kim out to find a knuckle hub at Kragen's, then he went to his office to make his afternoon customer calls. And he'd gotten to twelve people, telling them their vehicles were ready, when he saw Kim hurrying back from Kragen's and skidding the Speedway service truck to a halt on the floor. Earl and Ian walked to it as Kim hefted a box from the truck bed, and Ian felt his heart sink, for he knew Kim had mistakenly asked for the complete steering knuckle assembly instead of just the hub.

Earl showed Ian a hard-weather eye.

Ian asked him, "You think Kragen's will take it back disassembled?"

Earl broke open the box on the floor. "We do a heck of a lot of business with 'em."

"Oh, I'm sorry," Kim said.

And Earl said, "No muss, no fuss."

Quitting time in fifteen minutes. Ian left them for the Mechanics and found the night service manager there and still in his fishing clothes, his starched white shirt on a hanger hooked on a left finger while his right hand forced potato chips into his mouth. Lamar sagged against a doorframe, grayly creaming the grease from his hands while faint sounds of the Grateful Dead issued from his headphones.

Ian took the coffeepot off the hot plate before the dark ooze boiled down to black blisters. He then put the white paper coffee filters back in the box and put the box up where it was supposed to be.

Mike walked in and heaved himself into a hardwood chair just across from the night manager, frowning at Daryl until Daryl frowned back. And then Mike shouted, *"What?"*

"Nothing."

"Don't push me," Mike said.

Daryl looked for a half-friendly face. "Ian!" he said. "You the honcho?"

Mike said, "No; he's wearing the White Shirt because he's the maître d'!" Mike shook his head. " 'You the honcho.' "

Daryl said he was going fly-fishing up near Flintwood, and Lamar said he thought they had a forest fire up there. Daryl said they did, but it was put out by now.

Ian was tossing milk cartons and trash into a green plastic bag. He said, "The fire was in Briarcrest. That's sixteen miles from Flintwood."

Mike got irritated again and said, "Is there *anything* you don't know?"

"Compared to you, I guess not."

"Ho-ho," Lamar said. "Two points for Ian!"

Mike said, "You're sucking up again, Lamar. I hate that." And then he got his lunchbox and went out.

But Mike was waiting by Ian's black Chevy Blazer when Ian finished his paperwork and headed home an hour later. "I need a ride," he said.

Earl had been the first to do that, right after Ian was named the White Shirt. Earl gave him his whole history as he watered his lawn and fertilized his plants and put two orangish tomatoes on the kitchen sill. And at their six o'clock dinner, Earl had gotten up and mysteriously went out to the front porch so his sweet wife would have the opportunity to say, "You know, Earl really admires you."

Then Lamar asked for a ride to his house, let Ian hold his high-school basketball trophies, and then worriedly paced with a child in his arms as Ian examined his blueprint for a fatally flawed carburetor system. Lamar told him, "Why we don't talk much, you and me, is I'm shy." Then the two of them put headphones on and hunched over his shortwave radio as Lamar gingerly tuned the dial to Amsterdam, Frankfurt, and Moscow.

At Kim's apartment Kim held his little boy against his chest as Ian played a Nintendo game, journeying to the Castle of Ordeal, where he challenged its three perilous floors and got the Tail as a token of his courage. "Your hair's dirty," Kim told his boy, and the kid hid underneath a pillow.

But Mike stayed quiet until they were in his neighborhood, when he said, "I been hanging around gas stations and auto-parts shops since I was fifteen years old. Won the

Soapbox Derby when I was ten, and my old man didn't quote unquote 'help me' with it either. Which is why you can go ahead and fire me anytime you want, Mr. White Shirt. I'll land myself a mechanic's job wherever they happen to be hiring. At better pay, too, most likely."

"You have the talent. They can't take that away from you."

Mike got out, but halted on the sidewalk and asked Ian if he wanted a beer.

And Ian walked into a half-empty house and took a Budweiser from him. Mike chewed an Excedrin as he got a plastic funnel, trickled Jim Beam inside a Dr Pepper, and vigorously shook the bottle. Where the sofa used to be, Mike sat with Ian on the floor and frowned at his wife's handwriting on a letter. After a while Mike handed it to him. Ian quickly read it and handed it back. "I'm really sorry, Mike," he said.

Mike asked, "What the hell's in Michigan?"

And Ian said, "Motown. Wolverines. Cars."

A Hazard of New Fortunes

With his father's accidental death and then his mother's heart attack nine months later, Ethan Glazier inherited not just their handsome west-side town house but also the ski condo near Sugarbush that his mother had come to loathe, and in July, when it still hadn't sold, he rented a Jaguar and drove up to Vermont to change real estate agencies and have a weekend away from the heat of Manhattan.

The condo took up the third-floor servant's quarters of a nineteenth-century summer manse constructed by a shipbuilder with eight children, but the architects who renovated it sought the look of a mountain lodge and added timber joists, a communal sauna and hot tub, racks near each kitchen entrance for skis and poles and snowshoes, and wood-burning stoves in all the living rooms. The first-floor condo was an investment owned by a prosthodontist in Boston who was seldom there. And on the floor just below Ethan was his father and mother's closest friend up there, a registered nurse named Sally. She was his age, give or take, his mother told him, and it was such a pity she'd never married — potently insinuating that it was high time, at thirty-six, *he* did. Sally worked at a medical center somewhere and lived alone with a Siamese cat that he heard her talking to as she left the house that Friday evening, the voice so high, hopeful, and, face it, smarmy that Ethan decided not to introduce himself.

Even in July the first night up there was cool enough that Ethan sat in his father's wingback chair in a red flannel shirt, with a juice glass full of Glenmorangie single malt Scotch and a good H. Upmann cigar, paging through the nineteenth-century American novels his late father had taught at Columbia, listening to sick-at-heart jazz, or just watching flames consume the crackling pine limbs behind the fire screen. Or he walked the rooms in search of his mother's shakily handwritten notes to the weekly ski season renters: "We recycle — bottles and cans in green bin," "This switch to stay on," "When leaving, please turn thermostat to 60°," "Be mindful: your floor is another's ceiling."

Ethan looked at the oak flooring and imagined Nurse Sally on a sofa with the cat, silently watching the ceiling as he shifted from one instruction to the next, his shoes mindlessly telling stories of his restlessness and sorrow.

On Saturday morning he ran his ritual five miles along the two-lane highway out front, changed into handyman's clothes, and drove into Sugarbush to sign a listing agreement with Snow Country Realty and to find in a hardware store the scarce lightbulbs for his mother's refrigerator and clothes dryer.

The hardware store clerk was in his sixties and wore a green carpenter's apron and a name tag with "Allan" sloppily printed on it. His hair was unnaturally black and slick with oil, and his mustache was of the kind that suave actors favored in the forties. As Ethan hunted the lightbulbs, the hardware man stayed at his side, skeptically watching his hands.

"I'm not trying to steal from you," Ethan said.

Allan sneered. "Not with me watching you, you won't."

Ethan lost it. "Have you any idea how *wealthy* I am? I could *buy* this fucking store!" Allan just smirked, and in his fury

Ethan thought about galumphing out in his hiking boots, but the lightbulbs were indeed hard to find, so he paid for them with cash. After he'd gotten the change, the hardware man tried to shake his hand in a no-hard-feelings way. Ethan ignored the apology and walked out.

When he got into the rented Jaguar, he flung the brown paper sack with the two lightbulbs onto the right bucket seat. And then he added the thingamajig that he stole just not to be caught stealing. The quesiness in his stomach calmed and his hands no longer shook. The thrill was gone. So soon.

On the way back to his father and mother's condo, Ethan paused at a highway intersection and for the first time since last summer took a left instead of a right. He turned four more times, and then was on a gravel road in the shadows of jack pine and spruce. Here and there he could see houses tucked far back in the woods like hutches in a fairy tale. It was noon, but dark as evening. His father would have used the word "gloaming."

On "the fateful day," as his mother used to put it, Ethan was in Manhattan and had asked his father on the telephone how he'd spent his morning.

Reading for his fall seminar, Edgar had said. William Dean Howells. *A Hazard of New Fortunes.* But his eyes were sore now, he'd said. "I'm going to the pond."

"Are you healed enough?"

"It was just a hernia operation."

"What's Mom say?"

"Oh, she's mad at me," his father had said. "We get on each other's nerves up here."

Ethan parked and locked his luxury rental near a forest service haul-away pile of fallen timber. Hiking along a ski trail through shade and sudden chutes of sunlight, he heard the shushing noise of the falls and headed toward a sound that was like a tuner just missing a radio station. And then he was in a hot clearing where gray rock hillocked around a green pond. Water from a brook crashed in at one end and cascaded out the other in twin falls. Clouds of weaving insects hovered in the shade. Ethan hunched down to feel the coldness of the water, and then reached farther to feel on his hand and wrist the first hints of hidden currents swarming underneath the surface.

At first Ethan's father was reported missing, as if he were some Alzheimer's guy on a wander, but the next morning a retired Coast Guard scuba diver found him in the seersucker beach shirt and swimming trunks that he called his "bathing costume," five feet under the surface and still held as upright as a pillar by the force and menace of the undertow. Ethan imagined his father as he was when he lectured onstage, shifting his weight from foot to foot but otherwise ramrod straight, his head never glancing up as he patiently enunciated each word on the page.

There was such an insistence in his voice: *I'm going to the pond.*

In a liturgy of remembrance, Ethan cupped water in his palm and sipped it.

And his mother? Congestive heart failure. She was fixing deviled eggs in the kitchen, just underneath the oven soffit and the hokey Ozarks plaque that read BESS AND EDGAR'S HIDEAWAY. Nurse Sally heard the fall and found her too late. But it was the coroner who'd phoned him.

Looking at the kitchen floor, Ethan recalled his freshman lit course at Columbia and found Albert Camus's *The Stranger* in his father's library. The opening paragraph read: "Mother died today. Or, maybe, yesterday; I can't be sure. The telegram from the Home says: YOUR MOTHER PASSED AWAY. FUNERAL TOMORROW. DEEP SYMPA-

THY. Which leaves the matter doubtful; it could have been yesterday."

C'est moi, Ethan thought. *The Stranger.* And he was finishing screwing a lightbulb in his mother's "fridge" when he glanced through the kitchen window into a wide green backyard fenced like a frontier fort with tall maples. Sally was reading as she suntanned in one of the white Adirondack chairs. She wore a fluorescent-pink bikini that revealed a great deal of a fit, cocoa-brown, amazing body that his mother, of course, had failed to mention. She crossed tanned feet with painted pink toenails on the facing Adirondack chair, and Ethan went down to say hi.

With false bonhomie, he called, "Nurse Sally!"

She shielded her eyes from the sun with her book: *Edith Wharton's Ghost Stories,* edited and with commentary by Edgar L. Glazier of Columbia University. She smiled with recognition and said, "We finally meet."

"Which is your favorite?"

She looked at the book. "I haven't read any stories yet, just your father's introduction."

She was not his age; she was in her forties. She had a short, efficient, blonde haircut and a semipretty face that hinted at a constellation of acne years ago, but she was right out of a skin magazine otherwise, with sleek legs glistening with suntan oil, a hard, much-exercised abdomen, and breasts that were like large brown globes beneath her pink bikini top. She seemed unsurprised, even pleased, when his gaze fell onto her chest, and then she got his attention again by asking, "Would you like a wine cooler?"

"Sure."

She wedged his father's book beside her right thigh and flipped up the wickerwork lid on a shaded picnic hamper with her right hand. And Ethan was stunned to see a thalidomide-damaged left limb that seemed only forearm, with no hand except for a childish, functioning thumb and what looked like three pink fingertips. Another thing his mother failed to mention.

"Caught ya," she said. She handed a frosted bottle to him.

"Was I gaping?"

She ignored that. She lifted her feet off the facing Adirondack chair and said, "Have a seat." She got another wine cooler for herself and squeezed it under her sad little arm as she twisted off the cap. The Siamese cat was romping in the yard, lost in some imaginary safari. "Aren't you tired?" Sally asked.

Ethan sat. "Why do you ask?"

"Weren't you up at four?"

"I'm a lousy sleeper. Was I too loud?"

She shook her head. "I was just getting in. I have strange hours in July with so many nurses on vacation."

They drank their strawberry coolers and she talked to him just as so many had at the funerals. With a slight Vermont accent, Sally told how she and his folks used to play croquet out here. And have cookouts. And they snowshoed along the Mad River sometimes. She seemed to forget Ethan was his mother's son and acquainted him with how regal, intelligent, and feisty Bess was.

Ethan was already tiring of the conversation. With tedium he said, "She reminded people of Katharine Hepburn." And he heard his mother chiding, *Oh, Ethan. Can't you be civil?*

Sally noted, "They thought it was such a *pity* you could never make it up here."

"The world always got in the way."

She hesitated a second before asking slyly, "Would you be offended if I took off my top? I hate the tan lines."

Was this her hedge against the handicap, to give men just what they wanted? "The more the merrier," Ethan said.

She smiled and in a double-jointed way reached her right arm over her neck to unhook the back, and then her magnificent breasts lolled free.

She'd turned him into a goofy teenager. Ethan said with too much urgency, "You have a fantastic body, Sally."

She was superior to that, saying, "Thank you."

"And no tan lines."

"Elsewhere there are."

Ethan glanced elsewhere, and she caught him doing so. "Do you work out?" he lamely asked, and wanted to sock himself.

But she went with it. "I have a gym in my second bedroom. You can use it if you'd like."

"I'm afraid I seem a trifle unhinged. Just so you know: I *have* seen breasts before."

She laughed. "*Exactly* the sort of thing Edgar would say!" She told Ethan his dad was such a wit, such a card, he always found a loony way to tickle her. And he was so smart. She could ask him anything and he'd have the answer.

Ethan felt unengaged. And strangely wronged. He told her, "He wrote a Saturday column for one of the Long Island papers. Called himself 'Mr. Know-It-All.' "

"And you write, too, don't you?"

Ethan shrugged, his lethargy and misery gradually increasing. "Ephemera. My job is selling airtime for ABC."

"Still?"

"Still. But three friends and I are buying a chichi saloon on the east side. I might end up managing that."

"Well, I guess you can afford to now. The only child and all. You must have a fortune just in real estate."

"Oh yeah," he said. "I'm a tycoon."

"I just wish you weren't selling this place."

"Why's that?"

"I just thought it would be nice to have a guy I like above me."

The frankness of the innuendo caused Sally to flush with embarrassment and turn away. She drank the cooler as she looked at three swallows soaring and darting over the yard. Ethan watched a teardrop of perspiration scrawl its way from underneath her left breast and down her side. She smeared the wetness with her child's arm, and then she felt his doting stare and smiled uneasily.

Ethan found himself trying to determine what a normal man would do in this situation. "I feel a little silly," he said. "Sitting here with my clothes on and all."

She seemed to wonder if that was an

offhand invitation. "Are you going inside?" she asked.

"I have some odd jobs to do." He finished the strawberry wine cooler and stood and stuffed the still-cool bottle in the hamper. "Nice talking to you, Sally."

And then it was her turn to stare.

When he got up to the front landing, he glanced back down into the yard. Sally was still there, but the fluorescent-pink bikini top was on and her face was in her right hand. Lovesick and forlorn.

But Ethan just inserted the key in the lock. *Cold as ice,* he thought.

At six he searched the kitchen wine cellar and found a wonderful Château Pichon-Longueville cabernet sauvignon that he was uncorking as his telephone rang. "Hello?" he asked, and hated his tone: anxious, wary, no confidence.

"Hi," Sally said. "I was just making piña coladas and wondered if you'd like to join me for happy hour." The effervescence seemed practiced.

"Wow!" he exclaimed, and he again saw her crying in the yard. "In other circumstances I'd be there for sure," he said, buying time, "but I was hoping to make it an early night, and booze gets me too jazzed."

She said lamely, "I have sodas."

"Could I ask for a rain check, Sally? You're the tops, and I had fun talking to you, but I'm really winding down."

"Just a thought," she said gaily, and then she hung up.

Hours later he'd finished the Pauillac and was watching a Red Sox-Yankees baseball game when on a hunch he lowered the volume and heard the same game below him. He changed channels to a Saturday-night sitcom and walked out onto the deck, hearing, just minutes later, Sally's television switch to the same show. Holding up his remote, he pressed off the power, and this time it was only seconds before he heard the sudden silence from her condo.

She called again around midnight. Ethan was in his father and mother's king-size bed and Sally was slurring her words. She said how sorry she was to wake him and that she'd had too much to drink but she wanted him to know, because it was very important, that Edgar, his dad, was in love with her. Wanted to have a torrid affair, to put it bluntly. Well, no, not torrid. Very decorous, of course. But my how he flirted. So cute. Couldn't get enough of Sally. Won her over.

And so elegant. Called her "My dearest." Caressed her like she was . . . what's the word? Tapioca or something. Carefully. And he'd kiss her little hand. The other one. The freak one. Was Ethan still listening?

"Yes."

"I'm drunk, I'm drunk. Okay? But this is the secret. Secret you should never ever tell. We's going to meet at the pond. And have sex. The first time for us. We has it all arranged. But he wasn't there. Waited for him. In my nurse whites. Cursed him for being a coward. And all the time he was there. Underwater. Couldn't save him. So I'm not responsible, am I?"

"No."

She was crying. "Oh, I'm so soused. But it's all so sad, Ethan. And I been carrying this inside for months. That we were going to meet at the pond. And he drowned. I'm so lonesome for him, Ethan. I'm . . ."

She was still talking as Ethan softly hung up the phone.

Sleep was impossible. Ethan wandered the condo, holding a Beck's beer bottle by the neck, until he found a literary reference book and flopped into his father's wingback chair. Looking up William Dean Howells (1837–1920), he discovered that *A Hazard of New Fortunes* concerned the establishment of a new magazine by a gauche and ignorant millionaire who was in conflict with a socialist reformer in New York at a time of great economic and social upheaval. There were no nurses in it. Sex was not a feature of the plot. In fact, Howells, whom the book called "the dean of nineteenth-century American letters," was "hampered by a fastidiousness that forced him to avoid erotic passion and the sordid side of life."

Like Ethan's father.

Ethan remembered a dining room scene from his childhood, his father in his fifties and fuming over an English Department professor whom he called "a thoroughgoing cad." Ethan had been boy enough to sneak off to his father's dictionary. *Cad:* one who behaves in a dishonorable or irresponsible way toward women. Ethan had fantasized all night.

And now he had no fantasies, no strong desires, not even the lust for life that fires the foolishness in old, dying men. Ethan's mother once sighed and said, "Your father cares so unselectively."

A child of his age, Ethan, she knew, cared too little.

At noon on Sunday he held himself together

by getting into his running shorts, anklet socks, and New Balance shoes and headed shirtless on a hot and hilly ten-mile run along the Mad River. Soon after the one-lane bridge where fishermen hung their lines and tourists took snapshots of the river water crashing and knolling over hidden boulders, the forests gave way to green pastures and milk cows and wide fields of oats and hay that a soft wind seemed to roll through like a child at play. Willing each stride, no ache in his joints or lungs, he let his forearms fall and shook his hands to loosen his muscles. *A thoroughgoing cad.*

Around mile four he saw just off the highway an old, black, wood-sided Ford Country Squire station wagon, listed to its right in high weeds alongside a horse fence that fronted a peeling red ranch house. At first he thought the station wagon was just strangely parked, but then he saw a kid of fourteen or so in a Red Sox shirt and blue jeans, worriedly staring into the tailgate window. And Ethan noticed the gnarled right fender and skewed headlight, steam trickling from the radiator, and a mustached man tilted to his right inside the car, as if he were permanently stalled while reaching for something in the glove compartment.

Ethan halted and shouted, "Is he okay?"

The kid just looked at him with fear and shook his head.

Ethan hurried across the highway and down into foxtail weeds that were sawing in the breeze. He peered at the driver through his cracked side window as he tried his door, and he was stunned to see it was the hardware store clerk who was onto his shoplifting. Allan was wearing a green plaid shirt and green twill trousers, and in his reaching right hand was a partially crushed Budweiser beer can. His face was snow white and his teeth were oozing blood. Otherwise he was still as a picture.

The kid was now on the passenger's side and focused on the man's face. Ethan looked over the roof at him. "Have you tried all the doors?"

"They're locked."

"And the tailgate?"

The kid nodded.

"Has someone called for an ambulance?"

The kid shook his head.

"Will you do that?"

The kid ran off to the ranch house.

Ethan hunted for a minute before he found a weighty rock and smashed it against the tailgate window, a little surprised that the window glass didn't shatter immediately, that it took some concerted pounding before a softball-size hole broke out. And then he forced his hand in and found the handle and got the station wagon's tailgate open.

A Mazda Miata was heading toward him and he realized the driver was Sally. Ethan desperately waved his arms at her and she frowned, then steered off the highway and hurried out. She was wearing sandals, tight shorts, and a man's white oxford shirt, its sleeves rolled high enough to free her malformed hand.

She was in nurse mode as she asked, "When did it happen?"

"I don't know. I didn't see it. Probably just minutes ago."

She crawled into the cargo area of the station wagon and over the rear bench seat, where she knelt in the footwell and got to the man. She felt for a pulse in his neck and cradled Allan's head in her childlike left arm as she tilted his chin and started mouth-to-mouth resuscitation. Ethan crawled in and crouched behind her, watching in awe as she inhaled air, dipped her head, and forcefully exhaled into the older man's jauntily mustached mouth. She did that over and over again, and Ethan had time to imagine his father held with such romance. Sally reviving him. Images he hated strayed through his mind. *But it's all so sad,* she had said last night. She looked at Ethan with adrenaline shining in her eyes, blood smeared across her mouth. She gasped, "I can't do what I need to do this way. We've got to get him down on the ground."

Ethan clambered forward and reached over the front seat to the door handle and jerked it, then backed out of the station wagon's cargo area and hurried around to the driver's side. His right hand found the hardware clerk's left ankle and he saw his black, rubber-soled shoes and his cool, white, hairless shin. With discipline he gripped a green twill trouser leg in his other hand and tugged Allan's weight from under the steering column until he could gain a firmer hold. Were he a religious man he would have said a prayer for the hardware clerk, that heaven would receive him and that he would rest there in peace, for Allan was dead, of that Ethan was certain.

Ethan heaved him by his knees and Allan slid out halfway, and then Ethan was able to lay the hardware man's limp body in the weeds. Three or more cars had stopped and their passengers were silently ogling the drama, but staying far back as if afraid of getting anything on them. Elsewhere a passerby had put out a fizzing red flare in the highway and was guiding traffic away from the nearest lane. And then an ambulance and three emergency medical technicians arrived. As soon as the rectangular doors swung open, Sally yelled, "We need an ambu!"

"We got it," a female technician said, her stickler's face communicating that she did not mean the resuscitator but the entire situation.

Ethan stood back while they all crouched over Allan, Sally trading the medical information she'd ascertained with the technicians, who were trying to stimulate the hardware man's heart with a defibrillator, suction fluids from his mouth and throat, and find another breathing aid in their intubation box. The male technicians both looked like ski instructors, tanned and fit and mustached. One who was carrying a trauma box asked Ethan, "Were you hurt?"

"No. I just got here first. I didn't even see it happen."

"Was he alone?"

"Yes." And he added, "His name's Allan."

The guy nodded and went about his duties, shifting about with deliberation and unhurried efficiency. Ethan could tell from their looks that the hardware clerk was far gone but that they'd try to bring him back because you heard of it happening on occasion, and it was what litigation forced them to do.

Allan was strapped onto a collapsible steel stretcher while the female medical technician continued breathing into him with the thruway. And then the two men hoisted him up and gingerly slid him into the ambulance. The female took the technician's seat and the doors were slammed shut. No one switched on the siren when the red and white ambulance eased onto the highway.

The onlookers were quietly talking among themselves and Ethan saw a little girl gawking at what thalidomide had done to Sally's limb. The girl averted her stare when she saw Ethan's.

Sally stood next to Ethan, trembling as she wiped Allan's blood from her mouth with a Kleenex tissue she'd found in her car.

"You were a real hero there," Ethan said. *Jeez, listen to me,* he thought.

"My training," Sally said.

"I felt so useless."

"You always do when someone dies." She shoved the tissue into her front pocket. "Are you going to go on running?"

"Are you heading home?"

"Sure," she said, as if she wasn't but would.

Ethan fitted himself into the front seat of the Miata as Sally examined her face in the rearview mirror. Without emotion she said, "When I put my mouth on his, it filled with blood and I could feel chips of his shattered teeth."

"Horrible."

She got them onto the highway and said nothing for a while. Ethan was naked but for his running shorts and he noticed her noticing that. And then she blithely asked, "So, what did you do last night?"

Ethan scrutinized her, mystified. "Stayed in. How about you?"

"Went to work," she said. "I have strange hours in July with so many nurses on vacation."

"And you didn't call me?"

She smiled. "What are you, an orderly?"

She'd blacked out, he thought. She had no memory of the phone call. She tuned to a hard-rock radio station that silenced Ethan until they got to the three-story house in which they were owners. She turned off the ignition.

"This is so weird," Ethan said.

"What is?"

Ethan wondered where he should start.

"I'm thirty-six and I have a fortune and fine prospects, and life is not good. I feel toxic. Cruel. Cynical. Stagnant. Immature. I'm never going to be one of those jolly guys on bowling night, but this? I think about death constantly. Won't ride the subways because I hate going underground. I even find it hard, writing, to form words where the letters reach below the line. My father told me that just before he died William Faulkner said, 'It all tastes the same.' Call it yuppie impotence. Call it window shopping. But I'm outside, looking in. And it all tastes the same."

Sally gently touched his hand. "Are you seeing anyone?"

Ethan said, "Oh, I date around."

She laughed. "Psychologically."

Ethan rolled to his left side, his face nearing hers, and shocked Sally by softly caressing a breast. But she took no offense and did not shift from it.

"Tapioca," he whispered.

In her confusion she smiled. And then she pressed his hand tighter with her sad, child-like arm, and she asked in a hushed voice, "Oh, Ethan. What do you want?"

"Kiss me," he said. "I'm dying. I'm dead."

She kissed him. And she tilted his head

just so, and he felt his lungs fill with her hot, essential, dutiful breath.

THE THEFT

While he was waiting in the kitchen, the police sergeant got out a Marlboro cigarette and hunted a match. His name was Dunne, and he was assisting the Burglary Investigation Unit of the San Jose Police Department. He was mustached and gray and thirty-six years old, dressed in a stiff navy-blue uniform whose pleats seemed sharp as paring knives. Dunne opened a dessert service drawer and then a drawer with torn coupons and hand tools and batteries in it. Dunne stared at the hand tools for a good while before closing the drawer again. At last he went to the stovetop and held his cigarette inside a puttering ring of green and blue flame. He turned off the gas flame and took a hard drag on the cigarette as he looked at the fresh pumpkin-orange paint on the kitchen walls. Chatter was loud on the radio handpack attached to his belt so he turned it down. He exhaled gray tobacco smoke. She'd put wineglasses in the kitchen sink, the four rims all stained with pink lipsticks.

She finished her shower and hurried in, holding shut a white terry-cloth robe as she considered the policeman. Her blond hair was wetly brown and the tracks of the comb were still in it. She seemed surprised to see him there, though she'd heard his voice and invited him inside when he called to her from the kitchen porch. "Took a while," she said.

"Wasn't an emergency, just a burglary. You weren't in danger, were you?"

"Skip it," she said. She tilted away from his too-interested attention and sat down on a kitchen chair.

"Just tell me how it happened," the police sergeant said.

Linda sighed. "Like I told the flake on theft detail, I was just coming back from the grocery store. I parked the car in the alley and carried the stuff up the back porch steps and inside and he must have followed me."

"Was the door unlocked?"

"Sure. I mean, I unlocked it. With my house keys."

"You have them?"

She tried to remember what she'd done

with them and then turned to check the ajar kitchen door. She stood up and frantically peered at the kitchen table, the white pantry countertop, and the child's kneehole desk that she usually put her mail on.

"Are the house keys gone, too?"

She looked at him with panic.

"You opened the door with your house keys," the police sergent said. "Your hands were full. You may have left the house keys in the door and carried the groceries inside."

"Yes; I suppose so." She gazed at the door. "That's really terrifying."

"You could change the locks again," Dunne said. He tapped the jagged ash from his cigarette into his palm, then carried the ash to a wrinkled grocery sack on the floor.

She asked him, "Aren't you supposed to be writing this down?"

"Sergeants get rookies to do their paper-work, that's one of the good parts of the job."

"Congratulations," she said.

"About time," Dunne said, and looked at the furniture in the front room and hallway, then leaned against the kitchen doorway and crossed his forearms and ankles. "What else?"

A flock of sparrows flushed up in the yard and she followed their flight until they'd completely disappeared in the east. She said, "You'd think you'd have a feeling that an unfamiliar person was in the house with you, but I didn't. Everything seemed so normal until I heard the spring on the back door."

Dunne walked over and pushed open the screen door to hear the noise. The iron spring was orange with rust and rang slightly as it dragged against the wood.

"Like that, but not so much," Linda said.

"You could hardly hear it."

"Right."

"You looked behind you, though."

"And nobody was there," Linda said.

"And?"

"And I put away the groceries. Wind, I thought."

"You heard the door. Was that him sneaking in or him sneaking out?"

"I have no way of knowing."

"When did you notice your purse had been stolen?"

"Exactly?"

"You reported a theft at a quarter past three."

"Well, I suppose I hunted around for fifteen minutes or so before I was positive that I hadn't simply mislaid it."

"Any idea of the contents?"

"My checkbook. Wallet and credit cards. Lipstick. Kleenex. Hand cream. Junk mostly, except for the wallet. And there was just a few dollars in that."

The policeman took his cigarette to the kitchen faucet and killed it with a jolt of water. "Was it expensive, that purse?"

She perused him and said, "Extremely."

"Was my picture still in it?"

She shook her head.

Dunne peered out through the four-paned window just above the kitchen sink. A fat, aproned woman was kneeling in her garden next door and putting in flower bulbs with a trowel. She sat back on her haunches and shaded her face from the sunshine. "I'm trying to imagine how you must have felt," Dunne said. "You must have felt like there was a ghost in the house. Haunting you. Watching every move you made. Stealing your purse and your keys. And you didn't even know it."

"You're enjoying this, aren't you?" Linda asked, but from the hard intensity of his frown she could tell he was not.

A half minute of silence passed between them, and he said, "You've painted."

"Yes."

"Looks nice."

"And then the rent went up."

"Much?"

"Fifty bucks."

"Still a good deal," he said.

Linda stood up and got a diet cola from the Hotpoint refrigerator. She snapped it open and sipped from it. She asked, "Was it a coincidence that you came?"

"I heard the address on the radio."

"And you decided to give it your personal attention."

He turned up his handpack and heard a rookie patrolman reading information from motor vehicle registration papers, and then he lowered the volume again. "Shall I figure it for you?"

She sipped her cola. "You're the cop."

"You got a guy thinks you're hot stuff," he said. "You knew him once maybe, but he isn't getting anywhere with you now. Wants to, though. Would like to let you know he's still around. Looking out for you. And then he sees you getting your groceries. Wonders about talking to you, but doesn't. Hangs out, just waiting for you to get into your car. Still doesn't make his move. And so he follows you here. You surprise him. You stun him, probably. Here he's been on your tail for an hour and you haven't seen a hint of him. And you've been the only thing beside himself that he's looked at or thought about.

So he steals your purse like a kid writes his name on the sidewalk, just to say he exists."

"And he takes my house keys to tell me he'll be back."

She could have counted to one hundred in the silence, and then Dunne asked, "So how are things?"

"Getting better."

"Yeah?"

"Yeah."

"You happy?"

"Up and down. You know."

"Having fun?"

"Off and on."

"Seeing anybody?"

She shrugged.

"Any chance?"

"Who knows," Linda said.

"Okay," he said. "Your purse is in the milkbox outside." He put his hand in his pocket and took out her house keys and handed them to her. "You watch it," he said.

And she said, "You."

The Sleepwalker

She watches his slow decline as she would a fire at home, on restful evenings, opera softly emanating from the stereo in another room, perhaps a glass of cool pinot noir at hand, and he patiently staring at nothing at all, lost in thoughtlessness, as silent as smoke, as the flames eat away at the charred wood, feasting on all the good of it.

He was once so many people: a hardy farm boy, wild seaman, a cook on a Portuguese fishing boat, a roughneck on oil wells, then an oil driller himself, an inventor, a father, the owner of restaurants and farmland and commercial properties, yet ever laughing and lovable and in awe of learning. And now unlearning more with each week. Reminded of his accomplishments, he smiled as he said, "*I* did that? Well, I'll be goddamned."

And now he is a wanderer, bewildered by unfamiliar rooms, finding his way outdoors in raw weather without a coat and needing neighbors to guide him back to an address he can't recall. And a toddler, too, forgetting etiquette, getting into mischief, eating ice cream for breakfast with his four-year-old granddaughter, who tells him he can, who gives him permission.

The loneliness is the hardest part, the memories that she can no longer share with any meaning, or saying things of importance and realizing they will not be recalled, and fearing the probable time to come when she will be feared, a wife to a man for whom husbanding has ended. She is becoming increasingly a stranger invading his littler portion of certainty.

Some nights she hears him walking from room to room as if hunting his history, his mind, the hurly-burly life he's lost. She aches to think what it must be like to be him, to be helpless, puzzled, surprised, infantile. Hundreds of faces without names. Recognitions of him that he is not equal to.

But he finds his wife sleeping on the frilly daybed in the feminine sunroom at the front of the house and he looms over her like his old self and in the sentience of that night he says in his sudden and momentary wakefulness, "I know how hard all of this is for you. And I appreciate what you're doing."

Then he retreats into the hallway and back into his illness. But those words stay with her and are enough.

My Kid's Dog

My kid's dog died.

Sparky.

I hated that dog.

The feeling was mutual.

We got off on the wrong foot. Whining in his pen those first nights. My squirt gun in his face and him blinking from the water. And then the holes in the yard. The so-called accidents in the house. His nose snuffling into my Brooks Brothers trousers. Him slurping my fine Pilsner beer or sneaking bites of my Dagwood sandwich when I fell asleep on the sofa. Also, his inability to fetch, to take a joke, to find the humor in sudden air horns. To be dandled, rough-housed, or teased. And then the growling, the skulking, the snapping at my ankles, the hiding from me under the house, and literally thousands of abject refusals to obey. Like, *Who the hell are you?*

You'd have thought he was a cat.

When pushed to the brink I shouted, "I'll cut your face off and show it to you," and the small-brained mammal just stared at me.

But with the kids or my wife little Foo-Foo was a changeling, conning them with the tail, the prance, the peppiness, the soft chocolate eyes, the sloppy expressions of love, the easy tricks that if I performed I'd get no credit for.

Oh, we understood each other all right. I was onto him.

And then, at age ten, and none too soon, he kicked the bucket. You'd think that would be it. End of story. But no, he had to get even.

Those who have tears, prepare to shed them.

I was futzing with the hinges on the front-yard gate on a Saturday afternoon, my tattersall shirtsleeves rolled up and mind off in Oklahoma, when I noticed Fido in the California shade, snoozing, but for once a little wistful, too, and far more serene than he usually was in my offensive presence. I tried to surprise him with my standard patriarchal shout, but it was no go, so I walked over and prodded the little guy with my wingtip. Nothing doing. And not so much as a flutter in his oddly abstracted face. Surely this was the big sleep, I thought.

She who must be obeyed was at the mall, provisioning, so I was safe from objection or inquiry on that account. I then made an inventory of my progeny: Buzz in the collegiate east, in the realm of heart-attack tuitions; Zack in the netherworld of the surf shop; Suzy, my last kid, on her bike and somewhere with her cousin. Were I to bury Rover with due haste and dispatch I could forestall the waterworks, even convince them that he'd signed up with the circus, run afoul of Cruella de Vil — anything but died.

I got a green tarpaulin from the garage and laid it out on the front yard, where I hesitated before using my shoe to roll Spot into his funeral shroud, then dragged him back into the Victory garden where August's dying zucchini plants were in riot. With trusty spade I dug his burial place, heaped earth atop him, tamped it down with satisfying *whumps.*

I was feeling good about myself, heroic, as if, miraculously, compassion and charity had invaded not only my bones but my soft muscle tissues. I fixed myself a tall glass of gin and tonic and watched the first quarter of the USC football game.

And then pangs of conscience assailed me. Hadn't my investigation of said demise of

Precious been rather cursory? Wouldn't I, myself, closely cross-examine a suspect whose emotions were clouded, whose nefarious wishes were well established, whose veterinary skills were without credential? The innocence of my childhood had been spoiled with the tales of Edgar Allan Poe, so it was not difficult to conjure images of Scruffy clawing through tarpaulin and earth as he fought for one last gasp of air, air that others could more profitably use.

I trudged out to the garden with aforementioned spade and with great lumbar strain exhumed our darling lap dog. Considering the circumstances, he seemed none the worse for wear, but I did detect a marked disinclination to respire, which I took as a sign either of his inveterate stubbornness or of his having reached the Stygian shore. The latter seemed more likely. I heard in my fuddled head a line from *The Wild Bunch* when a critically injured gunman begs his outlaw gang to "Finish it!" And in the healing spirit of Hippocrates I lifted high the shovel and whanged it down on Harvey's head.

To my relief, not a whimper issued from him. I was confident he was defunct.

With care I shrouded and buried him again, committing earth to earth and dust to dust and so on, and with spritelike step conveyed myself to the kitchen, where I made another gin and tonic and, in semi-prone position, settled into the game's third quarter, the fabled Trojan running attack grinding out, it would seem, another win.

I was shocked awake by the impertinence of a ringing telephone, which I, with due caution, answered. It was my wife's friend Vicki, inquiring about the pooch, for it was her assertion that Snip had fancied a taste of her son's upper calf and without invitation or permission to do so had partaken of same within the last twenty-four hours. Even while I was wondering what toxicity lurked in the child's leg and to what extent the poison was culpably responsible for our adored pet's actionable extinction, a loss we would feel for our lifetimes, Vicki insisted that I have the dog checked out by a vet to ascertain if he had rabies.

Cause of death: rabies? It seemed unlikely. Notwithstanding his surliness, there'd been no Cujoesque frothing or lunging at car windows; but my familiarity with torts has made me both careful and rather unctuous with a plaintiff and so I assured my wife's friend that I would accede to her request.

Off to the backyard again, my pace that of a woebegone trudge, and with aforementioned implement of agriculture, I displaced the slack and loosened earth. This was getting old. With an accusatory tone I said, "You're doing this on purpose, aren't you," and I took his silence as a plea of nolo contendere.

My plan, of course, was to employ the Oldsmobile '88 to transport my burden to the canine's autopsy at Dr. Romo's office just a half mile away. However, upon my settling into its plush front seat, it came to my attention that Zack — he who is but a sojourner on this earth — had not thought to replenish the fuel he'd used up on his trip to the Hollywood Bowl last night. The vehicle was not in a condition of plenitude. Would not ferry us farther than a block.

With Buster lying in the altogether on the driveway, not yet unsightly but no calendar page, I went into the house and found an old leather suitcase in the attic, then stuffed the mutt into the larger flapped compartment before hefting Shortcake on his final journey to those veterinary rooms he always shivered in.

I am, as I may have implied, a man of depth, perspicacity, and nearly Olympian strength, but I found myself hauling my heavy and lifeless cargo to Dr. Romo's with a pronounced lack of vigor and resolve. The

September afternoon was hot, the Pasadena streets were vacant, the entire world seemed to have found entertainment and surcease in ways that I had not. I was, in a word, in a sweaty snit, and after many panting and pain-filled stops, my spine in Quasimodo configuration and my right arm gradually inching longer than my left, it was all I could do not to heave the suitcase containing Wonderdog into a haulaway behind the Chinese restaurant.

But during our joint ordeal I had developed a grudging affection for our pet; he who'd been so quick to defend my kith and kin against the noise of passing trucks, who took loud notice of the squirrels outside, who held fast in the foyer, hackles raised, fearlessly barking, whenever company arrived at the front door. With him I seemed calm, masterful, and uneccentric, the Superior Man that the *I Ching* talks so much about. Without him, I thought, I might be otherwise.

I put down the suitcase to shake the ache from my fingers and subtract affliction from my back, and it was then that my final indignity came. An angel of mercy spied my plight, braked his ancient Cadillac, and got out, his facial piercings and tattoos and shoot-the-marbles eyes belying the kindness and decency of his heart as he asked, "Can I help you with that suitcase?"

"I can handle it."

"Are you sure?"

"I'm just two blocks away."

"What the heck's in it?" he asked.

And for some reason I said, "A family heirloom."

"Wow!" he said. "Why don't you put it in my trunk and I'll help you with it? I got nothin' better to do."

Well, I did not just fall off the turnip truck. I would have been, in other circumstances, suspicious. But I was all too aware of the weight and worthlessness of my cumbrance, and so I granted his specified offer, hoisting the deceased into the Seville and slamming down the trunk lid. And in evidence of our fallen state, my Samaritan immediately took off without me, jeering and peeling rubber and speeding west toward Los Angeles.

I could only lift my hand in a languid wave. *So long, old sport.*

Our world being the location of penance and recrimination, it was only right that my last kid should pedal up to me on her bike just then and ask, "Daddy, what are you doing here?"

Waving to a fella in need of a shovel.

And then I confessed. Sparky's sudden death, the burial, not the exhumation and execution attempt, but the imputation of rabies and my arduous efforts to acquit his reputation with a pilgrimage to the vet's.

Suzy took it in with sangfroid for a little while but then the lip quivered and tears spilled from her gorgeous eyes, and as I held her close she begged me to get her another dog just like Sparky. And that was Sparky's final revenge, for I said, "Okay, honey. Another dog, just like him."

SHE LOVES ME NOT

She decided Cleanth's time for dying was long overdue and she enlisted me for the project. She was "The Beautiful Sabrina," high earner among the exotic dancers at Showgirls, just outside the Omaha city limits. Cleanth, her erstwhile husband, owned the joint. A series of bad breaks and misunderstandings that were almost completely based on my sleep disorder had deprived me of gainful employment other than my hardly-ever wedding gigs with my "Hot Hits of the Eighties" band, so Sabrina and me got in the habit of some consensual indoors recreation while Cleanth was oozing around his "All Nude Girls" and leering with his Halloween mask of a face, or he was hauling in hundred-pound Budweiser kegs, one in each hand, like they had no more heft than six-packs.

We'd end up naked and pleasured, watching *The Young and the Restless,* sharing a joint and whatnot, and she'd tell me hair-raising stories about the outlandish things her husband had done, was doing, and intended to do to the earth and its innocent creatures.

"But that's horrible!" I would say.

"Oh, Skeeter," she'd say. "You never seen a man so evil."

She could've been on afternoon reality shows, the tales were that extreme. Speechlessness would grip those practiced broadcasters just as so often it had done me.

And yet our screwed-up legal system let Cleanth go on living, unjailed and undeterred, while such as me have worn ankle devices and been lectured to and humiliated by our probation officers. The world is upside down sometimes.

Sabrina asked, "Won't you help me end it?" And then she clarified that she wanted me "to stop Cleanth once and for all" and in other words, like I was not catching on, that she wondered if I could kill him for her. "But make it look like an accident," she said. "Because he's got insurance."

"Are we talking, like, a fortune?"

"Six hundred thousand dollars."

My first thought was how we could parlay that insurance money into thousands and thousands of lottery tickets and have a significant edge on all those mini-mart losers. But Sabrina had her lovely violet eyes on a particular diversified small-cap fund that was zooming ahead of its benchmarks and whose exponential moving average was the envy of the umpty-umps on the Street.

I had no idea what that meant. My cellmate, The Professor, who is "helping" me with this reminiscence, says my having no idea is organic to the plot.

Whatever.

We there and then schemed a possible solution to our mutual problem, and of a night in January when Showgirls was shut down because of the Lord's Day, we all three ended up at their pink cinder-block vacation home on Quarry Lake. Cleanth and I were to go ice fishing that night, but first off, just before a late dinner, I offered him some dirty weed, which he was wont to overindulge in.

Enormous and mean are a scary combination. And Cleanth was as giant as a grizzly bear on its hind legs. He filled a doorway as good as the door did. Whereas I'm a lady's man, as fine-boned and handsome as an underwear model, if somewhat undersized. Skeeter, which is not my birth name, may give you a hint of it. So I was at a disadvantage in my homicidal designs, except that the marijuana was stolen by a hard-luck friend of mine from the Omaha Police Department evidence room and was reported to have been doused with a poisonous weed killer called paraquat, or bipyridylium for you chemists out there. Inhaled, the herbicide causes horrible injury not just to the lungs, but to the throat and soft tissues of the mouth. And soon, you die.

But not Cleanth. He took about six tokes and winced like a connoisseur and wondered aloud how much I paid for it. "Whatever," he said, "it was too much." And then he handed the joint across to me.

I stage-acted inhaling just a pinch and coughed that out.

Cleanth said, "Careful there, Skeeter. Don't want you to die. I'd have to explain 'traces of' to your mom."

I felt discovered for a second, but he seemed to be joshing and unaware of our plot as he finished the joint, betraying no ill effects. The bedroom television that he hadn't smashed was atop the living room one that he had, and he watched Animal Planet for a while, aiming his hand and making gun noises at all the trotting spaniels and beagles on the *Kennel Club* show.

"Would you like a piña colada?" I asked.

Cleanth nodded. "My throat's a little

scratchy."

Sabrina was waiting for me in the kitchen. Exasperated. She said, "Paraquat, huh?" She watched me shrug, and then she commenced cracking, mashing, and stirring together the ingredients of all the prescription drugs she'd collected from the girls at the club for just such an eventuality.

"What'll the pills do to him?" I whispered.

She had vodka and piña colada mix in the blender. "Well," she said, "he for sure won't get pregnant."

Was it my job to remind her? Seemed so. "Remember, we gotta make it look like an accident."

"I have a plan," she said. She was wearing a bloodred kaftan and underneath was nothing but Sabrina. She was so gorgeous I just had to believe her. She stabbed the blender on and spooned the powders in, then she poured the puree into a fancy glass. She had another premade in the refrigerator.

"Sabrina!" Cleanth yelled. "Skeeter feelin' you up?"

"Like always!" she called back.

"Skeeter!" he yelled. "Bring them kitchen scissors out. I got surgery to do on ya." But his tone betrayed he was kidding.

Sabrina gave me a shoo sign.

I considered the cocktails in my hands. "Hope I don't confuse them," I said.

She leaned in close to me, a jasmine perfume enriching the air, and so pillowy soft in her upper parts that I wanted to hang there forever. She whispered, "The vessel with the pestle has the pellet that is poison."

"Excuse me?"

"It's from some old Danny Kaye movie," Sabrina said. "The flagon with the dragon has the brew that is true."

I looked at both hands and saw that one glass was unlike the other, which I believed was her meaning. But as I carried the piña coladas out to Cleanth in a gesture of friendliness and generosity, I began to have hesitations, for I was a victim of a penitentiary education and had never been taught what a pestle or flagon was. There was no dragon on either one. And I'd already forgotten which hand I took the pesticide in. I held up my right hand and believed I detected a hint of pharmaceuticals, and that's the one I gave to Cleanth, who heaved the cocktail back in that get-me-drunk-now! way that he has. He wiped his mustache with his thumb, then, grabby-Gus that he is, took the other fancy glass of piña colada from me.

"I think they call that glass a flagon," I said.

Cleanth regarded it for a second, then me for a little longer. "Who cares?" was his reply. He held his stare on me as he swallowed what was meant for my enjoyment, and then asked me if I had a job yet.

I took both glasses and put them on coasters, fearful of their contents. "I have this sleep disorder . . ." I began.

But he just smirked. Crooking a finger for me to get closer, he said, "I have a solution for your sleep disorder." And when I tilted closer to him, he yelled, "Wake up!"

I couldn't hear for a while after that.

Cooking seemed necessary if we were to eat and pretend to be normal and, same as with housecleaning, Sabrina, the poor child, was never taught how. So I took over those chores, just as I always did ahead of our afternoon sexcapades, and made us some saltimbocca alla Romana with bruschetta and arugula salad. Chianti, of course, and seedless red grapes and Kraft cheese slices for dessert. Throughout our after-midnight repast Cleanth stayed alive as ever, so that Sabrina couldn't eat and she gave me a scared look when he went to the kitchen to screw off the cap on a box of wine.

She whispered, "Are you sure he drank it?"

Eloquent with Chianti, I said, "Uh-huh."

Cleanth hit his shoulder against the kitchen doorframe as he staggered out and fell down into his dining room chair. Spilling Chianti. "I got a gut ache," he said. "And my throat hurts. My lungs burn, too."

See? I wanted to tell her.

"Oh, sweetie," Sabrina said. She held a palm to his Cro-Magnon forehead. "Maybe you're coming down with something."

Cleanth's eyes widened and he smiled with his snaggled teeth. "We could have sex. I'd get well that way."

"Skeeter's here," she cautioned.

"Skeeter's another name for mosquito," he said, not for the first time. And his hands became overfamiliar with her.

In loyalty to me, she removed his hands and took some dishware into the kitchen.

Cleanth concentrated on his wineglass, tipping it in multiple directions, and then pitched it into the fireplace, where it exploded into a hundred shards. "She loves me," he said. And then he took up my wineglass and repeated the experiment with a similar result. But he said this time, "She loves me not." And he gave me an excruciating stare.

And just then Sabrina ran out from the kitchen with a skillet and whanged Cleanth hard in the back of his skull. She stood back as he scratched his hair with his left hand like he'd felt a tingle, and then she hauled off and whanged him again and his face dived into his bowl of grapes without so much as an "Ouch."

Stillness. Wide-eyed waiting from us two.

She held out the skillet. "Hold this," she said, and I just then noticed she was wearing oven mitts. She took one off and felt for a pulse in his neck. She said, "He fell on the ice."

"And hit his head," I said, quick on the uptake.

"And slid into the fishing hole while you two were ice fishing."

"And there was nothing I could do."

"It all happened so fast."

"And my sleep disorder kicked in."

She stopped to scrunch up her face unpleasantly. "Oh, Skeeter, no one believes in that."

"Well, that's my alibi."

"Help me get a parka on him and haul him out," she said.

Imagine dragging a sleeper sofa outside into the night and into the shark's teeth of a Nebraska winter, and you will have one iota of our hour-long struggles. Cleanth wasn't in the least cooperative, cold sleet afflicted us like needles, I had to half swallow a flashlight to find a zone of safe passage in the wee hours of that night, and I kept bruising my coccyx against the ice as my boots upended me. We finally found Cleanth's ice hole and with Sabrina by my side, as I hoped she'd forever be, we rolled the hillock of him into Quarry Lake. With the wrestling and final push, I lost my flashlight in his parka and Sabrina and I held each other in suspense as we watched its amber glow ease along with Cleanth in his slow cruise underneath the ice to his otherworldly destination. At last the flashlight gave up the ghost as he met his watery demise.

She left my high five hanging in the air as she trudged inside.

Sabrina uncorked a bottle of champagne and we toasted each other and kissed and slow-danced. No tune was necessary. And then she insisted, "Rip me, Skeeter. Rip me."

Wild with passion and excitement, I tore the front of her kaftan wide so that buttons skittered along the floor and Sabrina was there before me in her gorgeous altogetherness. We embraced. We kissed. She let me feel her up.

And just then the front door slammed open. Cleanth sagged against the frame in his wetness, hugging himself, his teeth chattering, looking miserable and too far gone to notice Sabrina's augmentations underneath my hands.

She was fast. She collected her kaftan around her and screamed, "Cleanth! What happened to you?"

Coughing, he said, "Don't know. I fell. Cracked my skull, I guess. Cold water woke me. Ceiling of ice everywhere. Would've been a goner, but I chanced on the fishing hole off Warren's dock and crawled out."

"Oh, I'm so glad you did, sweetie!" Sabrina said. "Here, let me turn up the heat and get you some blankets while you get out of those things."

I helped him wrestle out of a far heavier parka and knelt to unlace his boots. My fingers smarted with just that and I shook the freeze out of them. Cleanth looked down on me like he had not heard a good joke since high-school. "Where were *you*?" he asked.

I snatched the first excuse I could think of. "You traipsed off without your fishing tackle and told me to go back and get it for you. Don't you remember?"

"Huh," was all he said. Weed killer, chemical weirdness, skillets to the head, and ice water in his lungs had made Cleanth almost docile. But it did not seem a very practical solution to his ordinary regimen of meanness.

Sabrina called, "Skeeter? Will you come help me?"

She was in the bathroom. Whitish silt was swirling around in a water glass. "Sleeping pills," she said. "Eight of them."

"And?"

She was holding her hands behind her back as she nodded to it. "Take it to him. Tell him it's Alka-Seltzer."

I ought to have listened to the lyrics of 1982's "Maneater" by Hall and Oates. But I didn't, and I sashayed out of the bathroom with the sleeping potion, my fingerprints gumming up the glass, and singing to myself that blockbuster's refrain: " 'Oh, oh here she comes. Watch out boy, she'll chew you up. Oh, oh here she comes. She's a maneater!' "

"Stop singing, you little twerp."

"Alka-Seltzer," I said. "Down the hatch."

Cleanth did as he was told. "How'd you know I had a gut ache?"

"You said. Earlier. Nasty head bash on that ice, huh?"

His hand petted his injury. "Yeah. My skull kind of makes a crackling sound when I touch it." And then he slumped against me. "Real, real tired, Skeets. Help me to the bedroom."

I crutched him inside and Sabrina watched him fall backward onto their Amish wedding ring quilt. She lit a cigarette. We said nothing to each other. Like words would break the spell. His chest slowly rose and fell with his breathing. And then just his right eye opened, scaring me. But then he began to snore. Sabrina stormed out of the room like she'd had enough. I heard her thumbing numbers on her cell phone and I followed her out.

"Dutch?" she said into the phone. "It's not working." Dutch was the front bar manager at Showgirls. She listened to him and she looked at me. "Worthless," she said. Dutch said something else. She snapped shut her cell phone. "Says he'll be right over."

Dutch and Skeeter, we didn't see eye to eye. Understandably upset, I folded my arms and pouted. She blew smoke and sort of smirked at me. "On pins and needles, are you, Skeeter? Sitting down hard on the seesaw of life?"

"I just don't know what Dutch has to do

with it."

She tapped ash into a whiskey glass. "See if he's overdosed yet."

Walked into the bedroom. Walked out. "Still snoring."

She was in a mood. She stared out at the road, hunting headlights. We said nothing to each other for a while.

And I remembered how we first met. Even then I was living at Momma's and she paid me fifty dollars a week to handle laundry and cooking and tidying up. She kidded that I was her butler, but one night she joked, "Skeeter, you gonna make someone a nice wife." That emasculating comment frosted me. I needed to get out of the house real bad and I convinced Momma that my Narc Anon meeting had begun charging the regulars. She gave me a twenty and I headed out to Showgirls for some eye candy. Didn't know anyone there in those days, so I took a stool at the bar, facing the mirror, and fell for myself all over again.

And then I noticed a goddess on a nearby bar stool in nothing but the sheerest pink chemise and thong. Sabrina was trying to persuade a lout to purchase a hundred-dollar bottle of champagne if he wanted to continue the entertainment. He had the cash; more than a hundred was scattered out there by his elbow; but he was a glass-half-empty kind of guy and he loudly maintained he would not pay so outrageously for that which he hankered.

She was a good saleswoman. She tossed her hair and smiled and even let him tantalize himself with stray brushes against her femininities as she glanced at the mirror and watched me steal a fifty-dollar bill from his stack. I got off my stool with my Heineken and stumbled against her, and Sabrina's hand quickly hid the fifty of his I had tucked so deftly into her thong.

She found me later and smiled as she asked, "What's your name?"

I probably answered, "Skeeter," but I felt on the brink of something so grand that I could have blurted anything.

She said, "You've done time, haven't you."

"It was just a misunderstanding."

"Don't apologize. It's sexy."

"Well then, yeah," I said. "In fact I was executed."

She was not yet married to Cleanth, but he was even then jealous, and we heard him wrestling the lout off the bar stool and into the gentlemen's. We heard screaming and squishy thuds. Dutch sauntered over to the phone and dialed for an ambulance.

And Sabrina asked if I did yard work.

I ought to have said no.

She wrote down Cleanth's home address as she said, "His property needs mowing."

Each man, The Professor says, seeks out his own femme fatale.

Waiting for Dutch in that house on Quarry Lake, I sang Bee Gees hits to myself, and Sabrina went into the kitchen to avoid me. Around four in the morning, I hung out by the kitchen doorway just to adore her as she filed her nails. "The hard part was making it look like an accident."

"Oh yeah," Sabrina said. "I forgot."

"You limited my options."

Headlights swung their beams across the kitchen window and she stood up from the stool. "Here he is."

I called as she went past me, "You know that Rick Astley hit from 1987? 'Never Gonna Give You Up'?"

She scurried to the front door and jerked it open. Dutch loomed there, near as large as Cleanth, in a long yellow raincoat and sou'wester hat, welding goggles over his eyes, and Cleanth's Stihl chain saw in one gloved hand. He kissed Sabrina like I wasn't even there.

"Ahem."

Dutch scowled at me, fixed on his Peltor "Red Dome" hearing protectors, ripped the cord on the chain saw so it started snarling and chattering real loud, and walked with firm purpose to the snoozing object of his dislike. Sabrina stuck her thumbs in her ears, which made me smile at the antlers her eight fingers made. But then there was a sudden gurgle and a very wet noise, like paint was splattering the walls, and the noise of the chain saw ended. Hardly challenged.

Dutch walked out of the bedroom with blood sheeting off his raincoat and onto the floor.

"Well, sheesh," I said, feeling misled. "I could a done *that.*"

My ears were still ringing from the quarreling of the chain saw and Sabrina seemed to be giving me instructions that I couldn't hear, but I got the hint that I was to help Dutch with the disposal.

"Hold this, will you?" Dutch asked. And I took the chain saw from him. Watched Sabrina take his gloves. Seemed to me I was the only one getting my fingerprints on every dang thing in the house. Like I was the stooge.

Dutch reached out his right hand to my face. "What's missing?"

"Your thumb."

Dutch nodded toward the deceased. "Him. Caught me stealing a five-dollar bill.

This is payback time for me."

"Wondered about that hand."

"Well, now you know."

Sabrina went to some dry cleaning in their walk-in closet, tore the plastic off, then lined the inside of an empty cardboard box with it.

"Such efficiency!" I said.

My effort to lighten the mood only met with sneers. I shifted my gaze as Dutch carried over Cleanth's head and fitted it inside.

The headless body was wrapped inside the reddening Amish wedding ring quilt, which was a blessing, since either the Chianti or the saltimbocca alla Romana was making my stomach feel a little tricky. Dutch locked his arms around Cleanth's legs and I was trying to haul Cleanth's upper half with great difficulty until Sabrina joined in, now with overshoes and a parka on. We all three managed to get Cleanth's carcass on the floor. Dutch went on nagging me with orders and criticisms as we three dragged the giant outside and lifted him onto the bed of Dutch's pickup truck. Dutch went back in for the head as I hunted a pickax and spade.

I called shotgun, so Sabrina sat between us as Dutch drove farm roads into obscurity. She seemed to me to be favoring a guy who was only a front-bar manager after all, and as they hashed out their notions of what to do next, hurt feelings joined my sleep disorder and plum knocked me out.

Woke up to a slamming truck door and saw Dutch and Sabrina getting things ready for an interment. Had no idea where we were. The hole seemed to have been dug ages ago and when I questioned Sabrina about it she said, "Well, this was just in case."

Chill wind howling, Dutch flung into its final burying place the box with Cleanth's head in it. And then he shot me the evil eye as he asked Sabrina, "Shall I do it now?"

"Wait," Sabrina said.

Checked my watch. Half past six. Said, "We'll have sunrise pretty soon."

Dutch betrayed his I'm-about-to-be-hilarious smirk as he said, "Oh, did that just *dawn* on you, Skeeter?"

And I said, "I have a secret for you, Dutch. *No one* thinks you're funny."

"Bounced off me and hit you," he said. Like we were in fifth grade.

My face, I knew, illustrated a childish condition that Momma calls "petulance." I was imagining all the erasing we had to do back at the lake house and suspected it would be Skeeter alone on all fours with the bucket and sponge. Seeing my mood, Sabrina made a gracious effort to include me in the adult activities by having me help Dutch heave Cleanth into his cold, earthen grave. Then Dutch took the pickax and started chopping clods of frozen dirt onto the Cleanth-size mound below. Inside the wind, I was beginning to hear the faint sounds of traffic.

"And then what?" I asked.

Dutch looked up.

"You pin the murder on me. You say I killed Cleanth and then attacked Sabrina. She escaped my clutches and called you for help and you caught me hiding the evidence of my misdeeds right here. Are you going to kill me? Would seem to me you have to. Then what?"

Dutch smiled. "Sabrina and me are getting married."

She did not conceal the shock in her face. "We *are*?"

"Well, I ain't gonna propose at this instant," Dutch said. "But seems to me we had an understanding."

An altercation ensued in which I was just an amused observer as each side tried to firmly establish differing versions of their futures. I took up the spade and shoveled earth for a while, humming.

Worn out from arguing, Sabrina winced at me as she fired up a cigarette, and I mistakenly took that as a "Kill him" signal. I swung my spade right at his head, but Dutch deflected it with the pickax handle. We fenced like that for a while. Clanging and clacking and whiffing and oofing as Sabrina inhaled carcinogens with seemingly no concern over who was winning. But then I noticed her turn from our competition and hug herself from the cold as she looked up toward the sunrise. Even then in those peculiar circumstances, she seemed so beautiful to me that I stopped my flailing with the spade. It was a form of praise and worship that Dutch, too, found impossible to resist.

And then we noticed what she was noticing: commuters from farther west than Boys Town whizzing toward Omaha and their bloodless jobs and legal incomes and kindly ways of living. But three or four cars were already parked on the highway bridge and folks were staring down at us, horrified, scared, like we were their own destiny. A guy in a suit was yelling into his cell phone, alerting the Highway Patrol.

We were caught. Edging over toward Sabrina, recognizing the harm I'd done, and preparing myself for a guilty plea in the court of public opinion, I slung my arm around my gorgeous exotic dancer and gazed up at our overseers. Waved my farewell. Wishing them peace and happiness. Wishing them such love.

ACKNOWLEDGMENTS

"Wilde in Omaha" was first published in *Prairie Schooner;* "The Governess" in *Narrative;* "The Sparrow" in *Image;* "My Communist" and "My Kid's Dog" in *Harper's;* "Crazy" in *Vineyards;* "Wilderness," "Mechanics," "A Hazard of New Fortunes," and "The Sleepwalker" in *Epoch;* "The Theft" in *Witness;* and "She Loves Me Not" in *Tin House.* "Wickedness," "Playland," "The Killers," "Nebraska," "Red-Letter Days," "Can I Just Sit Here for a While?," and "True Romance" were selected from my previous collection, *Nebraska.*

My thanks to Santa Clara University for the gift of time in which to write; to Dick and Elizabeth Moley for their support for my work; to my agent Peter Matson and my Scribner editor Colin Harrison; and to the first readers of these pages: my wise old friend Jim Shepard, and my lovely wife, Bo Caldwell, my *sine qua non.*

CREDITS

"Wilde in Omaha," *Prairie Schooner,* Summer 2005.

"Wickedness," *Nebraska.*

"The Governess," *Narrative,* forthcoming.

"Playland," *Nebraska.*

"The Killers," *Nebraska.*

"Nebraska," *Nebraska.*

"The Sparrow," *Image,* January 2009.

"Red-Letter Days," *Nebraska.*

"Can I Just Sit Here for a While?" *Nebraska.*

"My Communist," *Harper's,* November, 2001, and in Peter Fish, editor, *California's Best,* Farcountry Press, 2009.

"Crazy," *Vineyards: A Journal of Christian Poetry,* University of Southern Mississippi, March 2010.

"True Romance," *Nebraska.*

"Wilderness," *Epoch,* Fall 1996, and Ellen Datlow and Terri Windling, editors, *The Year's Best Fantasy and Horror,* St. Martin's Press, 1997.

"Mechanics," *Epoch,* Fall 1997.

"A Hazard of New Fortunes," *Epoch,* Summer 2005.

"The Theft," *The Sound of Writing,* National Public Radio, 12 December 1993; *Witness,* Winter 1994, and Alan Cheuse and Catherine Marshall, editors, *Listening to Ourselves,* Doubleday Anchor Books, 1994.

"The Sleepwalker," *Epoch,* forthcoming.

"My Kid's Dog," *Harper's,* March 2003, and in Robert Shapard and James Thomas, editors, *New Sudden Fiction,* Norton, 2007.

"She Loves Me Not," *Tin House,* January 2009.

ABOUT THE AUTHOR

Ron Hansen is the author of eight novels, two collections of stories, and a book of essays. He graduated from Creighton University in Omaha and went on to the University of Iowa Writers' Workshop and Stanford University. His novel *Atticus* was a finalist for both the National Book Award and the PEN/Faulkner Award. His novel *The Assassination of Jesse James by the Coward Robert Ford* was also a finalist for the PEN/Faulkner Award and was made into a movie starring Brad Pitt and Casey Affleck. Hansen's writing has won awards from the National Endowment for the Arts, the Guggenheim Foundation, and the American Academy of Arts and Letters. He is currently the Gerard Manley Hopkins, S.J., Professor in the Arts and the Humanities at Santa Clara University in Northern California. He is married to the novelist Bo Caldwell.

The employees of Thorndike Press hope you have enjoyed this Large Print book. All our Thorndike, Wheeler, and Kennebec Large Print titles are designed for easy reading, and all our books are made to last. Other Thorndike Press Large Print books are available at your library, through selected bookstores, or directly from us.

For information about titles, please call:
 (800) 223-1244

or visit our Web site at:
 http://gale.cengage.com/thorndike

To share your comments, please write:
 Publisher
 Thorndike Press
 10 Water St., Suite 310
 Waterville, ME 04901

"In here," she answered. Now what was wrong? His voice resonated with excitement.

"News! I've got news!" he shouted happily. As he rushed into the yard, his face beamed. He must have a tent order, she thought. She had not seen him so happy in weeks. Maybe the boycott was over!

"What news?" she asked, holding out her arms to him.

"We're going home!" exulted Aquila, embracing her.

Priscilla began to tremble. She pushed her cloud of red-gold hair back and stared at his jubilant face.

"We're going home!"

"Rome!" she whispered. "Truly, Rome?" He kissed her, and swung her around playfully.

"Rome! To build the church, to build a life," he answered joyfully.